D0487591

BETWEEN LIVES

Bill James titles available from
Severn House Large Print

Double Jeopardy

BETWEEN LIVES

Bill James

Severn House Large Print
London & New York

This first large print edition published in Great Britain 2006 by
SEVERN HOUSE LARGE PRINT BOOKS LTD of
9-15 High Street, Sutton, Surrey, SM1 1DF.
First world regular print edition published 2003 by
Severn House Publishers, London and New York.
This first large print edition published in the USA 2006 by
SEVERN HOUSE PUBLISHERS INC., of
595 Madison Avenue, New York, NY 10022.

British Library Cataloguing in Publication Data

James, Bill
  Between lives - Large print ed.
  1.   Women biographers - Fiction
  2.   Spies - Great Britain - Fiction
  3.   Actors - Fiction
  4.   Detective and mystery stories
  5.   Large type books
  I.   Title
  823.9'14 [F]

ISBN-10:   0-7278-7527-2

Printed and bound in Great Britain by
MPG Books Ltd, Bodmin, Cornwall.

For Cynthia and Ray,
who helped with the landscape

One

Two deaths. And more or less at once people
started to tie them together, or try. They said
one caused the other. Louise thought this
doubtful: at least doubtful and maybe far-
fetched – melodrama. For God's sake, because something followed something else
timewise it didn't have to mean the first
brought about the second. She had an idea
there was a Latin tag that warned against
such sloppy logic. You could find classical
tags to warn against anything.

Now and then, when she heard people
bracket Andrew Pax's death with David
Gale's, Louise wanted to snarl the wise bit of
Latin to them, but couldn't remember it
properly. In any case, those she snarled it at
would probably not understand, though
even in the film game some folk surprised
you with their education.

Of course, Louise did see what people
meant when they spoke of a link between
Andrew Pax's grim end half a century ago
and David Gale's yesterday. She couldn't
believe in it, that was all. Or couldn't believe

in it totally.

'You're among the first to hear, Louise. I mean, among the *very* first. Before the media. I considered that only right.'

'Thanks, Ted.'

'I'm sorry it has to be by phone like this. Face-to-face would have been so much better. You've been close to David. Inevitably. He told me – oh, more than once, certainly more than once – he told me he could open up to you.'

'Yes.'

'As I see it – well, as I hope many, most, will see it – I regard it as reasonable to see it like this – as I see it, Louise, to go that crucial amount over the safe dose can easily happen. The craving for sleep grows frenzied. I've suffered myself like that. Plus, David's probably been drinking a lot lately. Justifiably. He's had a triumph. Adrenaline, Louise. This kind of accident could hit anyone – especially anyone who finds himself suddenly an acclaimed, wonderfully bankable cinema star. All right, all right, I suppose that is not quite *anyone*. No. We're all hoping the inquest is going to say Accidental.'

'It's a while since I saw him, but never a hint of anything like this, Ted. The opposite. He was so truly positive.'

'We have to think of things primarily from his personal and family aspect, primarily,

8

obviously, but obviously ... obviously, obviously – God, I'm stuttering. You can hear the nerves, Louise. Obviously, there also has to be ... *is* ... a commercial side. Louise, I loathe inquests. Christ, but what a stupid thing to say. I mean, does anyone *like* inquests? But, of course, there'll be the media before that. No controlling those sods. Their damned obsession with celebrity ... well, obviously thank God for it in other circumstances – I'd be the last to protest – but when that obsession is twinned with their other obsession – death – oh, God. Naturally, our Press Relations folk are looking at how to present it. I don't know whether you've got any ideas, Louise. Not quite your bag, I appreciate. Except you're used to putting things in their best light. I mean, going strong on, as you say, the positives. Featuring the *good* side of things, not the null. I'm not suggesting you spin, Louise, do let's be clear about that. But the positive. You know how to—'

' "Accentuate the positive". There was a song.'

'Yes, I admire that ability in you.'

'In my attempt at getting David's life into a book, I—'

'And a brilliant attempt. A wholly triumphant attempt, Louise.'

'I tried to show him full of fun and hope. The way the world thinks of him. It was based on what he told me: if you're ghosting a star's story it's *their* story, really.'

'You did catch his essence, Louise. A wonderful achievement. And I'd like to state this to you now – nothing that's happened invalidates how you wrote it ... helped *David* write it ... or makes it look, well, *inappropriate*. You wrote it ... wrote most of it ... you wrote it as you saw and experienced David, and how we all saw and experienced David. It would have been false to do it any other way.'

'In ghosting, it's the subject's voice that must come through.'

'Exactly, Louise. I don't want you to feel that this death in any way makes your presentation of him in *We're Rolling*—'

'I wouldn't say *my* presentation, Ted. This was David telling his own story – a kind of autobiography. I only—'

'Yes, a kind of, a ghosted kind. You were the one who made it *work* as a marketable book, Louise.'

'I—'

'And I don't consider that his death now in such an awful way contradicts the tone you established for this book – doesn't make it appear naively, deceptively bland. Not at all naive or deceptively bland. I'd challenge anyone who attacked *We're Rolling* as that.'

'Ted, I—'

'The publishers tell me there are forty thousand of these fine, hardback biographies in print, Louise – really fine hardbacks – plus very big paperback potential, obviously, and I'm assured they will sell, despite this terrible event, and that your royalty payments will accordingly be up to forecast. And we're also sure that David's superb last film will continue to bring the crowds in – the way it top box-officed from the start. *Broken Light* is established now, and not even something like this can hurt it. The original thinking – that the book sells the film and vice versa – still applies. Very much so. But an Accidental Death verdict would definitely be better.'

'You think that really matters, Ted – the mode of death?'

'Suicide – there can sometimes be a kind of grandeur to suicide – nobody would deny that. But with David's – if it *were* so – with David's, his comes after a stupendous public success. It would be a kind of insult to all those who loved his work, acclaimed it, paid lavishly to see it. Yes, an insult. Suicide is a word that might in some cases have provoked sympathy. A suicide like that woman poet's – the American–'

'Plath.'

'That was a suicide with some … well, *scale*. People wrote books on suicide because of it, penetrative, worthwhile books, reviewed in the *Observer*. David's is different – a kind of two fingers to an adoring world. I don't want to labour this, but you see my thinking? I

11

know you won't find it cynical. Our P.R. people were wondering, Louise, if we could do a substantial quote from you saying – well, saying what you've already volunteered to me in outline – saying there was never any indication of the kind of despair and defeat in David that might lead him to ... It's vital for us – for *all* of us, Louise – vital to get a more positive version of this death on the record before the media start their brutal, lurid speculation. They – that's the P.R. lads and gals – they feel a contribution from you would be very telling. You would speak not just as David's co-operator in his autobiography but as someone with a grand reputation in another, perhaps more esteemed literary area.'

'But as far as David was concerned I ghosted – really nothing more than—'

'I've always loathed that term, and more so now, obviously. Oh, I know you like to keep your two kinds of work separate – the full-blown "serious" biographies – say someone like that archbishop—'

'Cranmer.'

'And the other poet. Male.'

'Dryden.'

'Or, of course, more relevantly and current, Andrew Pax – you like to keep these apart from the "puff" jobs as I expect you'd call them – the kind of thing you did with David. Sometimes, I have to tell you, it peeves me a bit. Snobbish. In a quite valid sense you are David Gale's biographer, Louise. I think so, definitely. Surely, that's what it means on the title page of *We're Rolling*, when it says, "by David Gale, as told to Louise Summers". This is a joint work of true authority, and your distinguished name helps create that authority as much as David's. It's why we commissioned you. It would be irresponsible to let the reputation for accuracy and the status and potential sales of *We're Rolling* suffer because we failed to insist urgently enough and soon enough to the world that supremely gifted actor David Gale was hardly one to drop so far into self-hatred and hopelessness and arrogance – yes, I insist, it would be arrogance – a contempt for his public – to go so far that way that he would deliberately take his own life only a fortnight after world movie critics and audiences have hailed him in a magnificent lead part as Andrew Pax – comparisons with the young Gary Cooper, Olivier, Burton. I mean, even the *New Yorker* liked it – none of that usual refined smart-arse bitching and fucking loud Princeton irony. And only weeks after fans have queued in London and New York and Denver bookshops for him to sign *We're Rolling*, his life so far as fashioned and presented by acclaimed biographer Louise Summers. "His life so far." God, what a phrase, in the circumstances as we know them now, Louise. If we can provide *our* side of things ... and by that I mean all the team's side of things, including David's, were he only able to take part ... yes, if we can get our side of things in early and with proper force we might be able to influence not just public opinion and the cinema-going and book-buying folk out there and in the States but also reach this ... well, possibly damned awkward Coroner, as I hear, whose court will decide how David died.'

'Ted, I certainly don't mind being quoted as saying I heard nothing from David suggesting suicide.' And she thought it more or less true that she never did hear him hint at finishing things. Louise felt happy to do a late kindness. It was safe.

'Your response is appreciated, Louise. Our people will put it into terms which are caring, positive – your admirable word – yet tactful. We all have an interest in David's image, as much when he is dead as when he was with us and such a glittering talent.'

Louise could sympathize with Ted Burston. He had to cope with two related but not at all identical items: there was Gale's death; and there was the public relations presentation of Gale's death. And so, as often in his trade, he had to marry the pious with the hard-nosed. Louise thought she had done extremely well not to laugh even once as he

14

spoke.

The sense of farce continued to affect her after she came off the phone. She found that, as she walked about the flat, she was slightly bent over to one side; to a degree, cowering. While Ted spoke just now, she had had a vision of those thousands of stored plump hardbacks, in their ungaudy blue and gold jackets: a kind of thick, monstrous tower of abruptly obsolete, absurd books which, as she gazed at them in her fancy now, began to tilt and disintegrate from the top, as if about to break up totally any minute and bury her. Mad: she was not the one to be buried. A good ghost identified as much as possible with the client, but you did not accompany him into death. Ghosts dwelt with the living.

She felt grief for David, of course, of course. Perhaps she also felt a touch of guilt. There had been that little interlude and his sad pleas, plus the letter. Oh, yes, Lord, that – the letter. And even discounting this special, brief non-ghost and fleshly episode with him, she had always found Gale reasonably close to civilized, when drinking or not: civilized as cinema stars went. So, she could feel upset at what he had done. She could also feel angry. This death made her look an idiot, no matter what Ted Burston said. *We're Rolling* had projected Gale as the movies' hope for now, 1991, for tomorrow, and for ten thousand tomorrows after. The title, which he'd picked himself, said all that, was stuffed with optimism. This Life had him walking all over Kevin Costner.

And then Gale says with true Royal Academy of Dramatic Art timing, 'No thanks, I'll exit.' Thoughtless, selfish jerk. He was dead and so was *We're Rolling*, whatever the Coroner decided.

She tried to console herself. Smooth flattery was standard for a volume of this kind and nobody expected real, harsh insights. A ghostwriter was not hired to offer truth or even look for it. You were a temp on the star's publicity gang, and you thought *positive*, encouraged him/her to tell you what *was positive*. Journeymen and women in the ghost trade knew this and would not see Gale's death as a full career fiasco for Louise: reality banging in brutally on advertising. Even some of the reading public probably realized they were buying clotted blurb when they bought one of these alleged Lives. Marketing theory said they *wanted* it like that. The ghost made a star sound like a star, and Main Street cinemas survived on stars. Book customers knew the dark stuff was excluded, at least until restrospectives, as with Monroe or Grace Kelly. Fans probably realized the ghostwriter was not even told the dark stuff and would be discouraged from sniffing it out.

Just the same, self-destruction of someone

recently written up as the tops in vitality and promise was hard to accommodate. Colleague ghosts might feel sorry for Louise, but some of them would also enjoy a few long and helpless giggles at her disaster. She had had people on the phone already with their commiserations, the silky sods, although Ted said she was among the first to hear. Yes, very among. *It must be terrible for you, Louise. Where were you when you heard he'd done it, my dear?* as though he were her private Kennedy.

These mates rated worse than Ted with his creepy threats that, if she did not give dead David a wholesome, posthumous bill of mental health, the books and her income would stick, and the film might expire, too. Her telephone comforters wanted dense detail for their dinner-party tales, longed to measure up her pain and tie congratulatory ribbons around Louise's shame. On *her* dinner plate she had a cadaver. Oh, you prick-happy, corpsed sod, Dave.

Was it somehow a punishment? Very briefly last year she had been a bit more than his ghost. But for her, very briefly was enough. Some boredom, some genuine fondness for him, perhaps some curiosity, perhaps some fan awe, had produced the night or two together in 1990. Three. Then, to her amazement, he had been hurt when she tried to walk away. Louise had told him before things

17

started, such as they were, that she would not want to continue. Perhaps he was totally unused to those kinds of terms from a woman and thought she would change. After all, David Gale was the catch of catches. It broke him to see she meant it.

But she would not blame herself for what had happened. She meant to provide the kindness of tact and selective silence, and these must do. Hell, no wonder she preferred biographing the well gone, her other trade outlet. Hooray for subjects already dead, long before a book began. Say, Andrew Pax, her present interest. This was a proper literary task, not a hype anthology. When she worked as a serious biographer, not a ghost, she had what some critic generously called 'a unique flair for making the dead live'. Louise loved that idea. It put her into a similar category as the famous biographer Michael Holroyd, who said his work might help people continue a little beyond the grave: Shaw, Augustus John, Lytton Strachey. Some hope. At least this was a more genial view than Oscar Wilde's description of biography as body-snatching.

The argument over what biography could and couldn't do seemed to hint at another big, eternal question. It was about truth – pure, unbent truth. Did biographers have any chance of reaching it? Weren't they bound to edit, select, manage, slant the material of a life according to their own tastes and values? Such disputes about the worth or not of biography had buzzed for years. Cliché controversy. Now, though, Louise felt that the different problems faced in publicity ghosting on one hand, and, on the other, presenting a life like an impartial slice of history, might help her sort out these puzzles. Or make them tougher. Who said history was any more impartial than biography? Oh, God.

Two

Later in the morning Ted rang again to say a profile writer he knew from the Sunday heavy press wanted to do an extended obituary piece on David Gale. 'Something beyond what the dailies carry, Louise. This girl can get at the essence, yet playful with it. Pamela de la Salle. They need a column width for the by-line. I expect you've read her articles. Personally unprettyish and, yes, weighty, but I trust this girl. Though clever, she's intelligent with it. There's an edge to her work, yet she can be sensitive. I think she might be in this case. She's looked at *We're Rolling* and really flipped: says the organization shows a true professional brain ... meaning you, obviously – not just David reminiscing it to you. I felt you'd value this, as coming from someone in the business ... I mean, she's only a journo, yes, but gold leaf, and in the same general ballpark of careful words.'

Louise hoped Ted was not going to say he wanted her to talk to de la Salle. A writer writing about another writer's two kinds of writing – here comes fog.

'Look, Louise, I took it upon myself, in view of your remarks earlier ... I told her that if she wanted to visit you'd be happy to talk briefly. You see, she's fascinated by what she calls – and I think reasonably calls – yes, your "double role" in this.'

' "Double role" meaning that I—.'

'The David Gale ghost job in *We're Rolling* and then, with your other persona, as an accredited literary figure, your heavyweight and, I'm sure, learned biography of war traitor, Andrew Pax, the very man David so superbly played in his latest and last film, *Broken Light*. Perhaps I should say *alleged* war traitor, given the film's message. Your interview with Pam could be off the record for background or attributed: up to you. She understands this. Her piece will be a tribute to David, probably out before the full inquest, which is the kind of exposure for him ... for his dear memory ... the kind of exposure and favourable influence we want, as I mentioned. This is a girl who says she's a genuine admirer of David. Of course, they all try that shit to get our cooperation when the subject's tricky, but I've had our Press people go through all published newspaper items on David and they've been unable to find anything hostile or even sceptical about him written by Pam. All the really vicious stuff we naturally keep on disk and easily found, so we can get even. But in Pam's case, nothing. I accept her good intentions, Louise, and I believe the article will be a plus. What I mean is, this lump can write some fucking mordant prose. Fat girls do a lot of envy and grudging. Never, as far as I can see, though, any harshness to David. From her we'll get useful truth.'

De la Salle arrived not long after Ted's call, sweating a bit: the visible quantities on her brow and upper lip. Louise had certainly read and admired some of her work but could not recall ever meeting her. Unquestionably she was a name. 'As I see it, Louise, David Gale was a touch above the standard hack thespian, and topping himself probably shows depth, if we didn't already know it. The movie game's full of stars with vast personality kinks, but ever hear of one doing himself, herself in – except, that is, slowly by drink?'

'Carole Landis? George Sanders?'

'But rare. Until now, suicide was not on their agenda. This is what puts Gale up several artistic rungs. It's why I'd like to give him some wordage now.'

'He gets to be worthwhile because he killed himself?' Louise said. 'Gravitas of the grave? Ted thinks David devalued suicide.'

'Normally, I don't write about the movie tribe. They're puff-ball stuff. Gale's different – now.'

' "Nothing in his life became him like the leaving it," ' Louise replied.

De la Salle was seated deep in an armchair and waved her left arm – a banishing movement: 'I don't go in for quotes. My work is me and now, not Shakespeare's Malcolm.'

'The distributors think it was an accident.'

'Yes, we know that's rot, of course. Not just rot but stupid rot. No grandeur in accident. Accident is incompetence or helplessness or alcohol. Accident is Glen Miller drowned in an aircraft, like how many thousands in the war? I know you see the absurdity, Louise. The damn *feebleness*. What interests me, and what interests you, I'm sure, is the clear connection between the part Dave Gale had just played in *Broken Light*, and his decision that he couldn't go on. A *decision*, not some sloppy mischance. Why it was important for me to see you, Louise. Your, as it were, duality.'

'Ted said you'd focused on that. But I—'

'You're *the* connection.'

'I am? I only—'

'On the one hand you ghost the life. And I'd like to say that, as these Lives go, it's acceptable plus.'

'Thanks.'

'These books are usually shit all through, we both know that, but I did glimpse a decent phrase now and then.'

'Probably a quote from Shakespeare.'

23

De la Salle waved her arm again, protesting, dismissing: 'Oh, now don't go all hurt on me, please. Please. I admire your work. And it's the fact you're doing the first real, *thorough*, biog of Pax, as well as having ghosted Gale, that makes this such a ... such a *latent* situation.'

'*Broken Light* itself was a biog of Pax.'

'A *cinematization* of his life.'

'Plenty of scrupulous research went into the screenplay. After all, it was the script and the film that persuaded my publishers there could be a market for a full, book-form biography of Pax,' Louise said.

'Meaning the movie version wasn't adequate.'

'The film has to make a story.'

'Falsify.'

'Some believe fiction can get to the truth better than the recounting of fact. Supposed fact.'

'*Who* believes that? Ponce dons at Oxford.'

'The publishers and I came to think it would be interesting to look at Pax with—'

'With the kind of thoroughness and penetration you're rightly known for – when you're not doing star slurp. The kind of thing you give in your proper biographies wouldn't suit a commercial movie, nor the ghosted crap books, naturally.'

'My publisher thought the film might up interest in Pax, that's all. A book can look at some matters with more—'

'Exactly what I'm saying, Louise. This is a man hanged in war-time for a treason he might or might not have been guilty of.'

'The film says no.'

'Of course. It wouldn't have been made otherwise. What modern director does a picture saying the law was right, the Secret Service was right? Film-makers have to look progressive, liberal, brilliantly subversive. Quickest way to a pile and cocktail-party esteem. Eventually, they get their C.B.E., or even a knighthood, and turn into distinguished members of the higher system because they tried to tear holes in it. But what I want to hear is what *you* – you personally – what you think about Pax's guilt, or innocence.'

'I'm still researching.'

'But how does it look – at this stage? Overall. In general. The *feel*.'

'I'm still researching.' Stick with it. Of course, Louise saw that in some ways Pamela de la Salle might be right. There did seem something crazily too much about preparing a book biography on a man whose biography had just come out as a major, main-street cinema film. The only reason must be that some thought the film presented the tale badly: did it according to the politically correct, self-righteous, pumped up method of only-now-can-it-be-told

25

movies, not with a decent regard for fact. It was true, the film might get some interest going in Pax. Possibly people would want to learn more, in a balanced form, unjinxed by box-office demands and modish, phoney, public-interest revelation. So, enter Louise, in her weightier, literary, scholarly role.

De la Salle said: 'What we have is Gale playing a wartime spy – alleged spy – ex-Cambridge University Apostle, as their élite club was known, and with all the trappings, except gayness. The topic stays fashionable for some reason I don't get. Anyway, we're talking about a spy who's rumbled and executed at Pentonville prison in the hearty patriotism days of 1941 Britain. Hasty? Convenient? A distraction from bad battle news? The film suggests the lot. Louise, what I want to know is whether taking on this part – the dim, low-grade tragedy of it – the possible bungling that went with it – whether all these overwhelmed Gale. Whether they drove him to death, as Pax was driven to death, by others.'

'It was a part. He was a professional actor.'

'You'll tell me people play Lear and don't go mad.'

'People play Lear and don't go mad. People play the incredible shrinking man and don't shrink. Barrie Humphries plays Dame Edna but still has his balls.'

'This was an actor who'd been given only

26

gloss roles before. Suddenly, he meets a life that gets to him – gets to him and sucks him into identification: noble, manly, comprehensive, ultimately despairing identification. Were you shagging him at any stage, by the way? This would be like a *soul* thing, a humane, therapy thing. Not for publication, I promise. He *becomes* that life, Pax's life, you see. He becomes that life and finds he cannot live with it, Louise.'

Three

And then Ted Burston and those above Ted Burston reached a conviction that, really, suicide of a star could be seen in many ways as a plus – though not from his personal angle, naturally. Perhaps the self-destruction aspect should be emphasized after all, rather than down-played or even denied. Ted and the others might have been influenced by Pamela de la Salle's article, which had really patted David Gale on the back for his death.

'The general favourable response to David's extinction has amazed me as much as anyone, Louise, I don't deny it,' Ted remarked. 'And we know, definitely *know*, that hardly anyone was fooled by our well-intentioned statements claiming he would never see himself off.'

'It was an Open Verdict, Ted.'

'That misguided fucking twat, the Coroner, thought he was doing everyone a kindness, didn't he, Louise: the family and, yes, us, too? Benefit of the fucking doubt stuff. The law's like that. It's one thing you get to learn in this business – the public can surprise you with their shrewdness now and then. I'd definitely endorse that statement by ... is it Nixon? ... "You can fool most of the people most of the time but not all the fucking people all the fucking time." They *know*, Louise. They know David did himself in. Calculatedly. And they understand. They see sensitivity. They observe alienation. They love him for these qualities, revere him for them.'

Ted's thin but passionate voice banged triumphantly against the walls of his tiny office. It did not echo but seemed to cling for a moment to the masonry, so that Louise could mind's-eye the loud, breathy verbs scattered in black italic capital letters at separate places on the red and gold flowered wallpaper: *KNOW*, *UNDERSTAND*, *LOVE*, *REVERE*. She had had this kind of vision before in Ted's room. Last time it was when they discussed *We're Rolling* before she actually began. The words then were *TACT*, *POSITIVE*, *DISCRETION*, *POSITIVE*, *SOFT PEDAL*, *POSITIVE*.

Ted said: '*We're Rolling* has virtually sold out. There'll be an immediate reprint. It appears I was quite unperceptive, even crude, to imagine David had sullied suicide's sheen. People mention names to me where there was a similar actual aggrandizement of celebrity status because someone killed himself, herself, or virtually did so. Fine

29

precedents. I mustn't be blasphemous, but it's bound to put me in mind of ... well, no, I shalln't say that. But Plath we've already spoken of. Then James Dean through fast cars. Dylan Thomas through booze. Apparently Thomas wrote a poem, while he was alive – well, obviously – but about the dignity of death and the need not to panic or suffer intellectual breakdown because of its approach: "Do not go mental into that good night." '

'Plus Chatterton, Ted.'

'There you are. That's literature again, isn't it? You're more likely to be familiar with this kind of thing than myself. When I look at what *Broken Light* goes on box-officing regardless – I mean, records smashed here and in the States since it happened, plus Germany, Japan, Italy, giving the trade a wonderful start to the 1990s – I look at these figures and all I can do is smile at my early worries that David's death might be a setback. That is, a setback to *Broken Light*'s revenues and sales of *We're Rolling*. Clearly, the obliteration of a fine man and a talent, and the impact on family and friends are terrible. Esteem-wise, though, David flourishes. Possibly we'll rescreen some of his earlier work. There are quite decent moments in a few of them. I feel we actually *owe* the public that now. Suddenly, David's sort of mythic. Louise, is it absurd, but I also think of Gandhi. I'm not referring to the Attenborough job, *Gandhi*, though that only proves the point. I mean Gandhi himself – the way that after his death he took on even greater significance. Would Richard have bothered otherwise? Mythic. All right, Gandhi did not in fact commit suicide, he was shot, but he'd been fasting, fasted all his life – look at his poor legs, for God's sake – so he'd put himself into no real shape to survive a bullet wound. A kind of complicity with the execution, as I see it.'

'You'd like to amend the assurances we put out originally that David would never top himself, would you?' Louise asked.

Ted slightly rearranged himself inside his grey suit, obviously made uneasy by her bluntness. So, fuck him.

'And, to show the change of view, you want me to stick a really big *pro*-suicide chunk into the revised edition of *We're Rolling*?' she said.

'We'll try to organize a public campaign to clear Pax's name posthumously. It will help underline David's sensitivity,' Burston replied.

Four

How to flog the Apostles? Not the original Apostles. They were deep history. Let the Church handle that. Louise meant the *Cambridge* Apostles, who were only history, not deep history. Could she sell them? They fascinated her. Did ironies come bigger? In the 1930s some members of this supremely privileged university debating society acquired a towering fondness for 'equality' Soviet-style, and hence for treason. But was she able to put her fascination with such contradictoriness between book covers, so the Pax biography would pull readers, buyers – the way *We're Rolling* pulled buyers now?

These days, history – even recent history – was a tough item to retail. Who needed the past? The young middle-aged and everyone older had lived through so many upending events – the War, the Cold War and Wall, the collapse of the Cold War and Wall recently – yes, they'd seen such a welter of epic turmoil that those earlier days seemed too distant and different to be worth reviving. That was one good thing about ghosting rubbish: it dealt with now and the living, or the very recently dead. By contrast, authentic biogs had to market the tricky notion that what was over and gone should not lie forgotten and might even be worth shelling out for in hardback.

'Well, yes, I did see the film, as a matter of fact,' Lord Chate said. *Broken Light*? I can't remember when I went to the cinema before that, my dear – possibly *The Robe*, fifties? But, of course, *Broken Light* was, indeed, a special occasion for me.'

'It started memories?' Louise asked.

'As a matter of fact, I felt the poor young chap who acted Andrew did him remarkably well. Remarkably. There wasn't an actual *physical* likeness you understand, no, not at all, and I did think he looked a sight older than your standard Cambridge undergraduate of 1936 – say Andrew or myself – but perhaps these are quibbles. Yes, I'm sure, quibbles. I don't know whom that actor had spoken to about Andrew – not to me, at any rate – but he had many of his mannerisms absolutely right. But absolutely. Andrew in pursuit of an intellectual point – and he was often in pursuit of an intellectual point, I can tell you. In that kind of situation he could become exceptionally impatient, even un-civil. Even cruel. Never so cruel as to justify his own cruel end. But cruel, yes. His lips would thin and he'd plant his feet wide, like a gladiator waiting for the lion, and this gladiator expected to win. He usually did. In argument, I mean. Formidable. The actor – Grail? Gale?'

'David Gale.'

'I expect he was quite famous, was he? One ought to know him.'

'Reasonably famous.'

'He caught all that quality in Andrew brilliantly. But what a waste of a talent, his death. Such ability to capture someone's personality, someone he had never even met, and of a generation and setting far from his immediate knowledge. Didn't I read in the Sunday press the idea that Gale had grown so much into the character of Andrew that a kind of terrible closeness and shared despair grew, ending in the suicide. Far-fetched?'

'Pamela de la Salle. They have to get what they call an angle.'

'Or at first it seemed far-fetched. But then I did begin to wonder, you see.'

'An Open Verdict,' Louise replied.

'Yes, yes, quite. But is there really much doubt, my dear? Even the courts can be charitable sometimes. I don't know how bright David Gale was in fact. Did you come into contact with him very much, I wonder?'

'Pax was a classicist, wasn't he?'

Chate said: 'Almost all the very gifted ones *were* in those days. Or pure maths.'

'And Andrew was an Apostle, of course.

Strange name.'

He muttered what might have been a chorus, or might have been a curse: 'Apostle, Apostle – Cambridge Apostle, yes. Many of the most brilliant people belonged. That excluded yours truly, I'm afraid. They were choosy. You know about them? Of course, research is your trade. As a debating and learned society they go back to the beginning of the nineteenth century. Tennyson, I believe. And his famous pal.'

'Arthur Hallam. I did a biog of him.'

'People still want to read about the far past?'

'Some still,' Louise replied.

'And now Andrew's your topic. You like those who die young? And you're looking up all his old contacts? Well, grand to see you. I'm alone here most of the time. My children visit now and then, but only now and then. Plus grandchildren.'

Louise said: 'You accuse me of being hot at research, but in fact I'm not sure how many children you have.'

'The Apostles?' he replied. 'Secretive fuckers. Many from Trinity College, but also some others, like Andrew. A lot of the most gifted people turned very Left then. Gayness was popular. I've given in to that word at last. I hear Anthony Blunt was an Apostle, for instance. And Guy Burgess. Understandable, I suppose – the Leftness. People backed

35

the Spanish government in the civil war against Franco. And we had a terrible Depression. Soviet Russia seemed to offer answers. How quaint it all appears from here. Perhaps we could look at the grounds now. It's stopped raining. Warm enough to go coatless.' He stood up, then strolled easily towards the gallery window and looked out to ornamental gardens and beyond. He was in his seventies but still unfrail, still nimble. He had on a scuffed brown leather jacket and khaki cords. He wore plimsolls. 'God, if Andrew were here he'd scalp me for that sentence.'

'Which?'

' "Perhaps we could look at the grounds now." So damn lordly.'

'You *are* a lord.'

'He'd have laughed at that, too. Mind, he would not have objected to a real lord, a hereditary lord. There were a few at Cambridge in '36, and a lot more would inherit a title later. Their sort were part of the system. Andrew abominated the system, but not the individuals who rose in it. But *my* title is something lifelong only and for "services" to the public. Andrew would have regarded acceptance of that as vulgar, and as kowtowing. Paradoxical soul. You'd expect him to approve things which were vulgar – of the people. I was of the people, and my title comes for creating factories that gave work and not bad wages to the people.'

Louise did not move at once. 'I know it's been asked before, but do you think many of the traitor-spies emerged via the Apostles?'

'Ah, you're really stuck on them, are you? Come. It might rain again.'

'The film suggested—'

'That's where it was shaky in my view,' Chate said. 'A fudge.'

'Yes, I suspected that. It's why I wanted to do Pax's biography – to take matters on. But how exactly did the film fudge?'

He held out a hand to her. She reached up and took it and stood. They had been drinking Chablis and there was a smell of wine in the gallery and of something like pepper or chilli from his clothes. 'Oh, don't ask me the how of it all,' he said. 'Spectator from a distance, that's all. And I expect I've forgotten most of it. We're talking of nearly sixty years ago.'

He released her hand and they walked towards the gallery door. She said: 'Not brilliant enough for the Apostles, but brilliant enough to build your companies, land yourself a peerage and get a spread like this.'

'Other way about. I bought the place first. Then they more or less *had* to Lord me. Once it belonged to a marquis. I was just the kind of jumped-up success the 1980s adored. Thatcher was bound to get me a title. Plus I'd done my war service at lowly rank. In her gritty way she liked that sort of background.'

They passed a wall of paintings. To Louise, most of them looked dismal: very dark green landscapes in hefty wooden frames, the people in them lifeless, almost faceless. Perhaps the art had come with the house. He led her down a narrow, uncarpeted rear staircase and out on to an earth path, bordered with unkempt privet.

'Do you imagine we were a couple?' Chate asked.

'Who?'

'No, Andrew and I both chased girls.'

In a little while the path widened and became a paved walk beneath a pergola draped with wisteria and ivy. Somewhere out of sight peacocks screeched, a stupid, empty din that seemed so sharp with agony and was just show.

'But how did you even know Andrew Pax?' she asked.

'On the same staircase in our first year at Christ's. You must have discovered that, Louise. Research.'

'What I meant was, how did the friendship endure? It lasted far longer than your first year at Cambridge. Yet no link through sport, academic subject, politics or amateur dramatics.'

He stopped walking and seemed to stare up at a thick wedge of wisteria on a pergola cross beam. 'Don't know. Friendship can be like that, can't it?' At the end of the pergola they passed between two hedges – these neatly cut – and she saw a lily pond ahead bordered by flower beds. 'I detest this part of the garden,' he said. 'Such a cliché. All those fat lily leaves lying there on the water. Are you asking me whether we stuck together because I recruited him for Uncle Joe?' He had stopped again and stood in front of her, his fat old face deadpan and gaudy. The sun got a small glint out of the leather coat. He was hatless.

'No, no,' she said. 'We know who recruited him – if he *was* recruited.'

'Well, he *was* hanged.'

'You'd be the same age as Pax, a couple of youngsters straight from school. Not at all how recruitment was done. The recruiter would be older – a don. You must have heard of Roy Estham.'

He padded on ahead and pointed to some rhododendrons. 'The originals were planted mid-eighteenth century, it's alleged. My money doesn't go far back, my flowers do.'

'Of course, the film suggested Pax never was recruited – was wrongly executed.'

'I got that. I was overseas in the Army when they put him to death or I'd have gone down to the jail and waited at the doors with his girlfriend of the time, plain but very loyal and amusing off and on.'

'What happened to her?' Louise asked. 'A blank.'

'Or I like to think I would have.' Chate snarled at the pond as they skirted it. 'The film did have someone who looked as if he might be drawing Andrew into treason, didn't it? The don you mentioned. Yes, I think he might have been called Estham. But he could have been a composition of twenty Cambridge Parlour Pinks of the time.'

'The film's ultimate message was that Andrew simply had powerful, justifiable, very modish Leftist views and loathed the inequalities of those days.'

'Oh, yes, modish – at Cambridge.' Louise said: 'Perhaps he even loathed Cambridge, as a flashy example of those inequalities. Admired the Russians, but never worked for them. In any case, the whole situation was bonkers, as the film showed. When he's executed, January 1941, the Russians are the enemy, because of the 1939 pact with Adolf. By June '41, when he invades Russia, they are suddenly our brave allies and we can't do too much to help them.'

There was a bench up near the house and they sat down. 'More contradictions,' Chate said. 'In some ways Andrew *loved* Cambridge. It recognized his abilities and gave him a chance to do something with them. He had plenty of ego. But, yes, he was sickened by the class stuff, the snobbery. Plenty of that then in Christ's.'

'Oxbridge generally, I imagine.'

'C. P. Snow was at Christ's in our time, you know. Became a novelist later? And a Lord.'

'Yes, I've heard of him.'

'You see, the film, *Broken Light*, wasn't the first time the college of that era got fictionalized. Snow did a novel.'

'*The Masters*.'

Chate said: 'Andrew's attitude to Snow was interesting. Not simple, but typical. Snow came to Christ's as a research fellow in science, something like that. Vitamins. And he didn't really fit. That was the point. A class thing. He hadn't been at Oxford or Cambridge. University College, Leicester? He was deemed crude. Naff, it would be called now. One of Andrew's classics teachers, a lad called Peck, had a name for Snow taken from Aristotle. Andrew told me. I don't know the classics, but I don't ever forget words: it was the Apolaustic, from the *Nicomachean Ethics*. It means someone vain and fond of show, no real creativity.' He giggled throatily. 'You think I'm deliberately muddying things, do you, Louise – talking about Snow? You believe I'm holding back the real glimpses of Andrew?'

'Oh, of course you bloody well are. That's what friendship's about.'

'What I'm saying is that in some ways

Andrew was on the inside – might even have had a smile at the swaggering, learned abusiveness in Peck's label for Snow. And yet Andrew could also feel sickened by the snottiness of it. Or said he could.'

'And do you think that's all there was to it – just a hatred of rank, privilege – no actual treachery?' Louise asked.

'Snow's novel is a story based on a real situation at Christ's in 1936 and written up by him at once. Yet it was so close to fact it had to be suppressed until 1951 when the main people in the tale were dead.'

She thought about this. 'What are you saying – that a piece of pop fiction about Andrew Pax like *Broken Light* can get things more right than my efforts at supposed factual biography?'

'You should have stopped me, my dear,' Chate replied, '– me drifting off like that into side issues, if issues at all. No, not issues at all, are they?'

Five

Ted Burston thought it a pain that to get hold of Louise on a subject of urgency he had to ring her in Portugal. Of course, Louise would be out there collecting a chapter or two for her damn book on Andrew Pax. He hated dealing with freelance hacks who had more than one commission on the go. You knew they were thinking of something else, even while discussing *your* topic. This one – Summers – she did the Gale ghosting because it paid, but, really, was obsessed by her 'serious' work on Pax.

Always aim for exclusivity. But Summers would not wear that, and she was too big a name to get rough with. God, hadn't the business changed? Think how the studios used to keep total control of even the biggest stars, let alone some writer hired for a spin-off book.

He found it a special embarrassment to phone Portugal because he feared he might have to speak first to Clifford Deem. This was the counter-espionage officer who established a case against Pax in 1941, sent him to be hanged. Retired now, Deem lived with his wife in the Algarve, and Burston knew Louise had been invited to stay with them; she had left their number. *Broken Light* featured Deem quite big, and without kindness. In fact, the film stitched the bugger up. He was portrayed as a narrow-minded, ruthless hunter.

Before tonight on the phone, Burston had never talked to him. He sounded a surprisingly nice chap during the small exchange when Burston asked for Louise: an old-style, Cambridge-educated gent, gone a little native but still polished and obliging. Possibly he had not seen *Broken Light* and knew nothing of the job it did on him. Possibly, also, he did not give a toss about movies or much else. Some of these classy, ex-quasi-military people made a cult of *sang froid*. How we won the war.

'Louise, lovely to hear your voice,' Burston said when Deem put her on the line. There'd been a delay while something not quite in Burston's earshot went on in an adjoining room: a recitation of some sort? *Recitation?* 'Louise, I've looked at your revisions for the new edition of *We're Rolling*, and in many ways they're admirable.'

'You want more changes.'

' "Melancholy",' he replied.

'Yes?'

'This word appears quite often in the

44

amended version, what we'll call "the suicide version", shall we, if that's not blunt? I'm unsure about "melancholy", Louise, especially in multiple exposure.'

There was a silence. Burston said gently: 'Louise? "Melancholy"?'

'Mulling it, Ted. This was a quality I—'

'Suggesting someone wilfully bleak, defeated?'

'He killed himself, Ted.'

'And how are things generally there in the Algarve?' Burston replied. 'Can you talk?'

'Fine.'

The Deems must know Louise was associated with the film, so she might have met some enmity. She seemed all right and this reinforced Burston's belief that Deem did not care about very much now. What would he want with reputation, backwatering out there, affecting the lingo and lifestyle? Probably he was bright enough to know that most good tales need a villain, and his name had come out of the hat, that's all. If the prevailing liberal, open-society political tone hadn't taken over these days, someone other than Clifford Deem would have been picked as Mr Evil for *Broken Light*. No specific malice was meant. Public feeling about right and wrong did not stay constant. In Westerns, weren't the Indians once always the vicious, whooping enemy? Look at them on the screen today: naturally cultured, honourable, majestic, exploited. Moral values came and went, were aspects of fashion, and cinema had to adjust smartly, or where was your audience, let alone Academy Awards? Only think how Women's Movements wanted the mad wife in the attic as star of *Jane Eyre*, not Orson. There was a period when the secret service officer who saved the realm and destroyed one of its treacherous enemies could have been shown as an icon. Not lately.

Louise said: 'Melancholy was a quality I did actually observe now and then in David, though, of course, I kept it out of the original Life. It didn't seem a side of him fans would want in a star aiming to wow the world.'

'Right. So, why—?'

'Now, in our suicide mode, Ted, we're looking for early signs of what he would be driven to. Actually, I thought you'd suggested the word.'

'I just can't see "melancholy" as an outright positive term. Not in this context. And the Deems? Are they producing for you?'

'Oh, some.'

'Great.' There had been an early suggestion that Deem might come in as 'consultant' on *Broken Light* at a splendid fee, so preempting legal bother, libel hazards. Yes, a kind of hush money, and a standard safeguard when making factually based movies. But this could have led to scrutiny of the script by Deem and his wife; particularly his wife – an over-educated niggler, as Burston heard it. The film might never have reached production. He had advised against the consultant idea and it was dropped. Burston said: 'No, not an outright, positive term, Louise. And this is surely our brief: to present David's suicide as a glorious enhancing event?'

Burston was proud of that – 'glorious enhancing event'. You had to do it when dealing with writers. Whatever else, be flagrantly crude, be idiotic. D.L.O. had told him this, a decade or so ago: 'Ted, act moron.' At first, Burston had not been able to accept it. He feared that if you offended a writer's sensibilities by demanding some gross piece of script or revision, he or she would refuse, might even ditch the project. Their artistic pride was notorious. God, suicide as a 'glorious enhancing event'! He could imagine Louise chortling over this with colleague writers and all of them telling one another with tears in their eyes that it was 'so typical'.

But Burston had discovered D.L.O. was right. Most writers liked to be confronted with the outrageousnesses of the film trade's requirements. Yes, *liked* them, *needed* them. They felt safely and undeniably separate, while taking the cheques. Movie people could be regarded as brutally commercial, hilariously tunnel-visioned, hugely farcical. Writers knew themselves to be artistically, not commercially, driven, wide-ranging in their outlook, soul-blessed by the values of good literature. For the sake of survival, they occasionally needed to put up with *lumpen*, loutish functionaries like Ted Burston, whose excesses made them vastly quaint and therefore no menace to a writer's true Being. The Burstons had to be matter-of-factly humoured as part of the contract, that was all, then shelved.

Six

Ted Burston's telephone call had come as Louise was reading to Clara and Clifford Deem from the typescript of her book:

When Andrew Pax was hanged in the yard of Pentonville Prison, London, at 7 a.m. on January 2 1941 it brought to an end a process of investigation, pursuit, interrogation and conviction which had begun four years earlier and which was conducted more or less alone by one secret service officer, Clifford Deem, and himself a Cambridge graduate of Pax's generation.

The two Deems were sitting close together on a green leather settee, their Home Counties' faces eager and their eyes on Louise, like people watching a TV quiz and intent on beating each other to the answers. Clara said: 'It's the beginning of a chapter, is it? I like this method of telling things – the placing of the pay-off, as it were, first, and then the linear approach to it through flashback, I

49

assume. Professional. It's like that film, *The Pledge*, we went to in Lisbon, Cliff, where you see Jack Nicholson as a drunk while the credits show, and before you know what pushed him that way. I'm glad you called Clifford an officer, not at agent, as some have. "Agent" always seems to me a bit of a smudge. Cliff's a Cambridge double First, you know, plus a Blue or two. "Agent" doesn't seem plangent enough.'

Pax walked with calm dignity and in silence the twenty odd paces of stone-floored prison corridor to the door of the prison yard. It was then a further twelve paces to the fifteen wooden steps leading to the platform where he was guided on to the drop trap door and a cloth hood fastened over his face and head. The noose was then placed around his neck.

'Those numbers – so brilliantly precise, so authentic-seeming,' Clara said. 'It's the Ian Fleming Bond technique, isn't it: describe the background with exhaustive care so as to make the excesses of the plot seem firmly based and credible? Prose a bit encumbered with definite articles? I don't know about Pax's calm and dignity. We heard two changes of trousers, didn't we, Clifford? And then they gave it up as a bad job.' Her cheeks shone on the word 'trousers'. 'We also heard of frogmarching, and a long tussle on the steps. A warder's arm fractured, Pax's face bleeding, an ear possibly torn.'

Deem said: 'People put out these tales – the calmly dignified, and the other. Such accounts are purposeful. Wartime. Propaganda's vital. This was a traitor, so some would want him shitting himself at the end, because treachery is base and its practitioners must be shown as unclean. But this was also a country with good standards, worth defending, so it might not be *à propos* to make an execution sound messy and barbaric.'

'But for heaven's sake, which is right?' Louise yelled. 'None of the execution party are alive now, are they? Where do I ask?'

'Oh, *right*?' Deem said. 'You're OK on the paces, I expect. Right is another matter.'

'I stick to the trousers change,' Clara said.

'Right is what is right for your book, isn't it, Louise?' Deem asked. 'Not an absolute term. Your subject is Pax. He has to seem at least prima facie worthwhile – someone important enough to merit the kind of pursuit and so on described later in the chapter, I expect.' He turned to Clara and spoke ploddingly, like a teacher. 'Louise's readers wouldn't want him with dirty trousers in the second sentence of this episode. Books set up their own rules, require their own omissions. Who was it said all writing was a matter of editing out? Rushdie?'

'He didn't do enough of it,' Clara replied.

Deem said: 'To make Pax look insignificant or odious too soon would undermine the method of back-to-front tale-telling you spoke of. This is technique.'

The trip to Portugal was part of Louise's piecemeal work method. When doing a biography, she would check every section with its main sources, then rewrite it at once in what she hoped would be final shape, no matter at what point in the book it would eventually appear. She hoped freshness and energy would come that way. Then she would ask the source whether her final version was sound.

Louise had already visited the Deems once before in their villa on a hill outside Tavira. Now, she was back with the re-writes. Some of what she read they had provided on that first visit. And some of it came from elsewhere and she wanted their view of it – or, more particularly, his.

The Deems' nearest neighbour was a famed Portuguese professional soccer player in an enormous house a little above them on the hill, protected by a loud St Bernard. Clifford seemed proud of this proximity, though he had never met the star. Both Deem and his wife were convinced that to live alongside such a figure made them true parts of the Portuguese scene and brought reflected distinction. Deem, of course, possessed distinctions of his own, and the film had dealt with them in its coarse way. The book would deal with them, too, though maybe in a different tone. But Deem admired the footballer's eminence. It was simpler, safer, open and unpolitical and brought in more cash. Louise did not know a thing about soccer and, as far as she could make out, the Deems knew less. It was the man's *gloire* that tickled them and his secure spot in the local scene.

Louise thought she could understand Clifford's envy of the soccer icon. Deem might want escape. Perhaps he longed to be someone else, and thoroughly someone else, not just an ancient Brit plonked down on this foreign hummock to get some sun, quiet and olive oil cooking in retirement. The film demonized Clifford and, even if he hadn't seen it, he might have heard whispers, read reviews. In any case, perhaps he actually felt a bit like a demon himself, but wanted to ditch such self-blame by going native here, as native as he could; and as native as he could meant claiming closeness to the hero up the dirt road.

If Donald Pleasence had been younger and willing to wear a wig he could have done Deem, the savagely clever and determined persecutor, in *Broken Light*. They did put

Barry Cass in the part: Cass with that famed talent for portraying fixation in an off-colour cause. Hadn't he done Iago and Sandy Vallem, the charismatic evangelist?

'Are you going to read some more to us?' Clara cried excitedly.

'If you like,' Louise said.

'Oh, yes, grand. But rest a while. Let your voice recoup. Perhaps when we go back to the house.' They were in the garden. 'We love being read to, don't we, Cliff? Audio-book fans – very much so, *Crime and Punishment*, *Wuthering Heights*, some Anthony Trollope. Perhaps the life of the actor you did will get on tape. I'd like to hear that.'

Deem said: 'I expect you'll have to tinker a bit with his Life, Louise – in view of the death, I mean, if that's not gibberish. Portuguese papers gave it a lot of space. Gale was genuinely big-time, was he? Suicide's damned unsatisfactory. I lost a couple of people that way. It puts one's work into quite a different light. Even a broken light. But as you know, Louise.'

'Do I?'

'One or two people,' Deem replied.

'What sort of people?' Louise asked.

'These would be people one was quite closely involved with.'

'Cliff ran into all sorts.'

'How do you mean, "lost" these people?' Louise replied.

54

'That's it, lost them.'

'You were hunting them and they evaded you by killing themselves?' Louise asked.

'Some of that kind were very highly strung,' Clara said.

'Whoops,' Clifford said.

'Nervy,' Clara replied.

'I suppose in that sense, your lad was excellently cast, Louise,' Deem said. 'Edgy enough to kill himself.'

'It was an Open Verdict,' Louise replied.

'Clifford was never obliged to attend any inquest of those who gassed themselves after his inquiries,' Clara said. 'Or pills. There was no public side to his work, you see. Some folk have tried to define Cliff's skill. Well, the film did. In its way. I have to say, most miss the essence. That is, his honest savagery. It would be an intellectual savagery mainly, though occasionally spilling over. He was very rarely ordered to turn physically destructive. Not ordered to. As far as I know he wasn't. That's so, isn't it, Cliff?'

'People like Pax – they were kids: amateurs against a machine. I liked that,' he replied.

'But doesn't it sound McCarthyite?' Louise asked.

'I liked the assurance that the country could organize its own security.'

'But doesn't it sound McCarthyite?'

'You've got your stock of fucking labels and you'll stick them on, I suppose,' he said.

'We saw off those flibbertigibbets nearly half a century before the collapse of the Wall saw off their grab-all successors.'

'But if they were only flibbertigibbets, why pursue them to their deaths, one way or the other?' Louise replied. It was a clammy May evening and they had dined on braised goat in the garden. Now they were drinking coffee.

Deem said: 'One simply identified him, stalked him, finished him. None of it all that difficult. The film made things too complicated.'

'You've actually seen it, then? I'm never sure.'

'Didn't I tell you we had, last time?'

'Yes, but I thought, maybe politeness only.' Ted and Panopticon Films had invited him to the gala opening in London with expenses covered, but he politely declined. Indifference kept Deem away – that's how Louise read it.

'Saw the film in Faro,' he said. 'One or two quite good moments. Subtitles. Decent sense of period. The war and pre.'

'Clifford was never called up to the Army or anything,' Clara said. ' "Reserved occupation." Spy-catcher.'

'Did they pick you to deal with Pax because you'd been at Cambridge yourself?' Louise asked. 'Caius, wasn't it?'

'I had the feel of the place.'

'But you were never—'

'Not an Apostle, no. Wrong college, for a start.'

'Pax was at the wrong college, too. But exceptionally bright.'

'Oh, Clifford was bright. He went up very young.'

'Scholarship people like Pax and myself were two a penny at Cambridge.'

'They'd have been fools to waste Cliff in one of the Services by conscripting him,' Clara said. 'Obviously his kind of work could earn no decorations and he'll never get one of those fine obits in the *Daily Telegraph*: "Brigadier Vernon (Rusty) Coupland-Coup was awarded an immediate M.C. on the field of battle when as a young captain he-de-da-de-da-de-da."' She stood and walked to the edge of the garden. From there she could look down to orange and lemon groves and the strung-out village of Arco. It was as though she wanted to say that if Britain could not value Clifford properly they would seek their own place to be put out to grass on, thank you kindly.

The sun had gone and it became too dark to read outside. They went back into the house and sat among the Deems' bulky, shiny, any-period Portuguese furniture. The wooden pieces were no worse than the equivalent stuff in France or Spain, possibly influenced by elaborate monumental masonry in graveyards. Louise put her script open on the table, which was fashioned in some red-ginger timber and big enough for a banqueting hall.

Clara said: 'We remembered material we didn't give you last time, Louise. Gossip we got around the time and since said Pax was in a large cell, as much as twenty feet square, but walled only at one end. The other three sides were bars, so he could be watched in case of suicide attempts – our recurrent topic today, it seems. I don't know whether this clicks with what you've been told, Louise. Our version has Pax rushing about on the last days before he was stretched, throwing himself at the bars, clinging to them like a zoo ape, screaming confessions and denials, chucking up the really quite good food they gave him, although rationing was certainly in place by then. Genuine meat and thick cream with dessert.'

'But who are these facts *from*?' Louise asked. 'A warder talked to you? The hangman? The governor? A padre?'

'Remember, my dear, Cliff was in the information trade. We liked to know the truth. Felt entitled to at least that.'

'And *is* this the truth?' Louise said. Nobody replied. She began to read again, now some paragraphs about the selection of Deem by the Intelligence service – background Clifford had given her on the first visit. She felt both Deems become bored, so skipped ahead.

> The identification and then the pursuit began at Cambridge University in 1935. In this year, Pax, the gifted grammar-school boy with an Open Scholarship in Classics, arrived at Christ's College.

'Probably a member of the C.P. even then,' Deem said. 'You'll make that plain? Apostles of the thirties didn't understand any other kind of brightness. No, no, that might be overstating. Obviously, many of them were brought up in very successful capitalist, aristocratic households. But they were at war with all that now. They elected people into the Apostles who had Leftish views like their own. Of course. People who might be useful one day and who would permit no return of the Apostles' character to mere aestheticism.'

> Clifford Deem believed, and still believes, that Pax was already a Communist and earmarked for recruitment by Moscow when he arrived at Christ's. But now he was officially taken into the Cambridge University cell of the party. Such enlistments were a feature of Cambridge life in the 1930s, and par-

ticularly for the more gifted students. Many of the recruits were no doubt sincere, but it was also culturally and socially 'smart' to be a Communist.

'Fifteen steps up to a gibbet is a monstrous lot for a man to climb voluntarily and unpressured to his violent death,' Deem said. 'Did even Charles the first make it up fifteen when he nothing common did or mean?'

Some of the most distinguished undergraduates of the period were proselytizing Communists: for instance, John Cornford, an immensely promising poet, later killed fighting on the Government side in the Spanish Civil War.

Clara Deem stood and walked to a huge sideboard against the far wall, in the same glinting, ginger-red wood as the table. She rummaged there for a while and produced from one of the drawers what Louise saw was a tattered scrapbook with faded floral covers. 'Lighting on this the other day was what prompted more memories. Come see,' she said and, returning, placed the book open on the table.

Feeling somehow scared, Louise moved from where she had been sitting and stood alongside Clara, who began to turn the early pages. Mostly, they seemed to contain glued-in, old-style scenic coloured postcards of holiday resorts, names of the places in white or blue script at the bottom: Weston-super-Mare, Bognor, Looe, Mevagissey. Pencil or crayon sketches of pets were fixed on other pages. Louise saw several portraits of what appeared to be the same cat, two of a spaniel, and two of a large blue-grey Angora rabbit. The dog and the rabbit had their names printed underneath in curly, affectionate script: Cosmo and Algynon.

'Here,' Clara said. She had turned a couple more pages of child and baby photographs and stood back from the table. The book lay open at its exact centre. On the left page was displayed a piece of official-looking, close-lined, yellow foolscap paper. It had a small O.H.M.S. insignia top right. This sheet showed a drawing in purple ink which at first puzzled Louise. Possibly influenced by the animal portraits, she thought for a moment it must be a zoo cage.

Then she realized some details were wrong for that and suddenly saw this must be the death-row cell Clara had spoken about. It was well done: perspectives right and the three barred sides with what looked like exactly the same number of uprights and a regular distance from one another. Fore-grounded were a small table and straight-backed chair. Behind, she saw a bed and wash-stand with a closed slop bucket underneath.

In the area outside was another, bigger table at which two uniformed warders sat, both gazing towards the cage. To their left was a heavy door with an eye-level grille. This might lead to the rest of the prison and the execution yard. Inside the cage and clinging to the bars, feet off the ground, was a male human form in baggy clothes, its face a blank. But the hands had been skilfully done, although the scale was small. If it had not been for these, Louise would have had to agree with Clara's description of the prisoner as like a captive ape.

A quarto piece of faded, unlined paper was stuck on the facing page. It also carried an O.H.M.S. shield. Louise saw browned drawing pin holes at each corner. A few typed lines said Andrew Graham Pax had been duly executed at 7.12 a.m. on January 2 1941 and was pronounced dead at 7.26 a.m. There were six signatures, all bold and legible. Was that typist still around? How had the Deems acquired this piece of history? And why? To gloat? Deem was the hunter, after all, and Pax the hunted. This would show him trapped.

Louise and Clara sat down again, leaving the book open on the table. 'That dog Cosmo was a real caution, wasn't he, Cliff? Such moods!' Clara laughed for a while and then, as if unable to resist, stood once more and went to the scrapbook. She turned the pages back to Cosmo and stared at him, nodding and sucking her teeth with amusement. Obviously, she recalled many examples of spaniel moodiness. Leaving the book open at Cosmo, she resumed her chair. 'Oh, in those fairly simple early days of the war it was quite something – I mean, exciting, Louise – to be getting one's love life from a spy-taker. There were stupid folk who commented on Cliff's not being in uniform and around London so much, but one knew the whys and wherefores. I'm sure it appears an anti-romantic notion, but there *is* something crucial about the status of the man in one's bed: I refer to status in the generally recognized, current scale of things. I expect, for instance, the obvious intimacy entailed in ghosting for some of these star Lives would shift over into full relationships, would it, Louise? Status, you see. This must be gratifying for you, though your looks would bring plentiful offers, anyway, I'm certain.' She gave a congratulatory grin. 'Now do read some more, would you? Oh, would you?'

Among prominent Communists at Cambridge as well as Cornford there were James Klugmann, a talented modern languages undergraduate; and the don, Roy Estham, also a poet. Later Estham became professor of literature in Oxford and Harvard and, by an extraordinary turn, a member of the Order of Merit, one of Britain's highest distinctions. Estham, like some other prominent Communists, renounced membership of the party after the 1939 Russo-Nazi treaty, but is thought to be the recruiter who put Moscow in touch with Pax in 1936.

Clara said: 'There is a sense in which Clifford grew quite fond of Roy – another one who apparently took the terrible way out eventually. Yes, rather eventually.'

' "Apparently"?' Louise asked. 'Is there any doubt he killed himself? I've never heard it questioned before.'

'None,' Deem said. 'Clara's being provocative.'

'And yet it's so difficult to understand,' Clara replied. 'His poetry was the most fiddly pulp, true, but people don't kill themselves for that. They're unlikely even to realize it *is* pulp. Did Auden kill himself, for heaven's sake? This was the late 1960s when Roy did it – more than twenty years after Andy Pax snuggled under the hood. Admittedly, Clifford had to put the frighteners on Estham a little just before Pax's trial. That's right, isn't it, darling? But, again, nothing specifically physical. Just words, Louise. Estham's knowledge of the Cambridge C.P. and its Kremlin connections was unequalled. Clifford discovered pretty much everything about Burgess, Maclean and Blunt – even Philby – via Estham. Naturally, nobody would listen, until too late. Clifford was an officer, but a mere *field* officer, not someone in immediate touch with Cabinet people. Cliff didn't compel Estham to go into court and give evidence against Pax, but the insights he provided were vital.'

'Shame killed him,' Deem said.

'He had astonishing success. O.M. as early as his fifties. Only twenty-four of them at any one time. Queen's personal gift. Graham Greene? People of that calibre, anyway. And this despite the poetry. Did you ever read that rot-gut, volume-length thing, *In a Day's Redemptive Purlieus*, Louise? *And* despite his political record.'

'Yet guilt festered,' Deem said.

'Guilt at shopping Pax?' Louise asked. 'Or at landing Andrew in peril by recruiting him?' Much of what she heard now was new. She would have to re-work and expand several chapters.

'There were many positive aspects to Roy,' Deem said.

'Am I likely to deny that?' Clara replied.

'Did you know him well, then, Clara?' Louise asked.

'Naturally, someone like Cliff was never going to be an O.M. or anything else, and not just because he didn't write verse. His only reward had to be to see people like Pax stinking and roped. Or to hear of Roy Estham dead. Cliff went to Roy's funeral just to check whether he'd get holy ground.'

'I don't think you capture the Cambridge tone of that time at all badly, Louise,' Deem said. 'The Red cachet was well established by my day and it strengthened as the thirties went on and the Depression grew worse. Plus Spain and Adolf and Musso.'

Louise said: 'Two kinds of recruiting took place at Cambridge, did they? Bright boys like Pax were invited into the Communist network, and bright boys like you were invited into secret government service. Any mistakes? Were the destinations mixed up sometimes?'

'The C.P. was all right – impeccably be-haved, entirely modish, generally harmless,' Deem replied. 'We were interested in the contacts beyond.' He gave a large wave with one hand, encompassing at least Soviet Russia.

'How did it work, Clifford?' Louise asked. 'Did you target known key recruiters like Estham and follow up on the undergrads they seemed most interested in?'

Now Clara used *her* arm. She punched the air twice like a footballer after scoring and turned with a grin to Deem. 'Oh, that's lovely, isn't it, Cliff? Louise, do you realize it's the first time you've used his first name, though you've stayed with us twice – and very welcome to stay, certainly? Shows a pleasant ease in you at last. It would be a long way to come, come twice, and never call Clifford Clifford, regardless of what might have happened, and your views. I do hope there's more to Cliff and me than conduits for the life and Life of Andrew Pax. I've a curiosity about you, Louise. I don't know whether Cliff feels the same.'

Clara was a few years younger than Clifford. Tall and bony with her grey hair cut close, and roughly cut, she had big, confident grey eyes and would have looked a natural alongside him at Buck House if only he'd been invited to get the O.M., or even the O.B.E.

Deem said: 'Estham's suicide was a decent act. Late but decent. I don't mean only that slitting yourself in the bath gives nobody much clean-up bother. Principles. Late, though, in that he should never have accepted the O.M. Shoddy. Yet who turns down an O.M.? But having accepted it, he conscientiously recognized finally that ... He saw the farce of it, might even have felt he soiled a respectable Order. I can admire Estham. The poetry's a laugh, yes, but no real harm. I don't hold it against him, or anything else, really.'

Louise re-read:

Estham, like some other prominent Communists, renounced membership of the party after the 1939 Russo-Nazi treaty, but is thought to be the recruiter who put Moscow in touch with Pax in 1936.

The phone rang in the hall and Deem went out to answer it. Louise heard the receiver picked up. Deem said: *'Estou.'*

Clara leaned towards her and spoke quietly: 'Perhaps we shall talk later, you and I only, Louise. I try to make the best of it with Clifford, but—'

Deem reappeared: 'It's for Louise. Ted something. He said he missed us at the London film show, Clara. He'll wait. His firm's paying. I thought I'd recite a Roy poem.' He hit a pose, hands clasped in front of his stomach, feet apart. 'It's called "Breakdown of The Family". Nice piece of assonance.'

Thoughtfully, she's bought a plastic spade –
no bucket – at the beach shop for her lad;
and now she's beaming while he digs again
and flings the sand about like squalls of hail,
or ragged arcs of tracer bullets
from machine guns on the News.
She's glad that Colm,
at only eight, appreciates it's wasting

time to trouble over castle-making
when the towers are born to crumble, fondled
by this tabled tide. Why sweat to build?
Much saner, simpler, take your kicks
through flings.
She rather likes the package in the pining
pair of trunks just finishing a swim; she's
glanced about and thinks his wife looks dim.

'But what significance?' Louise asked. She
did not feel like hurrying to the phone.

'Oh, *significance*,' Deem replied.

'Is it symbolic?' Louise asked.

Deem pointed out towards the hall and
telephone. 'Ted Whatever sounds a nice
chap, Louise.'

'Well, yes,' she said, at last making her way
from the room.

Deem said: 'But you're right. So many do
sound nice.'

Seven

Burston had been pissed off when kept hanging on the line while someone seemed to croak verse not quite audibly, probably in another room. He'd waited, though, needing to get at her about 'melancholy'. When the recitation finished, he thought it might have been a sonnet, with part-rhymes most of the way through until the couplet at the end when there was a trite-sounding, perfect, chiming pay-off instead.

That's how writing was, wasn't it: had to impose its little comment, its point, its supposed truth in blatant form before it did an exit? Form took over. And, of course, the form would be made by whatever was the mode-mood of the here and now. Summers out there, doing the literary trek, thought she could come back with the unquestionable facts for her heavy dose of Pax. What she'd come back with was a version of those days, that's all. *Broken Light* was another version, with just as much chance of being 'fact'.

People like Louise Summers seemed to have trouble recognizing this. In the same way, she'd never really be able to see that the original packaging of David Gale in *We're Rolling* was now grossly inappropriate. Amendments suggested would probably strike her as absurd and comical. OK. Ted could play along, if it helped make her do them. His business was the moment, not alleged pure verities, and he thanked God he understood this. In the case of *Broken Light*, for instance, nobody was going to make a film these days to endorse the thesis that a spy had been rightly strung up. It had to be a corrective, a celluloid cry that injustice was done. You took the mode of the times, *these* times. Occasionally, Ted thought he, himself, would like to turn writer and do something about this whole situation – the movie, the Gale autobiog, the Pax biog – present it all in a novel. And that would be yet another take-it-or-leave-it-but-preferably-take-it-please version. He liked that epitaph Keats had done for himself: 'Here lies one whose name was writ in water.' That really got the temporariness of writers and writing. Wasn't everything writ in water, except for Faulkner's stuff, maybe, which was in whiskey? But, of course, epitaphs were chiselled in stone, and that's where people would read his name. Keats wanted it both ways – humility and *réclame*. Serious bloody writers were all the same, loved multi-meaning and evasiveness.

Ultimately, Louise had picked up the receiver and Ted was able to get in those carefully mulled thoughts to her about 'melancholy'. In his opinion it was a fucking *writerly* word and Summers could stuff it. Today had its own styles for saying things and they were good. He saw himself as their guardian, was proud to be their guardian. He felt the conversation with Louise would definitely go his way. He kept at it. 'You see, Louise, "melancholy" suggests a bit of a wanker – someone obsessed with himself and his own misery. David had this out-going, exuberant side, though, yes, it did prove to be outgoing and exuberant in a suicidal way.' He prized the insaneness of that. She'd be secretly tickled, and disarmed. 'But this is the kind of ... kind of *tension*, even contradictoriness, your revisions have to capture. And let me say I know nobody who could do it better, Louise. Was that old sod reciting doggerel just now? Is his head gone? They're really not giving you unpleasantness because of *Broken Light*? Or they don't talk of redress, courts, anything like that, do they?'

'I might have another look at "melancholy",' she replied. 'You'd prefer your term "exuberant", would you?'

' "Exuberant" is fair. Though, of course, "exuberant" is not necessarily linked to topping oneself, I see that. All kinds of

72

people have exuberance – bishops, hospital matrons, golfers with trophies – but it doesn't follow they're going to kill themselves. Hardly! I'm in your hands where words are concerned, Louise. You'll come up with something, I know. Yet I see this "melancholy" as sort of symptomatic of a wider fault – oh, no, no, no, "fault" is too strong a term – let's say a wider *problem* – yes, problem – a wider problem in the *tone* of the revisions, Louise. What we're after, isn't it, is the kind of noble glory that attaches to some few after self-destruction. The poet who was mentioned, for instance.'

'Dylan Thomas.'

'Him, but also the other you came up with. New to me and his name's gone, I'm afraid.'

'Thomas Chatterton. Suicide at seventeen.'

'Exactly. He's way back in history, right?'

'Eighteenth century,' Louise replied.

'That's all right, I don't mind the past.' He adored that bit of fatuousness, too. It would be crazy to let someone like Louise Summers know you'd heard of Chatterton, the 'marvellous boy', as Wordsworth called him; and had read his work long before the David Gale incident. If writers suddenly discovered you had learning they would see you as more similar to themselves than they'd thought; and then they'd feel entitled to discuss the subtleties of assignments, appeal to your taste and sense of decorum, instead of duly accepting the fucking orders and getting the job done as per. D.L.O. used to say, 'Once the bastards find out your bedside reading is *Finnegan's Wake* you become as much a nobody as they are, Ted.'

In fact, when Burston spoke of the increased public sympathy which would come from a re-written *We're Rolling*, he'd actually had in mind that stupendously touching portrait by Wallis of Chatterton in the Tate. It showed the young poet, wearing blue silk breeches and white shirt, poignantly dead on a couch, scattered fragments of his destroyed works on the floor nearby: the picture used on the jacket of Peter Ackroyd's fine novel, *Chatterton*. There could naturally be no exactly equivalent dust-cover picture of Gale on the new *We're Rolling*; but this was the kind of sad yet resonant image the book should seek. Incidentally, was *We're Rolling* a rather crudely bullish title in the new atmos? Burston thought a nice idea for the jacket would be a serious head and shoulders of David, with the faint sense of a gallows behind, though unoccupied.

'My feeling, you see, Louise, is that the urge to self-destruction should be linked in your revisions even more strongly, more explicitly, to the themes of *Broken Light*. Certainly you've part suggested this in the fresh material. And to someone like myself, familiar with the intricacies, the hints are effective, even telling. I appreciate the delicacy: the understated precision for which you are rightly famed, Louise. But I do think as far as the general, worldwide public are concerned – and we are talking about a massive potential readership which would include comparatively unsophisticated Third World countries – you know, film and book interest is opening up there more and more all the time – and as far as this kind of rather basic readership is concerned I feel that the undeniable connection between David's decline into top-grade despair and the appalling injustice of Pax's execution must be more boldly given. This pure communion between David and Andrew Pax – and I definitely do not see "communion" as too charged a word – this communion across the decades is, I'm sure you'll agree, a most moving and, indeed, majestic tragic theme. We must not let it slip away between the lines. Understatement is certainly a valid literary mode, but in a work like this, understatement—'

'Can go fuck itself,' Louise said. 'I'll take another look as soon as I'm back in London.'

'There's some time-tabling pressure.'

'A few days.'

'Don't you have a copy of the revised Life with you?'

'I think so.'

'Of course. You're attitude is always professional. None more so. It would be a real help if you could prioritize this and fax me corrections, Louise. We're talking enormous potential. I know you're engaged with the other project – Pax. Possibly, though, that doesn't have the same urgency. Not to be insensitive, I hope, but Pax has been dead more than sixty years. A few weeks' delay won't hurt the biography.'

'Well, I'll see.'

'Have the Deems got fax? There'll be one in the town. Truthfully, you get no aggro from them? Are they listening?'

'Great here.'

'It figures. He thinks he won, I imagine: saw off Pax, helped the O.M. prof to suicide, and now hears that an actor who played Pax as victimized saint has also done himself. Deem's laughing, but in a wry, dry, rather British fashion I should think.'

Eight

From his own time as an under-graduate at Caius College, Clifford Deem had already heard of the power-ful political influence on students of the literature don Roy Estham. He was a prominent leftist thinker who organized regular public meetings in Cambridge at which well known Socialist and Communist speakers starred. Estham was also an Apostle. Throughout more or less the whole thirties decade, this kind of vigorous left-wing activity and proselytizing by a university teacher were not regarded as in any way reprehensible or even unusual. Many Cambridge scholars held that this was the only respectable – in fact the only tolerable – political standpoint to take. Some of the privately wealthy and even 'landed' members of the university – both staff and undergraduates – actively supported left-wing causes, convinced by the weight of intellectual argument.

Naturally, dons like Estham realized that the security services would be interested in them. But they were so sure of the power of their case – and, at least in some instances, of the superiority of their minds – that they did not worry about being the subject of MI5 dossiers. Several, in fact, boasted of it, including Estham. This was a battle honour. It brought them status – status where it mattered, among their scholastic peers – and brought them even a kind of glamour.

Louise had rejoined the Deems in their sitting room after talking to Ted and was reading again.

'Oh, I love well-managed parentheses!' Clara cried.

Deem said: 'I don't know if you understand this, Louise, but when you've interrogated someone to breaking point he may develop a chronic dependence, especially someone as previously assured as Estham. You hold his soul. He needs to come now and then and see it's in good hands: checking his pledge with a pawnbroker. People like Estham think that because you've destroyed him you can rebuild him. They believe you know their structure and can stick it all together again. In a way, I suppose you *do* get to see how they're made. Mainly, though, interrogation's only a matter of pulling some tricks – not psychology.' He was sitting very upright in a leather armchair. Perhaps his back gave him trouble. That could happen to people who had been athletic. He had a round, snub, porky face, the eyes blue and hooded, not unfriendly but not warm, either. It was one of those faces that could have belonged to someone missing at least a bit in the head, or someone brilliant. Flimsy-looking pince-nez glasses hung on a bright pink tape around his neck. Louise wondered if she was ever going to understand him properly. He grunted: 'But my training was in how to take folk apart. No lessons on patching them up. This demolition firm wasn't also a construction outfit.'

'So, you must have seen a lot of Estham after Andrew Pax's execution?' Louise said. 'I hadn't realized that. A sort of friendship, regardless?'

'Regardless?' he replied.

'Oh, surely it's extraordinary. This dependence – given that you'd been an enemy.'

'I told you – routine,' Deem replied. 'Psychology casebooks are stuffed with examples.'

'Why didn't you mention any of this earlier?' Louise asked. God, if she hadn't come on the second visit she might never have heard it.

Deem said: 'Not something I'd want in your Pax biography – Estham's collapse. This is off the record now.' His voice took on unction. 'I've come to feel I can trust you, Louise.'

He was of a kind and of a trade who would trust nobody, not even when the trade was so many years away now. His eyes remained evasive beneath their thick lids. She felt baffled. 'But why keep it out?' she asked. 'It's interesting. Humanizing. And so very much part of the story.'

'Cliff would say, "Fuck humanizing",' Clara replied. 'If I may speak for him momentarily.' She smiled at Deem, requesting permission. He stared at her. 'Cliff believes he needs no humanizing, ta ever so. Simply, he wouldn't want you to publish things that might diminish Roy Estham because, don't you see, *his* status contains some of Cliff's.'

'When he turned he became our man,' Deem said. 'An investment. It would be unprofitable now – even now, an age after – unprofitable, yes, to make him look like a mental patient out on licence, required to report. Victory against a nincompoop is worthless. It implies there was no real danger from him.'

'And was there?' Louise asked.

'He would come to our house,' Clara said. 'Yes, often.'

'So *you* would see a lot of him, too, Clara?' Louise asked.

'He was so full of self-recrimination about shopping Pax,' Deem said. He crumpled his crumpled face a deal more and did an imitative whine. '"Was what I did right, Cliff? But aren't you bound to say yes? Tell me it was right, Cliff. Is it improper to ask that of you? But didn't I have an inalienable duty to Andrew?" Louise, in some respects it was grotesque, this Oxbridge tutorial voice, usually so one-up and lavish on vowel sounds, yet squashed into ghastly, quavering pleafulness.'

'One would hear some of it through the wall,' Clara said. 'I couldn't be in the same room. Even so long after the event, Cliff believed there had to be secrecy: decorum. I didn't always get the words, but I'd catch the tone of Cliff's replies, purring, comforting, deceptive. I knew he would be taking Estham gently over the makeshift ethics of betrayal, telling him in sweetly evasive and convincing terms what Roy longed to hear. There was something about Roy, something elegant, notwithstanding that fucking poetry, and something needy, of course. Needy, yes, yes.'

Deem stared at her again for a while. Louise struggled to understand what was being said. Deem spoke: 'Estham would go away after one of these sessions at our house

81

more or less restored, wounds bound up, identity salvaged, and he'd last like that another three or four months, collecting honorary degrees the way some men collect girls' pubic hair, and beautifully enunciating his tortuous truisms from platforms worldwide. Then he'd arrive on our doorstep once more, weeping, snot-flecked and soul-buggered. Start again.'

'I sent Roy Estham an early version of my drawing of Pax sweaty on the bars,' she said. 'I wanted to show him that I understood his grief and *Angst* and shame – the sketch being, well ... frank. We had a complex kind of relationship, Roy and I.' There was a vivid, eye-bright brazenness to her, the kind of fierce zest that would have been eerie in someone younger, but seemed all right for an old fighter making the best of things. 'But that was years before Roy's death. Oh, yes, years. It was not the kind of portraiture one could get spot-on at a first attempt, or even third or fourth. I don't know whether you've seen any of Roy's posthumous papers, Louise. Perhaps it was among them still. On the same kind of government stationery. It's not something I'd want to approach the widow about now, is it?'

Clifford said: 'Yes, there are at least two ways of looking at why Estham did himself in. Perhaps mixed, as I've suggested. The prevailing view is shame over betraying Pax and others to us, of course; people suppose this rankled, would not leave him alone, and was somehow sharpened by the grandiose absurdity of his O.M. But perhaps one also has to ask what "betrayed" means. After all, this was a don with influence over students. It might not be just the matter of giving Pax to the gallows. In addition, did he betray Andrew Pax and the rest by taking their natural, fashionable, juvenile, innocuous Red fancies and shaping them into the workaday stuff of active treason? Did he destroy this lad in more than one way? That, too, might make the award of the O.M. agonizing to him: it was after all for "merit" in his country's concerns. Nobody denies Estham's sensitivity. He lectured on Keats. Irony would enter his soul. He had self-awareness and a conscience.' Deem stopped, as if expecting Louise to question why he should give Estham any degree of praise. When she did not speak, he went on: 'They owned a place in Hampshire, another in Edinburgh and a villa in Corfu. Who can ever discover what the true motives for suicide are? This is generally a sweetly private moment between a man or woman and his, her knife, stove, razor, gun, pills. You're no doubt faced with the same obscurities in your film star. Oh, you and others will guess and theorize, but you can't in the least intrude. Not authentically.'

Clara said: 'He was familiar with deodorants years before they grew commonplace.'

'No, she didn't really send Estham the cell sketch,' Deem said.

Clara gazed at him, full of cheerful smiles. 'Cliffy hates to think I might be malevolent, Louise. I can understand. Well, would you like to be stuck on a foreign hill with Madam Malice? But I did send it. Was the drawing among his papers, Louise?'

'I don't remember it.'

'Destroyed by the damn wife/widow,' Clara replied. 'She would realize it put me very much one up. Knowing how to distress him.'

'Look, this is wonderful, living stuff – your motives for sending and the impact on Estham. It could be important to the book, Clara,' Louise said.

'Of course it could.' She spoke with throbbing enthusiasm, as though they were writing the biography in partnership and she had just come up with a clinching piece of research. Everything she did or said was performed with rich intensity. This was not just someone ageing and determined to show spirit to the end: Louise felt Clara had decided early in life to act animated. Perhaps she wanted to offset what might otherwise have been the dull solemnity of her looks. She had a long, pale, Virginia Woolf style face, and that snooty acreage between eye and mouth on each side of the know-all nose could have killed any attempt at liveliness, if Clara had not countered so hard.

'She didn't send the drawing,' Deem said. 'Clara teases. Clara dreams.'

'Which house did you send it to?' Louise asked.

'House?' Clare said.

'If they had three.'

'There were occasions when I thought he could be irreparably mad,' Deem said.

'And it was someone as fragile as this you posted the death cell drawing to, Clara?'

Mrs Deem wrinkled her drooping, long nose to signify humour. 'Oh, it was a jape, that's all.'

'What was?' Louise asked.

'Sorry?'

'Do you mean you sent it to him as a jape? Or was it a jape when you told me you'd sent it, but didn't really?'

'There you are then. As I say, I wasn't present at the sessions between Roy and Cliff, but one can deduce,' Clara replied. 'Obviously the essence of their discussion would be whether it was more wholesome to betray one's friend/protégé or one's country. You'll know that bleat from the old truffle merchant and boy-sniffer, Morgan Forster, novelist – another Apostle.' Now she made her voice give a pious, pronunciamento squeak: ' "If it was a choice between betraying my country and betraying my friend I

85

hope I'd have the courage to betray my country." '

Deem, correcting her in that pedantic growl again, said: ' "If I had to choose between betraying my country and betraying my friends, I hope I should have the guts to betray my country." '

' "Have the guts." Funny old locker-room language, isn't it?' Clara replied.

'Were you fond of Roy Estham, Clara?' Louise asked.

Deem said: 'The good interrogator is an opportunist and catches a moment, Louise. With Estham, the moment was the signing of the Russo-Jerry pact in 1939. Suddenly, he tumbled into patriotism, like Lucifer dropping from the presence of God. All the world looked different to him, including Pax, whom he happened to have made the way he was. Come June 1941 and Russia's a friend again. Estham would now like to change his mind once more. It was logical but not really sensible. I had to spend the next twenty odd years off and on telling him there are no political constancies only tides and *de facto* modes, and that it was one of these that killed Pax. What's fine as a creed one month is unspeakable the month after, or the month before. It's terrifying for someone like Estham to hear that all doctrines come and go. I told him to read an essay by Orwell on Dickens – remember it? Of course. This is a very political creature – Orwell – defending Dickens for not being political, because Orwell says, political values have next to no durability. Estham was once possessed by a brilliant faith in an eternal dogma, you see. His little house fell down, and so he kept coming back to ours.'

'And you gave real help, despite everything?' Louise asked.

'You've said something like that before. Despite what?' Deem asked.

'Despite his role as recruiter and so on,' Louise replied. 'And yours as his breaker.'

'Oh, all that. One tried to help him,' Deem said.

'Oh, did one, really? Really?' Clara fluted.

Again Louise struggled to interpret.

Deem said: 'I told Estham and retold Estham that his country had recognized him as a true son – the professorships, degrees, respectful treatment of his verse and eventually the O.M. A true son. I said this was clearly where his real affinities lay. In a sense I believed that myself. So many people could not be wrong about him. His temporary disaffection from Britain, his snaring of Pax and others, were quaint digressions. I stressed to him that to dwell on guilt was sentimental, fatuous. This would generally do the trick for a while. For a while. I couldn't be the only influence on him. Don't forget that, alongside the leftist upsurge in the sixties –

we all know about this – but there was also a strong corrective movement, preaching the hazards of Red infiltration in Britain. Late in the decade would come Ian Greig's frightener about university Commies, *The Assault on the West*, and the thinking was around well before that. His book, and the ones that followed, brilliantly formulated it, that's all. This kind of anxiety about the survival of Britain got to Estham, I know. He'd mention it. No irony, either. One could see that at times in the sixties he felt grossly culpable for furthering the Moscow cause, albeit a long while before. I'm no psychologist, myself, but I see him as having been intolerably split in his attitude to past behaviour, and hence the turn for relief to death.'

'Neat,' Clara replied.

Nine

'I will come to you in the night.'

To Louise the words sounded either breathily romantic or biblical or both: recalling the *Song of Solomon*, was it: 'Open to me, my sister, my love?' The words were whispered, but precise. Louise did not reply. To say 'OK' or 'Right' or 'Looking forward to it' might have seemed flippantly matter-of-fact. To say, 'No thanks, Clara,' was out of the question. Just 'Yes' could have been given a bit of throb and juiciness, perhaps, but Louise jibbed at that.

Then Clara quietly spoke again: 'In the night I will come to you.' Like this, with night up front, the thought was undoubtedly steamy: say pinched from Berta Ruck or *The Desert Song*. Now, Louise would have liked to giggle, but Clara was standing close and watching. Louise did a quick inventory, to check whether Clara had a hand on her anywhere. The two of them had just stepped into the wide, handsome panelled hall of the house. Giggling would have been off key here.

Louise had left the Deem chapters of her

biography on the table alongside Clara's jail-
house art: two attempts on paper to get at
what Pax was, lying close to each other, but
not comfortably. Lying and lying, both? Oh,
Jesus. In the hall she breathed a light, sweet,
cheery aroma of timber: cedar she thought,
but only because her mind had moved a
moment ago to the Old Testament, with its
quotas of cedars of Lebanon. In fact, she had
no idea what cedar would smell like, except
probably pleasant. How could the mind get
at the truth of *anything* if its processes and
decisions were so ungovernable?

Out of earshot, Clifford Deem was three-
quarters of the way up the bare polished
stairs on his way to bed. He stopped for a
moment, leaning on the banister rail, and
turned to stare down at Clara and Louise.
But it was as if he failed to see them. And
perhaps he did. The spectacles still hung on
their tape around his neck. To Louise, it did
not seem a matter of his eyes, though. More
his mind, and possibly his memory. She felt
he was wrapped in something that blocked
out Clara and herself. He reached up slowly
and touched his right cheek. Was he weeping? Louise could not be sure at that distance. Did ex-secret service officers weep?
That's what being ex was, wasn't it – useless
regret? But *what* did he regret: that he hadn't
disposed of more people like Pax and
Estham; or that he'd been so ferociously

successful?

As they watched him, Clara whispered: 'Please don't feel, Louise, that because you've taken him into the rough past you're responsible for this little breakdown. Oh, no, no. The sod will often put on these shows, especially when people are staying. Cliff has to think of himself as at least basically decent, and possibly even noble. It's got to be self-operated because no other bugger will ennoble him. People stopped on stairs always look dramatic. You'll have seen that in film-making. He can force real tears. In interrogations, when he was acting soft, he'd do that to weaken someone.'

She turned to full volume. 'You all right, Cliff?' He did seem to focus on her then. Deem breathed hard and started climbing again. They followed him upstairs. Clara went ahead of Louise and she saw her and Cliff kiss formally under a pale knights and beasts tapestry fixed to the wall and then go to different rooms. 'None of it can mean a fig to the Portuguese, Cliff, love,' she said, as he left her. 'They were neutral and have been since Napoleon, probably. Why we live here, isn't it? They are our people now and set our standards. The past really is a different country, as someone said. What do these folk know about the meaning of treason *circa* 1941? Nix. Isn't that so, Cliff?' But he did not answer.

In her own room, Louise switched on the pair of lights over her dressing table and brought a copy of the David Gale Life revisions from her suitcase. She'd need to start right away on a hue and cry for 'melancholies'. It was the same fine, big square room she had been given on her last visit, with more panelling and more ginger furniture. There was a bolt on the door but surely it would be brutally rude to use that against Clara, especially in her own home. It was not much of a bolt, anyway. In any case, Clara was probably fit enough to nip out to the garden, climb a drainpipe and come in through the window. 'Open to me, my sister, my love.' No, no, love was not the word. But Louise didn't mind offering Clara a little late companionship.

She read. It was vital to hit the right portentous note in these rehashed sections, and Louise had become rather more intrusive than a ghost should.

Yet about David Gale, even then, as he spoke of the brilliant projects provisionally scheduled for the next few years, one could, if one were alert to the undertones of his justly famous fine voice, and watchful of the shifts of expression in his thoughtful face – yes, one could detect a growing, even overwhelming, melancholy: a deep, unbreakable comradeship with despair. Of course, one might console oneself with the notion that these feelings were merely appropriate to the coming challenges of his career and assume he had taken them aboard in preparation. He longed to try some of the greatest tragic roles and was scheduled to play Antony next year in Camborallini's movie production of Shakespeare's great love drama. He was excited by new translations for the theatre of two tragedies by Aeschylus in which he would star, and by the prospect of taking the male lead – the Duke – in an all-British film production of *The Duchess of Malfi*, after completing *Antony and Cleopatra*. But this excitement did not conceal something in David Gale that went beyond the acting profundities required by such parts. It was as if he had lately glimpsed the appalling harshnesses and intractabilities of real ordinary life for so many people, and had been stricken by a melancholy that not even the glittering agenda before him could dispel. Perhaps if the signs of this melancholy had been clearer and had been countered by the help of family and friends, David Gale might not have been driven into the grim quandary where he felt he must end his life.

Well, yes, Ted could be right: the melancholies did ring out and gang up. Ted generally *was* right about the film trade and its spin-offs. How else did he hold the job? When she seriously thought back to Gale, and tried to recall what it actually was she spotted in him, she knew it had next to nothing to do with melancholy. It was terror. Louise had realized this when she did the original version of his Life but had, of course, kept it out – and out of the revisions, too.

Terror? Louise had seen he knew that protraying Pax in *Broken Light* was the limit of his skills: that he might never make it to such capable acting again. He had peaked. The Aeschylus, Shakespeare and Webster scared him inside out. Scared him suicidal. At twenty-seven he had grown sure he was starting to sink. It might be all right for a boxer to start sinking at twenty-seven, but an actor should be able to expect a future. He had pleaded with Louise to save him: he would ditch his wife. She had not totally understood why he thought she could do all that for him but, in any case, it was not her rôle, and she had told him. He sank further.

Naturally, he could not be described in either version of the Life like that. How would Ted like it if she re-rephrased this bit: 'one could detect a growing, even overwhelming, melancholy: a deep, unbreakable comradeship with despair' ... as 'one could detect a growing, even overwhelming, dread of failure that could have been conquered only, he thought, by leaving his wife and family and setting up home with the hired helper on this Life; as if by writing the Life I had won control of it and could give it direction'?

A crazed bit of fantasy to imagine putting that on paper, obviously. Ted would swoon, and justifiably, if she suggested it. Yet, that's how it had been. She saw similarities with what Clifford said about taking over the personality of Estham through interrogation. Something similar happened between her and Gale through the interview sessions for *We're Rolling*. Or it would have happened, if Louise had allowed it. Personality, character, could be as elusive and shifting as was fact, and just as hard to describe.

Instead of that dream piece, Louise experimented now in pencil on her jotter with replacing 'melancholy' by something more positive. How about: 'concern for Mankind everywhere'. She sketched the full thought as: 'one could detect in David Gale an overwhelming concern for Mankind everywhere: a deep comradeship with all in the world suffering inescapable privation and hardship.'

Then she added:

These new, mature insights had almost certainly come to him through brilliantly entering into the doomed career of Andrew Pax, in Gale's latest, triumphant film, *Broken Light*. Across five decades, this idealistic, victimized young man had somehow conveyed to David a scorchingly powerful sense of mission and selflessness; to the degree that Gale did not want to live on when he saw that such missions were always likely to be frustrated, and such selflessness mortally abused.

So-so. By-the-yard rhetoric? She moved on to the next 'melancholy': 'and he had been stricken by a melancholy that not even the glittering agenda before him could dispel'. Maybe, she could get away with simply replacing the one word here and would not have to re-hash a whole sentence or paragraph. 'Glittering agenda' was worth its place. Ted would like that as crap prose, but purposeful crap prose. Would it be all right if she took out 'melancholy' and substituted, say, 'empathic sadness': 'and he had been stricken by an empathic sadness that not even the glittering agenda before him could dispel'.

'Empathy' was probably still an OK word and un-bewhiskered. Again, Ted would like it. In line with his continuous role as smart but crude company man, he might pretend not to know fully what it meant, but, actually, it would resonate for him. Although David Gale was dead, by dwelling on his feelings for those victimized in life, his death would come to seem an assertion on behalf of others, not a collapse into sloppy, privileged *Angst*. Yes, that should do the trick.

All at once, from somewhere not far away in the house came the sound of shouting, and possibly even of some screaming. The noise was muffled, but Louise thought she could make out the voices of Clara and Cliff. Who else? At first, she read the sounds as raw savagery on both sides: cries that seemed to break uncontrollably from some terribly equal rage and pain. She might have felt like an embarrassed intruder and eavesdropper but, of course, did not. Instead, she listened hard, curious and thrilled. It was as though, after hearing all the clouded interchanges of the evening, she was at last getting something real. Occasionally, she could identify rasping phrases or words that stuck up out of the general, vague, snarling flow, like débris in a flood. Her own name was one of the words. Estham's was another. Both were yelled by Clifford. From him, too, she heard 'hijacked', 'mere tact', 'decorum', 'simple respect', 'puppet'. Some of these words, Clara repeated, perhaps mocking:

'decorum', 'simple respect'. She changed 'mere tact' into 'mere fucking tact'. She screamed 'minions', or it could have been 'millions', and 'trained' and 'fool'. Was Cliff demanding some tact and decorum in her behaviour, cursing her for having hijacked some of the earlier meeting and making him seem a puppet? And did Clara's answer declare she was nobody's minion and that however trained he might have been in some skills he remained a fool?

At the dressing table, Louise stayed hunched over her de-melancholized jotter and very still, afraid to go to the door in case Clara suddenly opened it. That was the thing about biography: people knew you had to nose, but not how much and ruthlessly you had to nose. They could get upset.

The din continued. Were they out on the landing? Would one fling the other over a banister rail, like film fights in Wild West saloons? Or did the noise come from one of the bedrooms? Perhaps a door was open. Why? The volume varied, and not only because the two were occasionally at top voice and sometimes only conversational: it seemed almost as if they moved about, circling each other despite age, like wrestlers or cats, changing the projection of their outbursts.

And then, suddenly, Louise began to feel that, despite what had resembled spasmodic, unpredictable spurts of hullabaloo, there

98

might be a pattern She did not merely mean that some words and phrases recurred. She half-sensed a timing, a shadowy structure to the exchanges, as if they had been put together for best effect by a dramatist. There was a nice pace to things and the climaxes and pauses and low-key moments came to seem organized. She certainly could not have described straight off how the modulating worked, not even if she had brought a stopwatch; but she grew aware of a rhythm, elusive, yet probably trackable if you made notes. Sitting around, waiting for stars to come off the set when she was ghosting, Louise had watched the development of many skilfully scenariod confrontations. She had heard directors and actors suggest an amendment here and there to the dialogue as written, so as to make the drama sharper, the interlocking neater, the passion rounder, the balance less obvious but stronger all the same. Inevitably she had come to learn how screenplays worked, or didn't, and how their sinews and skeletons functioned.

Similarly, these flurries from Clara and Cliff seemed efficiently put together. Had they been used before, with the intrigued listening guest's name adjustable? Clara had spoken of Clifford putting on a show. Did they both do that? For what? In another high tirade from Clara now, Louise distinguished 'betrayal', 'warranted', and then a cumbersome, screeched phrase, 'if so, absolutely mine, not yours'. What? Who? Louise waited for something more from Deem, but nothing. Or perhaps not nothing but a faint, weary, guttural, wordless reply. Deem weeping, weeping for the second time? She could imagine him face down on his bed, or crouched in a corner of the room, an arm across his face blurring the sobs. Weeping like that on the floor could make a fine fade to a scene, especially male weeping. She'd known a top actor thrown off a picture because his weeping fell short. Oh, God, what was true here?

The sounds subsided, falling to what seemed a steady, gentle buzz of ordinary talk, Louise thought there might even be some brief laughter. Then she heard what could be one of them crooning softly, a lullaby-type song, perhaps 'Berceau' by Brahms. The voice seemed to be Cliff's, though she was not sure. It caressed. Afterwards, silence came for a few minutes, and Louise turned to the typescript again. But it was a silence broken by the occasional sound of regular movement, and eventually by a series of short, emphatic, pleasure-filled gasps or groans. This time, she thought the voice was Clara's.

The talk purred again then for several minutes before tailing off once more into silence. This move from vicious combat to apparent contentment amazed Louise. Astonishingly, she found she was thinking of a scene in *The Postman Always Rings Twice*: that moment when Frank and Cora suddenly have to fuck after deliberately injuring each other, so it will look as if they were in the same car accident as her murdered husband. Violence and sex are one there. But, Christ, this was Clara and Clifford Deem, a retired couple, not Jessica Lange and Jack Nicholson in their horny primes.

If all Louise had heard just now was genuine it should mean, shouldn't it, that Clara would not be visiting tonight? Perhaps she had already done her visiting. They might have settled down until morning in Clifford's room. Or it could be Clara's. Louise picked up the revision pages again and flipped through them, circling more 'melancholies' in pencil for treatment some time tomorrow when she felt sharper and more creative. She must try to get the new alterations faxed by evening, or at the very latest next morning. She was returning to London the day after that, but Ted would not be happy to wait until she brought them then. Although she had spotted that many of his movie-boss grossnesses were put on to disguise a brain and taste, she also knew that he did love the urgency and clamour of faxes. Someone – possibly Darren Lee Old himself – must have instructed Ted that a dead star overlaid by melancholy was not, as the delicate boardroom term went, 'optimably projectable', and Ted would be restless until this was amended, though, obviously, not amended to the degree that the Life reverted to its former run-of-the-mill heavy optimism.

Without knocking, Clara entered Louise's room and closed the door quietly behind her. She was in a long tulle nightdress which rustled busily across the board floor. Over this, covering the upper half of her body, and worn instead of a dressing gown, she had on what looked like a soccer shirt. It was striped green, gold and amber and woven on the chest bore a large badge showing a castle and old-fashioned bridge. 'He's sleeping now, poor ancient warrior,' she said. 'Round-faced men look grand asleep, have you noticed? Strong, animal-like. I hate to see someone bony and with drawn cheeks and big eye sockets lying still, don't you? It brings back all those terrible 1945 photographs. We're damn lucky he *could* sleep tonight, aren't we, Louise?'

'Did all this trouble him, Clara?' She spoke 'this' roundly; it was to take in the Pax chapters downstairs and their discussion of them. 'I'm sorry I have to bother him with it – well, bother the both of you. Old crises. But it's so as to get Clifford correct in the biography.'

'Oh, correct.'

'It's important.'

'Roy Estham was like that,' Clara replied.

'Like?'

'Narrow-faced. That Belsen look when he slept.'

'I haven't got much on Estham's looks.'

'I don't know whether you've thought at all about getting things "correct" from my point of view,' Clara replied. Her voice was off-hand, or tried to be, but the weight on 'my' jarred the eardrums.

'Of course. It's the same as getting it correct for Clifford, surely,' Louise said.

'Perhaps the Pax story could be amended after Clifford's death. I suppose these Lives are sometimes changed.'

'Certainly. I'm rejigging David Gale at the moment.'

'But only after Clifford's death. I don't want him hurt now. What use?'

'Well—'

'Don't tell me "the demands of truthfulness",' Clara said.

'The demands of truthfulness.'

'We've reached an absurd sort of reversal, Cliff and I,' Clara replied. 'I have to do Roy down to some degree when I reminisce, so as to imply there was nothing substantial between him and me. Like saying I sent the drawing of Pax to Roy, which would obviously be a terrible act of hostility.'

'And did you really?'

'While Cliff has to plump Roy Estham up.'

'To make him a reckonable trophy?'

'That and—' She walked to Louise's window, where long net curtains shifted now and then in a small breeze. She stared very hard out into the night, like its owner.

'And because of Estham's death?' Louise asked.

Clara came away from the window and went and sat on the edge of Louise's bed. She moved gracefully. Louise remained at the dressing table. Clara said: 'His death, naturally. You'd have heard the yelling just now. Believe me, I don't want to take part in such set-tos. Cliff's not all that well. One of these nights he'll go under during a rage-in. Or the reconciliation afterwards. Porn videos are about his mark now. But, please, don't let that distract us, Louise. One groans vulgarly and rhapsodically and so on because that's how it is on the porno channels and his videos. Men have expectations now, even so old and with difficulties. And if he goes into a stroke it's a Portuguese doctor in the small hours, isn't it? They're fine, fine. The whole country's fine. But – yes, they're fine, fine.' She did some calm breathing. 'I wanted no confrontation. Well, you saw me send him off in friendly style to his room, didn't you, Louise? There's still a lot to be said for Cliff, and, in any case, he's all I have. If ever the evening's conversation's been about Estham, though, he will not rest. He'll start bellowing the name and other names – perhaps our guest's – and I go to him, simply to achieve silence. Eventually. Of course, he knows I'll turn up. There's a ritualistic side. Habitually he'll accuse me of having "hijacked" Roy. He means that he, Cliff, rebuilt, recreated, Estham and it was only on that account that I could find him worthwhile. He says what he calls "mere tact" and so on should have stopped me. That is, regard for his – that's Cliff's – skills. He accuses me of falling for someone else's "home-made hand-puppet". Obviously, I give all that sort of shit back to him, with knobs on. There's bullying built in to these Cambridge people, you know. The sods call it intellectual rigour. You spit back or get minced. Heard of F. R. Leavis? Of course you have. I mean, Louise, mere fucking tact! What's it's supposed to signify? I tell him that if there was any betrayal it was warranted, at least in retrospect, by his behaviour. Or more exactly the behaviour of minions who did his dirty work.'

'Dirty work?'

'And I let him know – again and again – that any credit to be derived for rehabilitating Roy was absolutely mine, not his. Not sure it's true, but you know how ruthless one gets in battles with a spouse. Come across the word "eristic" at all? It's argument designed to get victory, not truth. Do you believe in truth, anyway?'

'This was an affair with Estham that lasted how long?' Louise asked. 'Until his death?'

'Look, Louise, one's sex orientation can come and go, don't you find that? If one's lucky. I mean, even in the space of say an hour, and yes, less.' She leaned forward, stretched out a hand and touched Louise's wrist, but very briefly. The movement made the football shirt glint. A full team wearing this strip under stadium floodlights would be gloriously blinding. 'Until his death, obviously,' Clara said.

'Were you still ... well ... close?'

'Of course.'

'Why it was done?' Louise asked.

'Done? What?'

'The death. He killed himself because you two could never—'

'The inquest did say he killed himself,' Clara replied.

'Yes. I've seen the papers. While of unsound mind.'

'Of course it did. There'd be an expectation that someone like Roy would go that way, wouldn't there? Recurrent, intolerable attacks of mounting shame, despite Cliff's therapies. I'd never question that for years Cliff did sincerely try to restore him – to keep him alive and ungibbering, regardless. Then a shift when he saw how things were.'

'Which things?'

Clara turned back the bed clothes. 'I think all I want is to lie alongside you for a while. Not more than two hours. There'll be nothing invasive, unless, that is, you regard getting into your bed as invasive. Just for the warmth and the smell of another woman. You're not hopelessly deodorized, for God's sake, are you? It was a novelty in Roy, but a deadener now.'

'Fine,' Louise said.

'Mainly I came to talk.' Clara pulled off the football shirt, climbed into the big bed and lay on her back. She had the sort of face she herself would probably not like to watch when it was asleep: not quite skeletal, perhaps, but definitely different from the round kind she preferred on the pillow. Louise was longish in the face, too, and with deep eye sockets. Perhaps she had better stay awake. Louise undressed and put on pyjamas. Clara sat up and made a thing of watching. That was probably all right. Oh, certainly it was all right. When Louise cut the lights and climbed into bed, Clara stretched out flat on her back again. They hardly touched, but Louise was aware of Clara turning her head towards her, perhaps sniffing at her arms, neck and shoulders. That was all right, but nothing further. Clara said: 'Clifford himself was almost exclusively an intellectual soldier, I'm fairly sure of that. But he had all kinds of dapper people working for him, as you can imagine, Louise. These were lads actually trained to fool a coroner now and then, peacetime or not. God knows what they were like in war. But, look, dear, you've probably got enough trouble with your own suicide.'

'My own?'

Clara sighed: 'Gale. Talking of close, you might have been very close there, I imagine, and then suddenly he's gone. It's a hell of a problematical area, self-destruction. But perhaps there's comfort in recreating the Life. Perhaps there are other comforts, too.'

In the night Louise awoke. She had no idea how long she had slept. The room was still totally dark. She reached out to Clara but found she was alone in the bed.

Ten

'Video party this morning?' Deem asked.

'Fine,' Louise said. The porn? Would he get an extra kick out of watching with a young-ish woman guest? It seemed a reasonable, opportunist way to extend Cliff's latter-day pleasures, though he also seemed still able enough at night as actual participant, despite what Clara said. However, she would refuse to watch anything with dogs, cage birds or charcuterie.

'This won't be the first time I've viewed it, I assure you,' he said. 'Plus in the cinema. Not a negligible piece of work by any means. Certainly it reaches out. Yes.'

'Oh, *Broken Light*?' Louise asked.

'Of course,' Clara said.

'The film people kindly sent us a tape of the film,' Deem said, ' – to compensate for missing the London opening.'

They were taking a Portuguese breakfast of coffee and sweet cakes at the long ginger table, with Clara's scrapbook and Louise's Pax chapters still spread conjoint at the other end from last night. She felt a terrible unease about the chapters now. This was the thing with writing: you worked on a piece until it seemed pretty satisfactory and even final: you were proud of it, loved the look of the neat lines of type and the texture of amassed paper; and then someone said something or didn't say something and the pages were suddenly shit. They looked different, felt different, weighed different: weighed more, because they were dead-weight now. She had two loads of pages with her like that: the Pax chapters and the Gale Life. Excess baggage on the plane?

Cliff was in a battered drill suit today and open-necked white shirt. He looked more or less spruce and eternally British. You could see why we won an empire and let it slip. He said: 'We didn't show you any sights last time, Louise. So, a trip to Tavira this afternoon, concluding with a drink at the teachers' café in the square. But work a.m., possibly? We can stop the video here and there and discuss. That might be useful to you. We'd have three versions of events, then: yours, the film's, mine.'

'And bloody mine,' Clara said.

'Certainly,' Deem replied unhesitatingly: not a blink. Why did Louise expect a blink? 'Although you were marginal, Clara,' Deem said, 'you're entitled to some input, no question. Is that the term these days: "input", Louise? From these four facets perhaps some moments of authenticity might emerge.' He gazed out fondly at the morning sunshine. 'What I have to consider is, if I were living in Devon now, a speech of that length would put me into a great wrack of coughing. Portugal's my salvation, my medic.'

'Tavira, grand,' Louise said, 'if you're not giving yourself too much bother. Perhaps I could fax some material from there.' She had awoken early and done more pottering on the Gale pages. Instead of 'majestic and humane in his ultimately overpowering melancholy' she had written:

Radically affected by his role in *Broken Light* as the tragic young Cambridge graduate Andrew Pax, David Gale pondered a world darkened by intransigent error and hasty callousness and decided with the honesty he was famed for that he no longer wanted a part of this world.

Ted might see that new phrasing as a happier curtain-up to self-annihilation.

There was a separate television-and-video room, small but reasonably comfortable. This arrangement recalled that quaint epoch when television was only an adjunct of life, not its basis: when people suspended their usual activities to watch a specific programme for an hour or so, rather than sitting there and swallowing whatever the set force-fed. Perhaps here it was still only an adjunct, and Clifford and Clara spent most of their leisure elsewhere in the house spitting at each other. On the wall over the TV set hung a portrait in oils of a long-faced, agitated-looking girl of about twenty. Louise saw a resemblance to Clara, but could not decide whether it was a picture of her done many years ago, or perhaps of a daughter. Louise's research said the Deems had three children, two girls and a boy.

As soon as the video started it became plain that Clifford and Clara had in fact never watched a minute of it before. Like the TV room, their lie came from another era, an era when politeness mattered: Cliff's vintage did not openly spurn a gift, even one he knew would kick him in the balls. There could have been no trip to the Faro cinema either. This was the first time they had seen *Broken Light* screened anywhere.

But the politeness did not reach very far: Clifford laughed continually at the film, beginning immediately after the titles, and especially when *Broken Light* tried for suspense or poignancy or moral weight. He folded over on himself in the big brown leather armchair, as if keen to reservoir his merriment for eventual full expression, make sure it did not trickle away in minor giggles.

Louise found herself looking at the pink, hairless top of his narrow head. The pince-nez spectacles hung down straight on their tape. This view made him seem pathetically vulnerable, yet the laughter suggested mighty arrogance. She was bewildered again.

Cliff's amusement appeared real, not nerves. She did feel he overdid it, but only slightly. This was a movie aimed at all age groups and all genders, here and abroad, so of course it would appear mostly fatuous to someone who had lived through the events it covered. Think what real troops would make of *The Winds of War*, or what real rats would make of *The Wind in the Willows*. Louise herself found *Broken Light* half fatuous, and, after all, she knew the period only from reading and interviews with survivors like Cliff and Lord Chate. This was cinema, and cinema had its own brassy imperatives. These had not much to do with satisfying the one or two surviving relics of the period on accuracy of fact or tone, but with humouring the critics' tastes and getting a clear, politically OK tale over to ticket buyers worldwide.

For the opening, Rowdy Shindale, *Broken Light*'s director, had pinched excellent tricks from a couple of classics. Behind the credits he ran 1930s black and white actual news-reels, as Woody Allen employed fifties

113

footage at the start of *The Front*, backed by that *Fairy Tales Can Come True* number. For *Broken Light* Rowdy had music of a wistful, escapist pre-Second World War song, 'Red Sails In The Sunset'. The news clips showed hunger marchers, dole queues, Royal Ascot, Baldwin at the Palace, the Queen launching an aircraft carrier, a TB ward, children in a slum school and wearing slum clothes. David Gale's name shone big over the stilled winding gear of a shut mine. Imogen Cruse's billing competed with Edward as Prince of Wales grinning boyishly on someone's yacht in what could be the harbour at Antibes. Young women in light clothing and sun hats bobbed about the deck behind, occasionally gazing adoringly at his back and the camera. And then, as the film proper was about to begin, the news pictures were dropped. Rowdy switched to a series of rapidly alternating shots of the Kremlin and Cambridge colleges, and of Russian peasants and gowned 1930s Cambridge undergraduates, while a narrator gave the period background, like the teachy voice that launches *Casablanca*. The music had changed to 'Jerusalem', but reproduced very quietly, apologetically, ironically.

Cambridge, England. Moscow, Russia. What was it in the perilous, war-shadowed 1930s decade that linked this world-famed university – alma mater of so many brilliant men and women – with the ruling centre of the Soviet Union, Moscow's Kremlin? For centuries Cambridge and its colleges had represented wealth, aristocratic poise and glitter, educational élitism. Moscow, on the other hand, was the working heart of the young Russian people's democracy. These two cities seemed parts of different worlds. And yet something drew them close, even fatally close. A political revolution was taking place all over the globe. It had begun with the violent Bolshevik upheaval of 1917 in Russia. Now, powerful waves from that storm had begun to spread and to eat away at the long-established foundations of privilege and social class. Nowhere was this more apparent than at Cambridge. And nowhere were the dangers of this process seen more vividly than in the brief life of a Cambridge undergraduate of those days, Andrew Pax.

Just before Pax's name came up, the background to the words returned abruptly to newsreel. The music was cut. A small crowd stood outside heavy prison doors. Through a wicket two warders appeared. One of them pinned a notice to the door.

The camera went close. Headed 'Declaration of Sheriff and Others', the paper contained a printed statement, with spaces for the name and further details to be entered by pen in capital letters, as if there were so many hangings at London jails that a proforma was needed.

We, the undersigned, hereby declare that judgment of Death was this Day executed on ANDREW PAX in His Majesty's Prison of PENTONVILLE in our presence. Dated this SECOND day of JANUARY 1941.

Deem muttered throughout most of this. 'My word – the between-the-lines certainties in that commentary!' He stopped the opening of the film proper at the moment when David Gale as a youthful Andrew Pax arrived on Cambridge station with his luggage. Gale was at least eight years too old, but they had done a capable teenaging job: softening facial skin, getting his fair hair to flop languorously across his face, and swathing him in a three-yard ra-ra-ra, all-boys-together striped college scarf. Thirty-odd years ago Michael York might have graced the role. Gale had very efficiently brought a fine naive glow into his eyes, like pure youthful scholarship on the march. He lost a stone or so to become almost gangling for these early scenes.

Deem said: 'You'd think it was just a choice between types of architecture, wouldn't you? Which buildings deserve your loyalty – King's and Trinity, built with all that vain expense, fine intelligence and forbidding, ecclesiastical grey stone; or the jolly Kremlin minarets?'

'They need quick, visual symbols, Cliff,' Clara said.

'One gets no notion in this introduction, Louise, that people's views of Moscow as political pathfinder of the world might have changed a bit since the Wall came down.'

Louise coughed, grew hot and bothered. She said: 'Cliff, they couldn't even have attempted the film before the Wall came down, because they didn't – Well, look, they didn't know...' She squirmed in her armchair. 'This is a sensitive point, Cliff, but—!'

'Oh, you mean the way secret Soviet security records began to emerge – even before the official opening of KGB archives?' Deem asked. 'You're saying the film people didn't know earlier that Pax was not in their records as an agent, and that the courts and the hangman and I were wrong? Hence it's safe to make the movie?'

'Sounds cruel put like that.'

'But?'

'Yes, along those lines.'

Deem groaned theatrically. 'You can't

117

really believe, Louise, that people schooled to decades of absolute secrecy would all at once tell everything. The Soviets had worked out a contingency procedure years ago in case of catastrophes like reunification. First, fillet the files. Even in defeat – especially in defeat – this crew would reveal only what's useful. The rest? Torched. It still helps them to show Pax a martyr, for God's sake. Do you imagine you'd get the lot if our people went all Freedom of Information and put MI5 and MI6 papers on display?'

'Hard to credit, Clifford – the destruction or concealment of so much,' Louise said.

'They'd have their long-established list of Most Urgents.'

Louise shrugged. 'Well, the people doing the film believed what the files told them. Or didn't tell them. That's the point.'

'Is it?' Deem asked.

'It enabled the film to be made. Seemed to supply a theme.'

'Seemed. Oh, great,' Deem said.

'Louise, do you mean it's all right for a jolly warhorse like Cliff to be destroyed for the sake of a piece of fiction posing as fact?' Clara asked. Her long refined face looked more than sulky now. It was stricken.

Deem jerked up into his very upright posture in the armchair and turned to glare at her: 'I'm not fucking destroyed, you dim cow. Haven't you noticed I'm still around and cheerful and solvent and awkward? If she wasn't here we would never even have known what's in this film.'

'What's that mean, dear relic?' Clara asked.

'I'm not sure,' he said. 'How can an unwatched piece of movie tosh destroy me?'

Clara punched the air. 'Oh, God, is this Berkeleian dung? "If I haven't seen it it doesn't exist." But you will be seeing it now. And others have seen it. You'll know what they've seen, Cliff, and how their view of you is shaped. That's what I mean by destroyed.'

'Perhaps we shouldn't go any further with the video,' Louise said. 'I'd hate to be the cause of distress.'

'What distress?' Deem replied.

Clara said: 'When I say destroyed, I also mean, of course, Clifford, darling, you got no O.M., like Roy. Not even a leaving present. And never will now. I'm stuck with someone totally ungonged and badly pensioned. It's all on account of slanted publicity like this. Oh, a disgrace.' She seemed about to weep and put out her hand and gripped Louise's wrist briefly again, as she had done last night. She was wearing an old blue-grey dress in what might be real silk, and the sleeve whispered cosily as she moved.

'Fuck Roy,' Deem replied.

'Well, so you did, didn't you, darling?' she asked with great sweetness. 'Or your gifted bravos did.'

'So did you.'

Suddenly Louise longed to get out of the room, get out of the house and the town and on to a plane home. Escape, escape. It often appealed to her. She had come here looking for information, but now this information foully oppressed her; and at the same time eluded her: she did not know what she should believe and could see no way of establishing what she should. God, but didn't she feel nostalgic for the lovely dead safety of her Hallam research: the subject himself entwined in yew roots and contemporaries all comfortably gone, too. The Deems were old, but unspeakably lively. No, not unspeakably: they spoke too fucking much.

Just the same, Louise made herself sit still and let herself come clean: 'Look, excuse me, but – Christ, I'm losing my bearings with all this. The turns of mood and meaning.' She touched her brow. 'I've started to hyperventilate.'

'People do here,' Clara said.

'Always when they visit you?'

'In Portugal,' Clara replied.

'Occasionally I feel the conversation could be – well, as if prepared. I mean, your side of it, obviously. The two of you. Mine, hardly. Well, hardly mine. Oh, listen – I'm rambling, stumbling, you see. It's not at all typical.'

God, she would have liked to get a quick turn with the deodorizer that Clara so much despised post-Roy.

'Obviously you can't say any of this about Estham's exit in the Pax book, Louise,' she replied. 'Wholly unproveable and very libellous. Cliff would have to sue. And for all I know the laddy who actually did the wristy on Roy is still alive. Is he, Cliff? You're in touch with your little helpmeet? More than one? Louise, he/they could sue, too. Probably he's in distinguished retirement somewhere, chairing charities, which would mean big damages for loss of cleanness. Of course, time will solve your problems there. You'll outlive the sods and can write what you like then.' A mixture of regret and matter-of-factness moved into her voice. 'You understand, do you, that I only tell you these things to show how absolutely Cliff loved me, wanted me, prized me? This kind of recollection is damned important when you're stuck out on a hill in a foreign country, your most vocal neighbour a St Bernard.'

The abrupt sadness among all Clara's belligerence tore at Louise. 'Yes, I do see that,' she said.

'We always mark Roy Estham's birthday,' Deem declared. 'A small formal dinner, French wines, not Portuguese. I read aloud one of his shorter poems, although Clara

121

thinks the whole oeuvre piss. She fucked him but found his work negligible. A puzzle, really? I don't know: presumably cricketers who can't make the county side have wives who fuck them. Our dinner seems simply the decent thing to lay on for a man who eventually behaved right by our country despite his education; and then did what could be seen as the right thing for his personal values, taking himself off without fuss down the plug hole. He had those brief moments with Clara, true, but one can't dismiss his whole life because of that. I suppose she's told you all this already, has she, Louise? Was she into your bed last night, supping up your skin bloom, confiding? Did you sleep before she did? Possibly a mistake, my dear.'

'You mean I might have missed something?' Louise replied. 'Damn.'

'Roy could only be a blip to our relationship,' he said. 'I felt no long-lasting enmity.'

'How could you? Roy didn't long-last, did he, you disgusting sod,' Clara said. 'You contrived that, with assistance.' She wagged the sleeve again, this time dismissively in the air: that fine classy sound of lovely stuff.

Deem ran the video and they watched without talking for a while. 'Ah, this is me, this is me,' he shouted in his low, bubbling voice. 'I recognize the epic determination. This is me lurking around King's, isn't it, casing people as they leave an Apostles

122

meeting? God, but I'm steely-eyed and malevolent. Who did you say this is doing me, Louise?'

'Barry Wight. Very up and coming.' The film showed Wight playing Deem playing a tourist at Cambridge and seeming to gape at the spires and the prime roof guttering as disguise for his snooping.

'He's got your chin, Clifford,' Clare cried. 'I've always said you can read a lot in chins. Dame Myra Hess.'

Deem stopped the video again. Now, the camera was on a group of young men spilling out into a quadrangle from what was supposed to be King's: might actually be King's if the college had cooperated, unscared of a movie slur. David Gale was there as Andrew Pax, still looking boyish and to date untramelled by heavy politics or Estham or Clifford. In another ploy pulled from *Casablanca* this scene had everyone in academic gowns and dark suits, to make it damn clear they were undergraduates or dons: just as in *Casablanca* all the military and the Prefect of Police wear a full chest of medals and salute one another, even on a binge night out at Rick's café. In movies you bang them with visuals.

'Is one of those older ones supposed to be Anthony Blunt?' Clara asked, pointing. 'That cow-faced lanky lad?'

'*Would* you have checked on the Apostles

like this, Clifford?' Louise asked.

He snarled his answer from deep in the armchair, like an ancient wolf from its den, a wolf past pack leadership but still well up on nastiness. Normally, Deem would sit very straight, but he had slumped back now after the attack by Clara. 'Do you know any fucking thing at all about my kind of work, Louise? You're supposed to be writing a serious volume.'

'You wouldn't peep on the Apostles?' she replied.

'Some fart-arsing high-class chat soc, with soixante-neuf cock-sucking on the side,' Deem said. 'Am I likely to stand about in a raincoat like the Continental Op, risking my cover for that poncy lot? I was known in Cambridge, remember.'

'But your target was one of that poncy lot,' Louise replied.

'I had someone in the Apostles who could tell me who was saying what and who was snuggling up to whom. It's standard pro-cedure to turn someone inside an outfit like that.'

'Pax and Estham were snuggling up?' Louise asked. She pointed at the screen: 'This is Estham he's talking to now.'

Deem hauled on his spectacles tape and stared. 'They've done a decent casting job there, too.'

'Simon Claud Nolan,' Louise said. 'He

played Berty Mote in Stannard's *Stay Out Of The Park*. Nolan had an Oscar Nomination for Best Supporting.'

'Brilliant at getting the delicate smear of treachery into his face, wouldn't you say?' Deem asked. 'Plus he can suggest those obvious suicidal tendencies which were sure to hound Estham for decades and eventually triumph, regrettably. Yes, they're very clear.'

Clara gazed again at Clifford, but did not speak.

Deem said: 'They should make it an Oscar Award this time. Or half an Oscar. The bottom half.'

Looking at this frozen, silent picture on the Deems' big screen, Louise could see what the director had been after. Of course, Rowdy Shindale possessed every directorial grossness necessary for a fine, durable career, but he was also genuinely inspired at composition. Pax, just off centre of the group, looked unmistakably a sacrifice. Gale gave him both brain and doomed innocence. It was a beautifully technical performance. Clustered around Pax were the men of his own age, their gowns spread a little by the breeze and making a kind of funereal backdrop. Behind could be seen bits of stone college wall and part of a closed, handsome, stout old door. The effect was to make Pax look isolated and cut off from retreat. His seeming happiness would strike an audience as pitiable. They would smell catastrophe coming. He'd been laid out on the slab. He did not know it, although cinema-goers did. Cambridge would kill him.

There were two older men in the group: Nolan, as Roy Estham, and an extra playing the Blunt figure. Both looked friendly enough but also contentedly influential: charismatic shepherds among their flock, and one of the flock doom-marked already as the Pentonville scapegoat. No, Estham-Nolan did not appear suicidal. That might be just Cliff's special pleading.

Although Barry Wight's Deem was out of the frame in this group shot, Louise felt aware of that stalking presence, and an audience would be, too. Perhaps what Deem said was true and he had never personally tried spying on the Apostles. It did not matter. The film had the flavour right. There was a story to be told and *Broken Light* told it in its own occasionally spot-on ways. You could not say much more about any film.

'Estham was a Communist recruiter on a par with the very best – even John Cornford and Klugmann,' Deem said. 'Nothing wrong with that, of course. But it was what happened afterwards. The indiscreet step from politics to treachery.'

'Debatable step?' Louise asked.

'Yes, debatable. But not a pretty, bow-tie Cambridge Union debate or an Apostles debate. A blood and bone debate. I won.'

'Which Apostle talked to you, Clifford?' Louise said. 'I ought to know that. I don't want to follow the film, especially if the film is wrong about your method. So long after it wouldn't matter if you spoke, would it?'

He pressed Start again and let the video run, without sound. There was more Cambridge and then Pax in some sex scenes with a girl, played by Imogen Cruse. 'He liked both,' Deem said.

'Are you sure?' Louise replied.

'Apostles were secretive,' Deem said. 'It's a tradition.'

'But you told me one of them talked to you.'

'*I* talked to one of *them*. Ultimately I was able to convince him the Apostles merited no loyalty and that his country did.'

'How did you?' Louise asked. 'Apostles were so brilliant. How could you work on one of them effectively like that?'

Deem sat up straight again and turned the bright, hooded blue eyes hard on her. 'Oh, we were issued with a special booklet of instructions for dealing with I.Q. people.'

She felt herself redden. 'All right, Cliff. I was stupid. So, one of them did eventually talk to you – after *you* had talked so adeptly to *him*.'

'Yes, one of them did, but I don't talk about it to you.'

127

'Why? You're not bound by their secrecy.'

'He's dead. He was killed in the war. I don't disturb his bones for the sake of some damned trendy book.' Immediately Deem wrinkled his porky face into a small smile. 'Sorry, Louise. Your book won't be trendy, I'm sure. Or *merely* trendy. But I don't speak about that kind of arrangement, however long ago it is.'

Clara groaned and shifted impatiently in her chair. She said: 'When he talks like that – loads on the piety and rudeness – it's probably all balls. The film could be right and he snooped for himself. I can't imagine an Apostle grassing. Some interrogator said he found it easy to get information out of a Cambridge spy about espionage, but was brickwalled on the Apostles.'

'Now this is more authentic,' Deem said. 'Oh, yes!' He jammed his glasses on again. The film showed him on foot following Estham and Andrew Pax in a drab London street. Rowdy had all the right period props. Deem used parked vehicles, shop doorways and other pedestrians for cover. It appeared very pro. Estham occasionally glanced back, as if only he of the two of them feared they might be tailed. There was a glimpse of Euston station. David Gale had been made to look a few years older, was that stone heavier and a lot sleeker. 'Yes, this is pretty much as it happened, though we had six dogging them, actually, not just myself. That would be impossible. I'd do a stint then hand over, and so on. They mustn't get the chance to notice a constant face. But I can understand that the movie has to focus things. They want a single chargeable demon, don't they? Vital to show Cliffy Deem relentlessly gumshoeing this boy towards his rough death. Ah, the demands of true art!' For a second she thought he would switch off altogether. But his interest picked up again. 'These two are on their way to meet Estham's Soviet embassy contact.' He squeaked like a hamster: 'Yes, yes, oh, not bad at all this bit.' Estham and Pax entered a tiny, scruffy café, Estham ahead. An elderly, fattish, ill-dressed man was at one of the tables with a mug of tea in front of him. He seemed to pay no attention to their arrival.

Deem sat up even straighter and clutched at his brow. 'My God, Clara,' he cried, 'I've forgotten his name. Forgotten the Russian's name. What's happening to my mind?' The sun had edged into the little room and a beam entering as a wide shaft between two half-drawn curtains held his face like a searchlight. He looked distraught.

'This is nearly sixty years ago, Cliff,' she said. 'A lot of Russian contacts have come and gone. Fret not.'

'My mind's cracking? He was the centre of our case. It's disappeared.' His voice had fallen to a panicked whisper.

'Baku, wasn't it?' Louise asked. 'Like the oil field. Emmanuel Baku.'

Deem nodded a couple of times while watching the screen. There was no sign of relief or gratitude. He was too far into despair. 'Why couldn't I get it? Is there Alzheimer's in the air out here?'

The film showed Estham go to the counter and buy two teas. Then he and Pax chose a table on the other side of the café from Baku. They ignored him, just as *he* had seemed to ignore *them*. Apart from the three men and a woman behind the counter, the place was empty. The camera went outside again and showed Deem walk swiftly past the café, giving it hardly a look. He turned a corner and stopped, then doubled back, climbed a wall and came to a grubby rear window through which he could watch the three men. He would be out of earshot.

Deem laughed. 'Wow!' he said. 'Drama! Not impossible, but unlikely. Someone would spot you on top of the wall and call the police. In those days people did that, and in those days the police came. I was nowhere near. We had a girl already inside the café. We knew where they would rendezvous.'

'But how?' Louise asked.

'A very talented kid,' Deem replied.

'No girl is shown in the scene.'

'You don't say.'

'Was this another slag you and the rest of the brigade were fucking turn and turn about or oftener?' Clara asked.

'Is she still alive?' Louise said. 'Can you recall her name?'

'She married rich,' Deem replied. 'Three or four times. Mostly Americans. I heard Argentina last. Names slip, as you just saw.'

'But she'd be findable?' Louise said.

'Well, I expect *I* could find her, if I put my old mind to it.'

'*Will* you put your old mind to it?'

'She was a colleague, Louise. One doesn't do things like that.'

'This means at least he and probably others were definitely shagging her,' Clara said. 'He's afraid of complications, even now. I expect you'll understand why I've come to prefer—'

'Look at this,' Deem said, guffawing. Baku lumbered over and joined Estham and Pax at their table, but standing. Deem gave the film some sound now, though for most of the time he seemed to feel that whatever was said would be idiotic. Baku smiled largely. He had his mug of tea in the left hand and held out the other in comradely greeting. International affability resonated. Estham stood and shook the hand. Then, shyly, Pax did, too.

Robert Indimenda was playing Baku and said now in that big voice made to traverse

131

the steppes: 'Pardon. I Soviet engineer study bridges in your country. To build good bridges in my own country. I want talk to many English, learn their country, learn how speak. I Emmanuel Baku.'

Estham, also smiling, said: 'Yes, we are English.' He introduced himself and Pax. 'Please, sit down.'

'This is kindness,' Baku said. 'Railway bridges.' He waved a thick hand towards Euston. 'And all sorts bridges. We must learn. Your country – good bridges. Brunel.' He sat down.

Deem stopped the film once more, then rewound to the start of the café scene and played it again with sound, chuckling massively throughout. He let the film run, but knocked off the sound again. 'Baku's bridges,' he muttered. 'As significant as that one in the song at Avignon. The audience is being told this was an accidental meeting, yes?'

'It's what Pax said at his trial,' Louise said.

'Of course it is,' Deem said. 'Who believed it? Estham testified otherwise.'

'He was another Apostle you persuaded to turn,' Louise said.

'Cliff had a flair.'

'How did we know where they'd meet, if it was accident?' Deem asked.

'Did you?' Louise replied. 'Honestly?'

'I told you. We had a girl listening to them.

132

A crucial sequence for us. This was Estham introducing Pax to the Soviet embassy lad who'd be his contact and who was already Estham's, of course, until – well, until almost the end. Pax hanged, Baku back in Moscow just in time and Estham – well, Estham converted. They got Baku out late-1940 when he saw we were on to Pax. And on to Estham, obviously.' He shifted his chair to avoid the sun. 'We should be moving soon.'

'Did the woman give evidence?' Louise asked. 'So much of the trial was in camera. No available transcripts of most of it.'

'Naturally she did.'

'I'd find it such a help to talk to her, Cliff,' Louise replied.

Deem looked at Louise, his face suddenly very blank.

'You can't blame her for not believing you,' Clara said. 'You being you, with your inbuilt filthy training and eternal evasions.'

The film had turned back to newsreel for a few minutes and showed an Oswald Mosley Blackshirt rally in the East End, then a subsequent riot. Deem said: 'Estham brought Baku to the meeting because Pax was reaching the time when he could be useful. He would get his expected sparkling First soon after this, of course, and then go into the Foreign Office, one of the few grammar school people they let squeeze through. Estham naturally had some influence on selections, via other F.O. Cambridge people he'd nurtured. The Kremlin were always interested in bright Oxbridge boys who took that path, but especially boys from Cambridge. Pax was going to be among sensitive papers in a few months and working with powerful people.'

'I see you looking at our daughter, Louise,' Clara said suddenly, nodding up at the portrait.

'She's very beautiful,' Louise replied.

'No, not at all. Healthy, though. Our children divide two to one against Clifford,' she said. 'This one – Deborah – and our son, Rory, came to despise him once they discovered what happened in 1941. Viki, the other daughter, sees all that as just a necessary wartime briskness.'

'No, no,' Deem yelled. 'They do not look down on me, they do not, not Deborah or Rory. They understand history. Why do you say these bleak, tiresome things?'

Again Louise had the impression of a prepared set-to, or at least of old fighting ground. Was it modelled on one of those shouting matches in *Who's Afraid of Virginia Woolf?*, when Taylor and Burton war over their supposed absent son? Louise said: 'Yes, the court transcripts have been edited so much they're hopeless, of course, but I understand Pax pleaded that Baku simply became a good friend – a Communist good friend, true, and one who shared Pax's political views, but only a good friend – someone who could tell him at first hand about Russia, a country that had always fascinated Pax, and which fascinated so many of his generation. After all, Communism wasn't proscribed in Britain.'

'Oh, yes, it's about a generation all right,' Deem replied. 'I know what he told the court. I was there for most of it. I know, too, what was said at this café meeting. It's not much like the film script, Louise. Shall I tell you how the conversation went?' He frowned, as though needing to concentrate. 'Estham says: "Andrew, this is someone you will know as George." Baku always took the name George in Britain. These people have their fixed methods and habits, just like professional criminals. Estham went on: "George knows all that is necessary to know about you, and a lot more. You will not contact him, but *he* must be told how to contact *you*, at all times. That is, your private address each time you change it. He will have consideration and never contact you in Cambridge, nor in your place of work when you go down. He will explain to you now how those communications arrangements will be made. It is a simple matter of putting a Personal advertisement in *The Times*. I've told George that you are not interested in money for this service, but he wishes to pay you from time to time all the same, and will pay you something today, as a token. In due course, he will let you know the kind of material that would be most appreciated.'

Louise said: 'Oh, my Lord, Cliff, you reproduce this conversation word for word, yet couldn't remember Baku's name? And you were not even present in the café, you say.'

'It was central to the court proceedings. I went over and over the girl's notes. Naturally it's implanted still.'

'Are you saying Pax knew in advance that this meeting would take place? He wasn't taken there, unprepared, by Estham?' Louise asked.

'Of course he knew. Of course he knew what he was undertaking. Would we have convicted him otherwise?'

'Would you? You're telling me a woman officer could get close enough to them in a café to hear the detail of what was said? Said by people who were presumably on guard against surveillance. We're talking pre-bug days, aren't we?'

'A very gifted girl,' Deem said, 'a trained girl. She saw the money pass.'

'In a brown envelope, I'm sure.'

'In an illustrated book on the bridges of Brunel. I might still have it. Pax kept it. A clever-boy fool.' The video had reached a sequence with Pax, tense but confident, being interviewed for the Foreign Office post and then celebrating this appointment with his family and Imogen at a working-class pub somewhere.

'High fucking flier, isn't he?' Deem said. 'We'll see.'

Louise said: 'Cliff, isn't it possible that your woman agent would actually *like* to have her work made public now? It must have rated as very distinguished, yet she could receive no credit.'

'She received credit – from her superiors and colleagues.'

'Perhaps now she wants more,' Louise said. 'This is an old lady, possibly with not much left but a remarkable past; a remarkable past that is unrecognized. Couldn't you ask her? You needn't disclose her whereabouts to me until she agrees.'

Clara started laughing: 'You'd trust him to tell you the truth about her response? People like this woman and Cliff do not expect public acclaim, Louise. They got their satisfaction from the sound of the gibbet trap. It was an intimate little career.'

The film moved to what seemed to be Deem interrogating Andrew Pax in a prison room. To her surprise, Cliff kept the sound off even now, as if he still could not bear to listen to what the script did to him. Barry Wight played him as intermittently avuncular and splenetic in this scene. Cliff held his nose yet managed to giggle again.

Louise said: 'There's nothing in the Moscow archives about the three-sided café meeting.'

'I should think not,' Deem said. 'Baku's there, though, isn't he?'

'In the diplomatic section as an ordinary official in the Embassy commerce department: an engineering background.'

'Yes, they'd done a lovely job on his profile.' The film quietly ran on. They watched what could be another interrogation. This time it was Deem and Estham, and the surroundings very different. Both men had drinks. They sat at ease in a big, well-furnished room with heavily framed oil paintings on the wall and a table where newspapers and magazines were laid out. Louise thought it must be a London club. Although Simon Claud Nolan started the sequence cheerily, his head sank forward and his eyes lost hope as the conversation proceeded.

'That's not bad either,' Deem said. 'Nolan you say? He's good. Estham was so fucking feeble.'

'He had been sickeningly undermined,' Clara said.

Deem gave her a single finger, then switched off as the prison gates and waiting group of people came up.

'Oh,' Clara said. 'I thought I glimpsed you – your actor – in the ghoul crowd, Cliff. Did you get there, then, for the declaration? Are

138

they right on that? Crowing?'

He stood up. 'Well, now, Louise, we were remiss last time in not showing you a bit of the country. Clara felt the same, didn't you, darling? So, a little jaunt into Tavira for lunch? We'll introduce you to some other Brit settlers, but younger.'

Eleven

'Obviously, over the years I've tried once or twice to kill Cliff,' Clara said. 'In the circumstances it was the least one could do. I think you'll see that, Louise. Actually, twice. Closeness does give one chances. Both attempts a long while ago. Ah, yes.' Her voice shook fondly, savouring these distant memories.

'No,' Louise gasped. 'No, I *don't* see it.' Repeatedly during these last couple of days her hold on sense and balance would suddenly go. What was real? What was credible? 'Christ, of course I don't see it. Are you talking literally? You physically attempted murder?'

'Murder *is* physical, you know. But Clifford was trained to look after himself, and people don't forget those skills, Louise. He took a Double First in History and English at Cambridge, so you can imagine how useless in a practical sense he must have been to MI5 when he joined. In the thirties and forties they would school them, school them, school them, school these bright scholarly

140

nincompoops in a black airless room, teaching neat, patriotic brutishness, stitching self-protection into the nervous system with steel thread. He told me about it. Although Cliff's not young now, he would probably still see it coming if I had another go. These were people who had it inculcated that they were always in peril, especially from those nearest. Well, I probably shan't try again. I still grieve for Roy, but a bit of the rage has dried. Everything dries as we get on. Or leaks. We've made a surface. Cliff and I have settled into a decently temperate run-up to the pyre, and as long as we programme things right we each still get something from a shag now and then, in the cooler months and as part of a phoney reconciliation mode.'

Clara and Louise were strolling around Liberation Square in Tavira. Clifford had bumped into a Portuguese family he knew and stopped behind to talk. Clara pointed her aged little finger about fondly and said: 'We think of this as our Portugal – the riverside cafés, the fascinating stalls and sauntering crowds, the river Gilao itself and the lovely Roman bridge. I hate the whole fucking lot of it.' Revulsion made her tremble. 'My remarks about the attempts on Clifford is obviously another one of those little snippets you can't use in your book, Louise, or I'd have to deny I ever said it and make legal trouble for you. But it's embargoed only *pro tem*. When I'm dead you could safely do an update. I'd like that. I'd like people to know I loved Roy more or less deeply – oh, yes, definitely as much as more or less – and long enough to search for vengeance, twice. If you look at one of those big kitchen knives you'd think things might be easy when someone was asleep alone in dunes, but the training is needed, and how would a woman have got that at Cheltenham Ladies' College? Although all his crud verse prevented full devotion to Roy, verse was not his complete essence. I always carry a poem of his in my bag. Want to hear?'

'Well, I did hear one.'

'This is another.'

'Well...'

But Clara brought out a grimy, folded piece of foolscap. 'Written at a time when I'd told Roy that Cliff and I had abandoned sex. I can't remember whether that was true. Half true, maybe. The poem's called "Personal Pronouns" – just Roy's sort of dim pedantry.' She read in an emphatic, can-you-hear-me-in-the-back-row? voice, and a few shoppers turned and gazed at her:

Sometimes after hours of love she'll sigh
a while and say with soul, 'I just can't do
this to him any more.' To him. Get that.
She claims it's centuries since they made

142

love – that's mutually. So, in a way she's
right when telling me she can't do this
to him, but means – i.e., she means on
op of what she seems to mean – she
means she can't do this to me again,
not him, because it gives her wifely grief
to think how grievously he'd grieve,
suppose he ever knew. And what she
means by preaching that she can't do
this to him is not that from now on she
won't – because she never does do this,
to him.She means – and truly means,
I mean, almost: she means she must
not cause bad hurt by giving him this
 notional offence; so means to slam the
moral stopper on with me. This kind of
 kindness to him when, thank God,
he's in absentia – well, naturally – can
make her seem my kind of kindly girl.
I mean, I sometimes almost envy him.
'He gets your tender, comradely concern,
and everlasting sensitivity,' I say. 'I'm on
the side. I'd even like to be him now and
then and win your care.' 'Oh, yeah?
If so, I couldn't do this to you any more.
See what I mean?' she says.

'I like conversation in poems,' Louise said.
'It gets you clear of daffodils.'

Clara put the paper away. 'OK, so I
botched my vengeance tries, but I think Roy
would really have appreciated the efforts.

He'd understand I'd been serious, taking a knife out to the beach like that in a towel, and then the other time, too, with the car. If there's one thing Roy would hate, it's to be for ever considered a dirty suicide. He had some true glow and force, even before the O.M. And there was tenderness and patience. As to the O.M., he'd be unique, whichever way you look at his death: I believe no member of the Order of Merit before Roy had been murdered or committed suicide. I haven't done full research on this, but I do think so.'

'But tell me, tell me exactly, how your attempts on Clifford failed,' Louise said. 'It's important, Clara.'

'Important because you won't believe it without damn circumstantial detail? Oh, you scrupulous, fact-focused people,' she said, in a teasing but saddened voice. Then, suddenly, this bantering, gloomy tone went. She grew frantic: 'Oh, I'd love to come back to Britain with you.' She put her head for a second on Louise's shoulder. 'Please take me. Oh, please.' The change was startling, disturbing. Suddenly, all assertiveness had gone. Adulthood had gone: these were the whispered prayers of an infant, like a little girl pleading to be plucked from an awful foster home, and scared the adoptive parents will hear. 'I won't cry, but please, for the sake of my soul,' she said. 'Let me come.'

'Why not?' Louise replied. She made it hearty. 'Have a break. See the new, grubbier London. Cliff should be able to get by on his own for a week or two.'

'I meant for ever,' Clara replied.

Louise had guessed but needed to head her off.

'I've never said this to any visitor before, Louise,' Clara whispered. 'Believe me. I think we've struck a chord, you and I, despite age, despite everything.' Her manner was still juvenile. It was as if 'despite age' meant the reverse of what appeared: *she* was the child, Louise the adult. Clara had on a very sharp pearlized blue leather dress and blue lamb's wool cardigan, not the kind of outfit to back a child's voice. They paused near the First War memorial to the Tavira dead: 'France, Africa.'

'Louise, on the face of it I suppose it might seem quite cheering to know a man wanted one so much he would have a rival slaughtered in case one went to him permanently.'

'Well, I—'

'But this laid a compulsion on one, didn't it? If Clifford valued me enough to organize that death, *I* needed to prove I valued Roy enough to try for *Clifford's* death. I'd have looked less than Cliff, otherwise. Not on. Not on at all. There's a tough arithmetic to feeling. Possibly I *am* less than Cliff, but it is not to be admitted to him, is it? And I mean, how would he prove that – actually prove it? He has no decorations. Oh, true, he has triumphs in his past, – official deaths and so on, and not just Pax – but these could be seen as bread-and-butter only, routine to his job: a spy-taker takes spies and gets them topped. If I'd failed to try to match Clifford as to emotional connections he would have exulted. This is his training, too: dominate, get one up. Ascendancy.

'Exactly how he smashed Pax and then gravely – gravely – reduced Roy so he *wanted* the grave. I could not allow it. I would have felt less whenever I saw the children. You describe our daughter in the painting as beautiful. Kindly, but hardly so. Yet Deborah does have rights and is entitled to a mother with some edge to her.' She leaned on a balustrade, perhaps tired by the walking or by making her case. 'To mention vengeance is possibly to mask in crudity my impulses of those times. This was a matter, also, of looking after my living core. I needed Clifford dead for that. We've spoken of the mathematics of feeling. Well, an equation: to accomplish my properly realized life, Cliff had to be dead and done by me, not sickness or some contractor. I'd have liked the person or people dead he used on Roy, too, naturally, but I could not identify them and would have been unable to cope, anyway, of course – stalking pros on their own ground. Feeble-

146

minded to try. It should have been possible with Clifford, and it might have been, but for the implanted wiliness and his trained light sleeping and damned eternal luck.'

'How exactly did he defeat you – the attempts with the kitchen knife and the car?'

'My thinking is that you, too, are lonely, Louise. I picked that up when I came to your bed. It's in your gratitude, in the openness of your body. I see this as natural, in view of the loss of someone as close to you as the actor, and in such circumstances, my dear.' Very briefly, as before, she fingered Louise's wrist.

'I was his ghostwriter, that's about all, Clara. I didn't want more. That was his problem, as a matter of fact.'

'Take me with you,' she whimpered. 'Can't you see how much you need me? Come out of denial.'

'Did you try to find the people Clifford used?'

She gazed wearily down at the memorial and nodded her grey, grey head slowly a couple of times, but not signalling a yes: it was sadness again. 'Ah, you're trained, too, aren't you Louise? You're trained to be sceptical of everything you hear. You're trained to seek substantiation. You still don't believe what I say?'

'Clara, are you afraid of Clifford?'

'But perhaps what I've told you is not relevant to your work on Pax,' Clara replied.

'Oh, of course it is,' Louise cried. 'Basic. If Roy Estham killed himself, as has always been supposed, it would probably imply terrible regret for what he did to Andrew Pax. And that will be a key part of my tale. Or it would have been, until you spoke. His suicide says so much about loyalty, fractured loyalty, shame; plus about the changes in public feeling, political climates and about all the off-on legalities of war, a debate which never ends and is so relevant today. Now, though, you put the accepted facts in question. It's crucial. You say he was assassinated. That would affect the whole drift of the biography. Please, Clara: all at once my work's got no bearings.'

Clara resumed her ordinary, worldly, deadpan voice. 'All security services are instructed in what is called "constructive suicide" – as an extreme recourse, yes, but everyone learns about it. That is, you get rid through apparent suicide of someone troublesome or spare and at the same time turn the death to your propaganda advantage.'

'Here comes Cliff,' Louise replied. He was walking slowly after them and they went back to meet him. He began to yell amid good-natured laughs: 'And did she ask you in her Baby Jane squeak to take her to Blighty with you, Louise, for pity's sake? Every bugger who visits gets it. Did she

148

make out she'd tried to kitchen devil and/or Volvo me and now dreads retaliation? Every bugger who visits gets it. Always she dreams of starring. Did you hear the blow-job poem, too? I love it. If Roy could have only hung on he'd have managed the Nobel.'

'He would have hung on,' Clara replied.

Deem put his arm around Clara's shoulders and hugged her gently, tenderly. It was a touching picture: these two old people full of off-and-on mutual loathing, and tales to blackguard each other. 'She has to turn Estham into something estimable, someone capable of true feelings, or what do all those years of bedding him on the reasonably quiet add up to, poor girl? Clara's so keen on moral status, aren't you, darling? At her age, people turn to stocktaking.'

On the other side of the square they sat down outside what Clifford called 'the teachers' café' drinking beer with youngish British men and women who taught English as a foreign language at that end of the Algarve. They seemed happy, boisterous, reeking with satisfaction at not being in Britain. The teachers obviously knew Clara and Clifford well and made a big and happy fuss of them. Clifford introduced Louise as a long-time friend and left it at that. The talk was a bit about grammar and classroom control but more concerned with holiday treks into the mountains and Spain and

Africa. When darkness came down, it began to get a little colder and he and Clara went to sit inside the café. Louise remained at a table with some of the teachers in the square. One of the women, a pretty, pushy, loud girl, with rasping Scouse accent that must have made things tough for her pupils, said: 'Aren't they super, C. and C.? We love it when they come to see us. They seem part of the old, better Britain. Like people on the Grand Tour in the eighteenth century, impressing everyone with British values. All Britain's got to give the rest of the world now is the language – why we're all harnessed here. And the language only counts because it's also America's language, Hollywood's language, international capitalism's language.

'But Clifford goes back to a different period, a worthwhile period. Those brilliant old drill suits. He's a retired diplomat of some eminence, you know, and held important posts when Britain still provided leadership in Europe and beyond. And Clara's a gem, too, in her own right. Very well read and devoted to him. She speaks beautiful English. Have you heard her saying "one"? Such a supremely suited couple. I can't help thinking of that poem, "Grow old along with me | The best is yet to be." It's rare, Louise. They so hate – so hate to be apart. But, perhaps I'm telling you things

150

you already know better than myself, if you're an old friend. Do you work? Are you in the Foreign Office, too?'

'I write historical biographies.'

'Really? A literary figure no less! Lovely. But nothing modern?'

'Too many problems. I prefer people like Arthur Hallam.'

'Ah, I've heard of him. He's the one who told stories about those boating kids in the Lake District, yes? *Swallows and What-d'you-call-its*. One of the girls named Titty, for God's sake. Yet interesting, I should think.' She paused. 'But that's wrong, isn't it? I'm talking about Arthur Ransome. Joke. I thought you might do an enraged, Brit tirade about the quality of English teaching abroad. You're too canny. Probably I've got it all wrong about the two C.s as well, have I? They detest each other?'

Twelve

Tired after the Tavira trip, Clara went to bed early. Louise remained downstairs with Deem, drinking tea and talking vaguely about Portugal and Cambridge and the awkwardnesses of biography: the frailties of information. This was *the* topic now, wasn't it? How could she – how could anyone – lasso truth and bring it back for people quietly to admire? Was there, in fact, such a commodity as truth? Everyone had their own truth, and it was liable to turn the truths of others into lies, bias, imagination, forgetfulness, self-protection – that above all. Who could sanely argue that a puffery book like *We're Rolling* was any less likely to get at truth than one of Louise's heavyweight studies? Abruptly, Deem stood and walked to the table, where Clara's sketchbook lay open still, alongside Louise's typescript chapters. For a while, he stared at the death cell drawing, ignoring the typescript. 'Pax asked to see me while awaiting execution, you know,' he said, without turning his head. 'I went, of course.'

In her armchair, Louise grew alert. 'No, I didn't know. There's no record of that.'

'Of course there's no record of it,' he replied. 'All sorts of records are missing.'

'The prison records are not at all bad, as a matter of fact, especially about visitors: most of them immaculately written in clerky pen.'

'He wanted to ask me if what he had done was right,' Deem replied. 'Bit like Estham, but reversed. I said I thought it was.'

'To ask *what*?' Louise cried. She stood quickly and went around the other side of the table. 'I can't talk to your back about something like this, can I?' She pointed at the disgusting drawing. 'Are you saying someone in the death house asks the man who put him there whether – regardless of everything – whether what he, the man in the death house, had done was actually right all the time, and the fact that he was awaiting execution by the State was merely ... oh, I don't know ... merely a troublesome hitch?' Her words galloped, almost ran away. She knew what this bastard Deem was doing. She had met it occasionally before. He wanted to tell her she was only someone who *wrote* about things, speculated about them, treated them – treated them in what she no doubt considered an appropriate way, but inevitably gave them the treatment natural to her and to the era in which she had grown up. Against that, he was someone who actually lived things. And, while living them, he encountered deaths. He was telling her that the distance between them was impossible to cross, even if he gave out a fragment now and then of how those things really were, if that was how they really were.

'Yes, I thought it was odd he should want to see me,' Clifford said. He took a couple of steps on the polished boards. 'Do you know, Louise, even now, I can still feel the roughness of the stone floor in that corridor to his cell, through the soles of these shoes, here, tonight? And I've got the disinfectant smell in my nose, and a kind of oily smoothness of the bars against my fingers when I touched them for a moment, waiting for the cell door to be opened.' He held a hand up and stared at it with a fine semblance of wonderment.

She glanced at it. 'Oh, Christ, you could have got all this from one of a thousand books about jails,' Louise yelled. 'The disinfectant smell! Everybody says so. It's like ether signifies a hospital.'

'From books?' he said mildly. 'Yes, Louise, you'd think in terms of books, wouldn't you? I've been in a lot of prisons to interview people, interrogate people. I suppose you might be right, and I'm merging many impressions. But these seem so clear, have always seemed so clear, and so clearly associated with Pax and death row. They had him in khaki Army battle dress – that hairy, heavy stuff. Possibly it was a black joke: as if they'd got him enlisted for Britain at last. A khaki sweater under the tunic. No shirt and no tie, of course. The usual thing about the trousers – too big around the waist, but no belt or braces allowed, so he had to hold them up with his hand. Like Nuremberg. Just the same, Andrew Pax had a presence. I don't mean the kind of rot one reads about: the nearness of death conferring stature and poise on condemned people. That's books, too. But he had a toughness, a bonny contempt for the State machinery that had put him where he was.'

'You were part of the machinery, and maybe the biggest part. A contempt for *you*?'

'Probably. Why not? Non-Apostle. And yet he invites me there.' Deem gave a baffled, sad smile. The porky face looked almost authentically given over to grief. If she ever wrote up this interview, that's how she would probably describe Deem at the moment, and nobody could contradict it. Except, that is, herself. She might think of contradicting it, or of leaving it out. Was the grief charade?

Louise said: 'My God, is this true? Can I use what you're telling me in the biog?'

'Is what true?'

'As starters, that you went there at all,' Louise said. She turned to the pages of her typescript on the table, picked them up and flicked through to near the end. 'Here's a

155

plan of the jail's ground floor. Show me where Pax was. Show me.'

'You'll have Clara down here if you yell like that.' He took the page, squinted and at once pointed to the correct spot on the drawing.

'That's damn easy, though, isn't it? You'd realize it would be right alongside the yard.'

'Yes, I do know jails.'

'There must have been a dozen people aware you were in the prison. You'd have to be let in at the main door, because prisons don't have side entrances. That means warders at that point, then more warders when you got to the death row building, and more at his cell. I've seen logs written by officers at every stage of a visit.'

Deem made his voice buzz with patience. 'Ah, you respect records, Louise, are wedded to them. You'd be trained to it. But this wasn't what the prison people would recognize as a "proper" visit. I had absolutely no role. Once he was convicted – in fact, once he was charged – there should have been no contact between us. And there wasn't, until he asked. It was done by a bit of connivance, a bit of stealth. And so, nothing entered in any daybook. This visit did not happen. People were no doubt ordered to ignore it. About an hour. Very tragic, very moving. As I say, Pax full of dignity, full of intellectual curiosity about his position and mine. Oh, yes, mine even more so. That excellent mind still ticking away.'

She felt engulfed by marvellously convincing and possibly bogus detail. He must have been at least a brilliant artisan in his trade and possibly an artist. 'Dignity? So how the hell does that square with this?' She pointed at the sketch of the Pax figure clinging to the bars. 'You talk about his trousers. Clara talked about his trousers, too, didn't she?'

'Come,' he replied. He held out a hand but did not touch her. Both of them went back to their chairs. He sat squarely opposite her, on the other side of their crazily wide, stone fireplace: like something from a history play. Despite his features, Clifford looked grave and honest. Long ago in his career experts would have trained him to manage himself to appear at least the second of these.

'I can say in the book that you answered his call to see him and that you assured him what he had done was right?' she asked.

'Yes.'

'You'll speak on tape?'

He held up both hands now. They floated wide apart before his chest, to signal how open he was. 'If you want to fuss with that. Do you think I'd withdraw it after you published, supposing I live that long?'

'People do disown statements. Print makes their words unrecognizable to them.'

'I'll put it on tape.'

She hurried to her room for the recorder.

Clara must have heard her moving about and opened the door of her own bedroom now and took one step on to the landing. Tonight, she was in very brilliant blue cotton pyjamas with some kind of heraldic badge in purple and gold printed on them. Like Deem she stood very erect. There was real grandeur to her. But Louise sensed something else there, too: perhaps miserable loneliness, perhaps a plea. 'Cliff giving you a load of shit, Louise?' she asked.

'Not sure. He says he visited Pax on death row.'

She was quiet for a couple of seconds, eyes closed, as if thinking back. 'Oh, yes, that's true,' she said. 'I think that's true. He's always said that. They didn't get on too badly, in the circumstances. Cambridge, you know. The place freemasons people. It's when he talks about Roy that he'll lie himself inside out.'

'But Roy was Cambridge, too, wasn't he?'
Clara shrugged.

Louise said: 'Perhaps you should come down. Put the other side.'

'Goodnight again,' she replied, then stepped back and closed the door.

Downstairs Louise spoke the date and time to the recorder. She wanted an official rigmarole, to deter him from lying. Stupid: this was somebody who had spent a working life in lies, and it would be as natural for him to

158

hatch them as spot them. Tape wouldn't scare him. 'Clifford Deem, did you see Andrew Pax at all after his conviction?'

'He asked me to visit him in his cell two days before execution. I agreed. Rules were bent to make it possible. He was very young. People felt sympathetic. He wished to discuss the ethics of his position.' Deem became fussy and insistent, speaking directly towards the recorder. 'The ethics, I say. He knew it was useless to talk about legalities. The law was going to take its course, and he realized it. I told him, yes, I thought he had done right.'

'But what did you mean by that? After all, you were responsible, more or less alone, for sending him to the condemned cell.'

'I was saying that, if his political opinions were what he said they were, and what I believed them to be, it would have followed that he must act as he had.'

'Treasonably?'

'Treason is a matter of law. As I understood him, he was not referring to the law. Suppose, for instance, there were a war with a Middle Eastern country. Would a British Muslim be justified – morally, not legally – in joining the other side? Pax meant, had he acted right by his own principles?'

'But those principles were wrong, weren't they?'

He turned his head towards Louise now. 'I

thought they were wrong. Wrong at the time. The country decided they were wrong at the time. The country was preoccupied with survival. Its laws were part of its fabric. That whole fabric was seriously menaced, from more than one quarter. And so the law had to be applied, as proof that the fabric remained intact. This is not what he was asking me, though. He sought some deeper consolation. I felt entitled to offer it.'

She switched off the machine and shoved her head forward at him: 'Listen, Cliff, is this you suddenly wanting to square your slippery fucking self with today's view of Pax's death?'

Seeming unoffended by this, he leaned across and switched the recorder back on. He gave her question a light-hearted, almost flippant, cadence: 'Is this me wanting to square my slippery fucking self with today's views of Pax's death? I suppose it's just about possible. Why should I bother, though? I am near death. I can expect no reward or recognition now. I do not even live in my own country. Where would "today's view" come in my reckoning? And yet it's true, when climates change one dresses accordingly. So, it could be. But what is today's view of Pax's death?'

'The film's view. *Broken Light*'s view.'

'This is a hack movie.'

'But hack movies are hack and commercial

because they chime with what the public are thinking.'

'It's the thinking of a *young* public, isn't it? They're the people who go to the pictures. What do the young know about war, Louise? What do *you* know about war? What did your actor friend know, or the people who gave him what to say and told him how to say it? None of you was there. None of you heard Hitler ranting and threatening us and our country and our personal safety, live on the radio. Remember that character in Martin Amis's *Money*?'

'You get all sorts of books out here, do you?'

'This youngster in the novel has been reading and come across Hitler. He says something like, "I can't fucking believe this stuff. Look how far he spread his violence." That's an Amis joke against his dimwit hero, of course. But the point is, such people don't even know about that "stuff"; and if by some fluke they find out, they can't believe it. None of them – none of you – were around to read in 1939 about Stalin joining up with Adolf, two skittish barbarians set on a breaking-and-entering spree worldwide. These kids in their cinema seats today watch another kid not much older than themselves dropped through the hatch, and they can feel nice and sad and involved in his fate: they see youth made to suffer for the errors

161

of their elders, and it's a message they thrill to, weep to. They'd gladly cough up the fat cost of the ticket, so that David Gale and those who ran David Gale could get rich and honoured by catering for the famous self-pity of the crêche.'

'For Christ's sake, Clifford, you don't sound at all as if you think Pax was right.'

'And then what Alan Bennett in his *Diaries* calls "fastidiousness".'

'You do get all sorts of books out here.'

'Remember it?' Deem replied. 'He says that the Falklands War made him able to understand how people like Burgess and Blunt might fastidiously "step aside" from patriotism. Burgess, Blunt and Bennett himself – they're all very bright people, though Bennett was Oxford, and the implication is that they see more and feel more sensitively than the populace. Clara mentioned E. M. Forster. He'd be another. Are patriotism and brainpower at variance? Perhaps, perhaps. Then there's Dr Johnson, of course, with patriotism as the "last refuge of a scoundrel".

'Now, Andrew Pax was Cambridge and very bright, too. If he believed Russia was the only future he might have been right to help her, even if at the expense of his own country – whose ways and whose government he had come to despise, perhaps understandably. A matter of taste. Yes, fastidiousness. I can see that, and could even at the time. But Pax was possibly more like John Cairncross. You'll have heard of him: the Fifth Man, as he came to be known, another brilliant Cambridge traitor, always top of the form. His magnificent brain told him he had a duty to help Russia, before the war and during it. But before the war, Russia was the enemy. People like Pax and Cairncross would not believe that. Their fine intellects would not let them. Pax was hanged to prove they had it wrong.'

'But in a sense he was right, wasn't he? Russia ceased to be the enemy as soon as Hitler went in in June 1941.'

'Of course in a sense Pax was right. That's what I've been saying, isn't it? What I told him – told him long before June 1941. Time did make him and Cairncross and some of the others right. But, you see, there was *no* time for Pax in 1941. As a matter of fact, we all wondered about how much time *we* had. And we blamed people like Pax for helping put us in that shit pit by their treachery: blamed and properly convicted him of it.' Deem stretched forward again and switched off the recorder. 'I think you'll have such a brilliant book, Louise, full of hot and exclusive insights.'

'But will they be right?'

'Ah, right. Where will we be looking at it from?'

Louise was booked to fly home next afternoon from Faro. The three of them had an early lunch in da Barraida restaurant outside Tavira, and then Louise would go to the airport alone by taxi. Da Barraida specialized in suckling pig. 'No, I shall not ask to come with you to London,' Clara said. 'Perhaps that was foolishness.'

Louise saw she yearned for a rebuttal.

'Yes, foolishness,' Deem said. 'We're too old to escape each other now, wrinkled by the same bit of foreign sun.'

Louise said: 'Clara, if you wished to come for a break and Clifford agrees I would love—'

'I know he made me sound some sort of discard in what he said about Roy last night,' Clara replied. 'So you wouldn't want my company, Louise, not even for a short spell.'

'We didn't speak of him,' Louise said. 'Her book is about Andrew Pax, Clara.'

Clara chipped away at her food, head down. 'Cliff's version of what happened to Roy is pretty well known, of course. It's what he told the court.'

'Yes, Louise will have seen all that. She's strong on research and records. It would have been tiresome to go over it.'

Clara looked up from the plate and began to intone. It was like another set-piece, but a solo this time. 'We had a phone call, Louise, late one evening. This was when we were living in Chislehurst, super suburbia, Cliff still employed by the Department, of course. He answered. Perhaps he was *ready* to answer. I tried to remember afterwards whether he seemed nervous and poised to get to the receiver first. I don't know. But he did get there. He replied very briefly to whatever was said and put the phone down. He told me it had been Roy, sounding distressed and in need of help. This would be very unusual. Unprecedented. Roy often wanted support, it's true, but when he did he would come to us, not ring up and summon Cliff. Roy was living in a big country place near Sevenoaks at the time, "Urals", or some such. He had recognition and decent money by then. Academe money. Literary journalism money. The poetry was still shit, but bang up-to-date shit, and on the whole it probably helped his career. Clifford said he must drive over there at once. I told him I would go, too. He didn't object, not for a moment. I think he wanted me to go, wanted me to see what was there, and what wasn't.'

Louise said: 'See what was there? But how would – Clara, do you mean Estham had told him on the phone he was going to kill himself?'

Deem said: 'This was a terrible experience for both of us, Louise. In my little trade I've seen violent deaths, obviously, but this was appalling, just the same.'

'The house had lights on when we arrived, but we could get no reply when we rang the bell. We discovered afterwards that his wife and children were away. Was she in cahoots with Cliff, you'll ask.'

Louise swallowed spit, could not ask anything.

'Two loads of jealousy, His and Hers,' Clara said. 'Clifford went around the back looking for a way in but apparently everything was locked up. So he smashed a window. He *says* he smashed a window and climbed in: told the court he smashed a window and climbed in. I didn't hear any breakage, but, of course, people like Clifford learned how to do that sort of thing quietly, so, yes, it was feasible. Just about. He came through and opened a bolted side door for me and we stood in the huge hall of the place and called out to Roy. Clifford made a really good show of this, his voice primed with anxiety.' She speeded up her concluding sentences, as if this part were a formality. 'Of course, we got no answer, so we began to search. Within a couple of minutes we found him dead in the bath. As everyone knows. He was arse-up, his face under, so he had done himself twice. Apparently. When eventually they drained the water and blood they found the blade.'

'It was very grim,' Deem said.

'There was no note,' Clara said. 'Well, naturally there was no fucking note. That's why he wanted me with him when we discovered Roy, surprise, surprise – not just to see him in such a mess but to find at first hand there was nothing for me. No message, no last thoughts. Cliff couldn't be accused of having destroyed a letter. I was there, to watch the discovery, take part in it. Or, I was supposed to assume it was a discovery for Cliff, as well as for me. This was the definitive end of Roy in a red bath, and the end of him and me. Cliff had won again, and had arranged for me to be there and witness the glory of it.'

'I have seen deaths like that before,' Deem said. 'They're among the worst to come upon suddenly.'

'Who made the phone call do you think, Louise?' Clara asked.

'You said it was Roy, *in extremis.*'

'No, I didn't. I said Cliff said it was Roy *in extremis.*'

'Well, of course it was Roy,' Deem replied. ' "I'm finished, Cliff, finished." Those whispered words terrified me. I gave them at the inquest.'

'Yes, you certainly did,' Clara said.

'But Clara imports her own venomous scenario, I'm afraid, Louise. She's still injured to the marrow, poor old clothes stand. I hope I can remain tolerant.'

'This was Clifford's bravo on the line to say it had been done,' Clara said.

Louise took some wine, needed some wine. 'Oh, Clara, how can you—?'

'Would you like your spouse to think more of someone you had personally cracked and diminished than of you?' Clara replied. 'See it from Cliff's side.'

'You actually know this phone call was—?'

'Perhaps more than one of them handled it for him. Yes, a scenario. And how! This was a very polished piece of work. What you'd expect. We are dealing with pros, after all – natural wit plus brilliant training. It was planned for Clifford to rush over and legitimately make a forced entry, fearing the worst about Roy, or to say he did. This would cover the damage done by his man or his team when he/they got in. You'd think operators of this calibre might have used a bit of plastic on the front door, but that doesn't work on a deadlock, Louise, and it can leave a trace, anyway. The straightforward old methods are best – as long as you can provide a happy explanation. After all, Peter Wright said that despite modern surveillance gear they hadn't found a better way to open envelopes than a steaming kettle. And by claiming to have broken in himself, Cliff could provide a happy explanation for damage. He would also require a quick look around to see his laddy or laddies had left no other evidence.' She smiled warmly across the piglet wreckage at Deem: 'Mainly, though, he wanted the phone call so he could get me there as a destructive punishment.'

'Yes, she was devastated that he left no word for her, though she seems so magnificently brave about it now, Louise,' Deem said. He stroked her fingers gently. The waiter watched and gave a fond, southern climates grin at this outburst of elderly affection. 'Clara has real guts,' Clifford said.

'Do you understand, Louise, why I don't want to stay?'

'I still see something quite noble in this suicide,' Deem said. 'Well, something virtually classical, of course. It takes real fibre, real sensitivity, to feel guilt on that scale over such a period. One may disapprove of the reason for his guilt and of the figure at the centre of it, Andrew Pax. Yet to go out like that made Roy seem more to me than just an addle-headed pimp for Moscow and long-distance adulterer.' He stood. 'We must get Louise to her taxi now, darling. She has things of moment in London tomorrow, I'm sure. I'd say we've all done damn valiantly on the pig.'

'Do you think Estham called you over there to implicate you, Cliff?' Louise asked. 'So it could appear as murder done up as suicide with you in the frame?'

'Oh, Roy wouldn't have the nous for that,' he replied.

In the aircraft Louise slept for a while and dreamed of Andrew Pax, but of Andrew Pax who at times became David Gale, and at times became an ape clinging to cage bars and grunting sentences from *Das Kapital*, as well as pleas for understanding and mercy. But when Pax was Pax, he was unmistakably Pax: the same podgy, insolently cheerful face she had seen in school photographs and Cambridge photographs and newspaper photographs during her research. He did not look especially bright, but he did look aggressive and sure of himself. In the dream, his eyes seemed jubilant with victory of some kind, his skin childlike, full of health and bounce. It was the sort of trump card face a terrified country might want to pull a bag over and get to the end of a rope.

For some of the time in the dream, Pax, dignified, even jaunty, paced his cell, holding up his trousers with both hands and talking the philosophical basis of his actions, as Deem had described, though talking them into a vacuum: Deem did not appear. The voice had a North of England rasp to it, which would be wrong for Pax and his London and Cambridge background, but which seemed fine for the embittered denunciation of capitalism he gave. It was during this

170

solemn pacing that Pax abruptly turned into David Gale, wearing the same battledress style clothes and still holding up his trousers. Gale went to the bars and, releasing one hand from his waistband, stuck it through in what seemed an imploring gesture: perhaps a need of human contact, perhaps a search for help. Now, Louise herself appeared in the dream, just outside the bars, and Gale's hand was reaching towards her, the fingers busy with longing. Gale cried in that thick filmic voice, 'Will you, Louise? Will you?'

Would she what? Touch him? Save him? The shock and the problem of it part woke her for a moment and she glanced about at the passengers alongside, afraid she might have made some horrified outcry while asleep. But they continued to read or themselves dozed. She realized that her dream was like all dreams, a hopeless mixture. There were new, strange visions in it, and also bits of what Clifford Deem had said, and bits of her reading and even of her cinema-going. David Gale prowling the cell was certainly from *Broken Light*, though they had not given him the humiliation of insecure trousers: improper for a star. There had been no reaching through the bars in the film either, as far as she could recall, and certainly not to herself! No crying out. She wondered if that sequence might have invaded her dream from *The Silence of the*

Lambs, when Hannibal Lecter stretches his arms so meaningfully towards Officer Starling. Films were powerful.

Louise slept again and picked up the dream. Pax as Pax was now busy around a Cambridge college. Someone bald and heavy and owl-faced appeared, and might have been C. P. Snow, though Snow in middle-age, not as he would have been in the 1930s. Pax seemed to be bellowing, shouting a defence of Snow at a gaggle of exceptionally effete and snobbish-looking men seated at a dining-room high table. 'No, he is not an Apaulostic,' Pax yelled, 'he comes from Leicester.' The scene faded then and reassembled into a Mastership contest at the college, with Pax once more shouting his views, but this time the view that Snow should be voted Master. Again Louise half awoke. She gathered that her dream was fiddling with the glimpses Lord Chate had given her of Christ's, and then getting jumbled with what she recalled of Snow's *The Masters.* Fiction had as much stature as reported fact. God, dreaming a life was pretty much like writing one: the same impossibility of control, the same unmanageable, warring, random currents from almost everywhere.

When she dropped off for the last time, it was Pax as Pax again, though wearing that booming scarf the costume people had given

David Gale. He was walking in what seemed to be a thirties hunger march. Or it might have been a combined hunger march and a miners' march for jobs. Poorly dressed people yelled unintelligible slogans and there was a hammer and sickle banner. Pax marched near the front, and looked not so much aggressive now as sad and responsible. From among trees skirting the road, a man watched, using field glasses off and on. He seemed to make notes on a pad, but the pad gradually became a wood-framed slate and the later writing was done in squeaking chalk. The face behind the pencil which turned into chalk was not clear, but the eyes seemed bleak and official. Deem? Barry as Deem? The march appeared to be led by an elderly, long-haired man in a wheelchair. Pushing the chair were a tall, beautiful woman with dyed blonde hair, and a man wearing a black leather coat. Occasionally this man called out something in the kind of abrasive Yorkshire or Geordie accent Pax had used. Oh, God. Louise roused herself and abandoned sleep. No insights would be achieved there: she could learn nothing about Pax from her subconscious, because her subconscious let in almost everything, including that wheelchair among the hunger marchers. This slice of the scene undoubtedly came from Anthony Powell's thirties novel *The Acceptance World*, which she had been re-reading lately in Penguin: the march actually illustrated its cover.

To keep herself awake, she brought out the typescript chapters of Pax's Life from her valise and began to mark with red Biro paragraphs for possible revision. For unavoidable revision. You could not trust your subconscious, but could you trust your conscious, either? And, more important, how far could you trust the conscious of others, or what they said was their conscious; others like Clara and Clifford, the two resonant C.s, but so rarely in harmony?

Thirteen

Before getting the campaign under way to clear Andrew Pax's name, Ted Burston thought it might be best to talk to at least one of the relatives. D.L.O. did not regard this as crucial. Perhaps it wasn't, not totally. But, at his level, D.L.O. occasionally lacked time or patience to look at projects in all their detail, and Burston often felt a duty to check against aspects that might turn out awkward. Didn't the firm employ him at a fine salary to keep an eye? This was certainly not to criticize D.L.O. It amounted to an admin matter, nothing more.

After all, the way D.L.O. went full-out after any idea was absolutely great, probably one of his main executive strengths. He would just surge through to what he wanted; and what he wanted was nearly always spot-on for the company. Didn't the firm employ Darren, at an even finer salary, for such flair? It would have been cruel and absurd to accuse D.L.O. of simply disregarding detail because he saw himself as such a big mind, such a magnificent, world-style eminence: in any business operation some details might turn out vital, and D.L.O. would obviously know it. The thing about Darren, though, was he believed that as long as he had the essence of something right – and he invariably did – well, often did – yes, as long as he had the essence right he considered he would always be able to bang the detail into line subsequently, given his unique skill and vim.

Or, preferably, perhaps, others – fucking dogsbodies, no doubt, in his mighty view – these dogsbodies, such as Ted Burston, could do that *for* him; given the ability of senior staff to deal with such spiky difficulties before they became overwhelming. Ted saw – on, as it were, D.L.O.'s behalf – that things could get tricky if objections to the campaign came from Pax's family once it was under way. By then, prominent figures might be involved and they would resent any taint via messy protests from relatives about, say, intrusion on private regret. The campaign was sure to attract big publicity and this must not turn grubby; otherwise, the company might be damaged, even though, of course, the company could not be openly connected with the campaign. And if the company were damaged Darren would be damaged, too. Burston knew he must quietly protect D.L.O. and his towering, careless ego. Yes, a duty.

On file from the very earliest planning days of *Broken Light* was a surviving sister of Pax, unearthed by the researchers. Her name was Elsie, which could have been acceptable when she was born, but did suggest a distant period now and some decline. Obstructive aggro from her must be unlikely, yet Burston wanted to make sure. This was Burston's nature – to make sure. Zoom figures like D.L.O. were too damn splendid for such plod, of course. Originally, it had been hoped the sister might provide insights on Andrew's character for the scriptwriters, though in the event she was not consulted.

He thought he might visit Mrs Elsie Gough immediately. Probably he would not need to bother D.L.O. by telling him at this stage. Possibly he would never tell him. If this old lady in Wales would simply give Burston a written promise to support the campaign – or at least not to fucking well fuck things up out of sheer bolshy negativeness – yes, that ... then there would be no reason for D.L.O. to know she had been approached. And naturally she would support it. What sort of woman would hinder the vindication of a brother across the decades, for heaven's sake? She might have taken another surname through marriage, but she would surely be grateful to see the honour of her original family restored. Someone of this age living in Llanidloes could not have much left to wish for, poor dear.

He rang her direct, not via the secretary. That was a basic courtesy when dealing with an oldie, who might suffer confusion with phones. 'Mrs Gough?' he asked. 'This is Edward Burston of Panopticon Films.'

'I believe you did your best in *Broken Light*.'

'Oh, I'm so pleased.'

'Panopticon? Wasn't it a kind of jail in the nineteenth century, built to such a plan there was all-round vision for the screws? Appropriate? That star, Dave Gale, the one who so tragically ... well, I was taught to regard suicide as the unforgivable sin, I'm afraid. The sin of despair, denying God's ability or even willingness to save.'

'Suicide is certainly dire.'

'But he had Andrew very accurately in the picture – that silly little intellectual whiz. Excuse me, I can't help feeling like that about Andy. I saw him not long before the hanging. With my mother. My father wrote him off, and didn't want to know. My father was religious, very. We all were. In fact I am still, I suppose, by today's standards. Where else for comfort? Where else for the rock on which to build, Mr Burston?'

'I know. Religion's quite a thing in Wales, I heard.' He considered that one of his best for brainlessness.

178

'My mother thought – well, this is flesh of my flesh. She had to be there. I expect you can understand.'

'Of course,' Burston said.

'Do you know, they strip-searched us for jemmies? It is not a proper thing, perhaps, to see one's mother naked, and especially not in a jail. Remember what Genesis says about Lot's daughters being privy to his nakedness? You know, at times I can still see that death-row corridor and cell. It's the kind of experience that would keep me, personally, out of spying for ever, I can tell you. Maybe that was what mother had in mind. To deter me. When you've bred one traitor you're probably rather concerned, Mr Burston. She went down and down after seeing Andrew like that, and then what followed. Naked in the search room, she still had a zing to her body – is it respectful to say this about one's mother?'

'Oh, yes, entirely.'

'I do hope so. You could see why she would be pestered by the gentry she was working with at the time on several wartime charity committees. Indelicate propositions endlessly, Mr Burton. She would mention them at home – to me, though young, not to father, naturally.'

'Sickening.'

'Of course, in those days the gentry thought they had a right to whatever they wanted, even those old enough not to be in the war and concerned with welfare.'

'*Droit de seigneur.*'

'We thought of it as more like David with Bathsheba in Second Samuel.'

'That as well.'

'Though, of course, mother never went with the gentry – none, I'm sure of that – as Bathsheba did with David, while married to poor Uriah.'

'Women have a path to tread,' Burston replied.

'But after Andrew's death she grew stoopy and her face turned void and wild, like someone hit permanently sick. Myself, it took me ten years to get over Andy's death. There was no therapy about in those days. You just held your nose and walked on. Do you know, Mr Burston, father disapproved of cinema – Plymouth Brethren, you see – yet I'm embarrassed to say I not only went to see *Broken Light* but was disappointed to find I was not in it. I don't mean in present person, obviously. Would I look the part now – this hair and rural dentistry? I don't think so. But perhaps you could have got some child star to be the *then* me. Oh, dear, vanity! I was about twelve at the time. Mother and I were so glad we went to see Andrew, really. It was quite a sentimental encounter. Andy had been trying to persuade the lad who hunted him to visit – the secret service officer, you know. He was in the film, of course. The one with unfriendly and friendless eyes, yet not unattractive.'

'Barry Wight – playing Deem. Barry's eyes are often useful. They both pull their weight.' Burston needed Elsie to consider him thick and not too dangerous.

'Andy wanted to speak with the officer about what had happened. This was so like my brother. He believed everything could be put right by intelligent talk. He was good at it. He did not seem to realize that not all set such value on words. Isn't it the *Epistle of James* which stresses the importance of works?'

'That area.'

'I believe this Deem did go to see him later. Mercy will out in the most unexpected circumstances, Mr Burston.'

'True.' This whole story was full of unexpected circumstance and minor, marginal people.

'Andrew was not in a good state. His tunic wet with tears and froth. Gibbering. And worse. But I realize you couldn't do all this in the film. That Gale had to look after what's called his image, I believe ... until he took those pills, that is. And an audience need a bit of dignity to go home with when they pay such a lot for seats, don't they, even in an out-of-town spot like this?'

'We've had a lot of feedback about

Andrew, Mrs Gough.'

'Feedback? Well, yes, I expect so.'

'Favourable. It's prompted some thought.'

'We stood outside the gates on that morning when the notice went up.'

'Heartbreaking, yet courageous.'

'My father was home on leave, but he wouldn't come there, either. A full staff sergeant. "That vile Christ's," he used to say. That's Andy's college, not blasphemous, you understand. But he was against it as name for a college.'

'Yes?'

'Father blamed Christ's and Cambridge. Well, I've heard him call them Sodom and Gomorrah. The bombing was still on. People had stern views. And Barbara, Andy's girl-friend, was with us at the gates, too, of course. As in the movie. She was lovely in the film, but not really like Barbara, not as I remember Babs, anyway.'

'Imogen Cruse.'

'Wonderful body. I wondered if she might be inclined to other ladies. But still lovely. There's a lot of that in the cinema business, I should think. We have to take a more open view of it these days, though I don't know what father would say.'

'We couldn't trace Barbara Priest. We simply had to guess.'

'You'd need a romantic angle, obviously for a film as long as that. I think Barbara emigrated soon after the war ended. The States? Canada? Probably there was a baby.'

Burston was dazed. 'What baby?'

'Andy never said a word nor Babs herself, but mother thought Babs was carrying and ma was good at spotting. People's mothers *were* good at it in those days, always on the watch for slip-ups because single-mumming was definitely not the game then. Well, they knew mother and father would be even more hurt.'

'Hurt? You mean the baby? Oh, they weren't married, of course, were they?'

'Carrying when we were outside the gates together. Then we lost touch. She stuck by Andrew while he was still alive and there was some hope. But then ... oh, just disappeared. I can't blame her. Such pressures in war-time. The enemy was the enemy. The enemy was everyone who looked the least disloyal. A young girl wouldn't want to be associated – not go on being associated when there was a future. And especially she would not want the child associated. I don't regret I went to the gates. The one who posted the notice was crying, but many people did have unfor-giving views then. Although twenty-four was young to be hanged, people much younger were getting killed. Andy was run over by a machine.'

'I wondered if I might call on you.'

'Oh? What point, Mr Burston? The baby?

Baby! Well, in his/her fifties now. Some new film possibility? A sequel? How could that be, though? I mean, Andrew's so dead in the film – that really foul sound of the trap – and the star's dead in life, as it were. Where do you go from here? The baby?'

'Wider issues,' Burston replied.

'I was brought up to consider wider issues.'

'I thought so.'

'I'm afraid my hubby thinks Andrew was rubbish, just like father.'

'So would he object if I visited to talk about your brother?'

'Oh, it's possible. But I was taught one should expect opposition in life and quietly face it. Yes, visit.'

'Fine.'

Burston wished she had sounded different, more combative, more eager to see the family reclaim its dignity. Despite the invitation at the end, she sounded almost casual. For God's sake, how many ancient women called Elsie in sodding Llanidloes were phoned by a film company? It was damn smartarse cheap of her to bring up that the name Panopticon could mean the Benthamite prison, as well as a source of novelties and wondrous sights. But he would go to call on her soon. Today, he was giving lunch to Pamela de la Salle but could travel to Wales before the end of the week. Lunch with Pam was a good routine, and he would not want anything to get in the way: the meetings had their uses for both. That had been an extremely unspiteful profile of Gale Pamela wrote after her interview with Louise, yet not exactly dull; and Burston would be able to thank her properly now; perhaps talk about other possible helpful articles for the paper, though nothing on the Pax campaign this early.

'Oh, the Gale piece,' she said. 'You liked? Thanks.'

'We had a lot of feedback.'

'Well, I expect so.'

'Favourable. There'll be a further edition of his Life.'

'You're re-hashing it?' she asked.

'Not so much actual changes as a few minor switches of tone here and there.'

'Christ, you're dismantling the first edition altogether, are you?' she replied.

'A few minor switches of tone.'

'Did Summers agree to scrap it as it was and re-write? No temperamental artist stuff? She's a bit hoity-toity. Quoting Shakespeare and such shit. But after all, only a bloody ghost, though a top one.'

'Louise took our point about the need for a slightly amended perspective extremely well.'

They were eating in a place Burston had discovered in Latie Street, Holborn. There

185

was a Peruvian chef who knew how to cook mutton, and do almost everything else beautifully, too. The restaurant was in a warehouse basement, though a big, airy basement, bright with paintings. They knew Burston by now, but made no tiresome fuss of him. D.L.O. also came here sometimes, and with quite major guests of all nationalities. It had been a true plus for Ted to recommend the spot to him.

'Was this a D.L.O. matter then?' Pamela asked.

'What?'

'Dusting up the Life.'

'Consensus. Discussion. It's how D.L.O. operates, I'm very happy to say, Pam. With Louise a key part of the consensus, obviously.'

She grinned, had a bit of a secret think and then said: 'Changes of that sort, on D.L.O.'s orders – I just wondered what would happen if he were moved out.' She held her broth up and went into a full smirk as she blew on it, a complicated use of the lips: 'So crazy if someone comes along as successor to D.L.O. and says change the whole thing back again to what it was. Do a bloody *third* version.'

He had been gazing at one of the surreal paintings, trying to sort out the body of a horse, but her words got to him all right. 'So, what's that mean, Pam – "if he were moved

186

out"? What someone "comes along"? What is this?' Pam heard a lot that mattered: a main reason the lunches were worthwhile.

'Oh, Ted, come on, you know.'

'No, honestly. Please, Pam.' Yet he did recall that moment when D.L.O. gazed fondly around his suite, like preparing for farewell, the way Thatcher looked at Number 10 through the car window just after she'd been kicked out.

Pam took some broth, as though unwilling to say more, sure he was stalling. Staring at him over the spoon, she was obviously trying to read his face. 'All right,' she muttered. 'If you say so.' She put the spoon down in her bowl: lots of significance. He felt afraid. 'A whisper around about D.L.O. Well, about Panopticon. I get this from our office in the States. Ted, you're really telling me it hasn't reached you? Now, honestly? Look, even I know about this, yet hardly ever touch movie stuff. You're playing loyal and dumb? Your loyalty's famed.'

'What from the States, Pam? I'm intrigued.'

'Please, Ted.'

'What from the States?'

'One of the biggies moving on Panopticon. Allied International? Entercosmic? Zone?'

He laughed a while, shaking his head slowly, pityingly. 'Oh, Lord, Pam, these tales come up all the time. The same companies –

Allied, Entercosmic, Bayzone. You really shouldn't listen to such old-hattery.' He began to eat again, oysters in hollandaise. He was at ease, almost.

'Panopticon looks very profitable now, after *Broken Light*, regardless of Dave Gale exiting.'

'We're doing all right, yes. So?'

'More than.'

'Just all right. And don't forget we're only the Brit outstation of Maydelle Movies, L.A.'

'But the tale says – oh, the usual way of things in cinema land – it says someone wants to buy Panopticon from Maydelle, but not buy the lad who made Panopticon a success. The tale says D.L.O.'s got to go. As ever, there's new brooming.'

'Yes, a tale.'

'And they don't like the Panopticon name. Did you know it was some sort of clink?'

He mopped up his sauce. 'Listen, Pam, this week I'm actually travelling all the way to Wales specifically on a task designed to strengthen D.L.O.'

'What's that about then, Ted?'

'This is a project. A decent project, of significance.'

'A D.L.O. project?'

'Any project in Panopticon is ultimately a D.L.O. project, isn't it?' he replied wearily. 'Leadership. Yet, with consensus, of course.

D.L.O. is quite dictatorial about the need for consensus. As it were.' Fucking brilliant: an oxymoron! The democratic despot.

'So, is the trek worth it? You know how things are in your game – and in mine, come to that.' She made a throat-cutting gesture with her large hand. 'Projects get swiftly beaten into nothing and die. Die with their author.'

'I see this as more than a project, as a matter of fact. A wider issue.'

'God. It's really doomed in any shake-up then.'

'Something that would stand above boardroom manoeuvrings.'

'Jesus, Ted, this is bad. Something political?' She winced. 'Oh dear, I know – you proposed this to D.L.O. yourself and he bit? One of your genuinely bright notions. Is this a move to get Pax canonized? Something like that? It is?'

'You'll hear about it first, when we're ready.' Her instincts were a raging pain.

'Can you see Charlie Nimm in Entercosmic touching Pax?' she replied. 'He thought Reagan was too Left. Or Faldave of Bayzone?'

They did not talk much through the rest of the meal, and not at all about those wispy rumours. It would be just like that greasy sod D.L.O. to keep things of this calibre from him. Jesus, but wasn't it disgraceful, hurtful, that he should learn it from a journalist? You let D.L.O. know about a great eating place and he'd still treat you as somebody far, far back. 'Are you going to write about this alleged deal?' he asked her as they were leaving. 'You wanted my reactions? That it? I've told you nothing, Pamela. You're wired, you bitch? Not that it matters. I've told you nothing, nothing, nothing.'

'Write about what?'

'Your takeover "tales".'

'They're only tales, to date. Of course I can't write about them.'

'Right,' Burston said.

'D.L.O. hasn't given you even a hint?'

'There's nothing to hint about. If we discussed Allied or Zone or Cosmic every time someone launched one of these reports we'd never have time to make pictures.'

He found Pam a taxi, claiming he needed a stroll himself. She said: 'Will you still do your selfless expedition into a far country, trying to shore him up, Ted?'

'What else?' Burston replied. 'Haven't I told you: I've heard nothing that alters the situation?' When she had gone he hailed a cab for himself. Back in the office he rang Llanidloes to cancel the visit. A man answered. 'May I speak to Mrs Elsie Gough, please. It's Edward Burston of Panopticon.'

'Well, you can fuck off for a start,' he said.

'I'd been given to understand this was a religious household.'

'Fuck off,' he replied, putting the phone down.

Fourteen

At home in the night no more dreams came to Louise, but neither did sleep, and on the next day she Air Portugalled to Faro again. This was getting costly. Her research budget might not stand it, and the Revenue would never wear such travel as necessary outlay: it was no part of a biographer's role to protect old ladies. But she must bring Clara back. It had been intolerably cold and harsh to ignore her plea. Christ, it could have been more than that, worse than that. In the night and very awake, Louise had seen – yes seen not dreamed – she had seen a woman in a pearlized blue leather dress and blue lamb's wool cardigan floating face down beneath the surface of a slow, wide river. There were no willows growing aslant this stretch of urban water, but there were a hell of a lot of big and big-toothed silvery fish about.

It had been mad of Clara to talk in Clifford's presence of how Estham died; or of how she said he died. As she herself had stressed, Clifford was trained in many hard skills. Of course, she might have said it all in his presence often before. This time, though, she had said it to someone who wrote and published. In fact, what Clara alleged was probably unusable for now: libellous, unsubstantiated, grossly speculative. Perhaps Clifford did not realize this, though; maybe suspected that Louise could smuggle a harmful innuendo or two into the account of Estham's death. Clifford might anticipate police interest, a re-opening of the file and demands by detectives for verification from Clara of what she'd said: yes, might anticipate them.

Louise did not telephone the Deems. Instead, she arrived at the long, gleaming white house in the foothills of the Serra do Caldeirao by taxi in the evening. She could get no reply at the front door but heard cheerful voices and occasional laughter. Louise went around by the side of the house and found Clara and Clifford sitting opposite each other at a white plastic picnic table, talking and Clara, head back, staring at the sky. It was warm still. A dozen Bass beer cans stood or lay on the table, some squashed, four or five perhaps unopened. Cliff heard and saw Louise first. At once he stood and beamed a welcome: a line from a Maya Angelou poem nudged Louise, about someone summoning up sincerity like a favoured pet. Clifford reached for a full can and eventually located one. He opened it and handed it to her. There were no glasses. 'Louise has returned for you, Clara,' he said. 'I'm not surprised.'

'Yes, so will you come with me, Clara?' Louise replied. She said it as matter-of-factly as she could, no gush; like an invitation to a shopping trip. Adoring the taste of beer through metal, Louise drained the can and enjoyed the deep belch she had known would follow, and the lesser ones that would dog that. Deem opened another for her. She took a mouthful or two. Things would start to look simpler soon. 'Cliff, I've got to have some names,' she said.

'Accomplices? Is that what you mean?' he asked.

'Of course,' she said.

He nodded a couple of times. She thought there was a kind of sadness to it. 'Louise has swallowed as gospel that gorgeous tale you gave her about Estham's death, love.' He walked laboriously to the middle of the lawn and brought a chair for Louise. 'There's plenty more Bass where this came from,' he told her, as she sat down at the table with them. 'We import by the gross. Remember Osborne's Archie Rice, Louise?'

Clara whistled towards the Milky Way. 'Oh, Christ, Cliff, you're so patronizing. *Osborne*'s Archie Rice. Do you imagine Louise needs a finger-post?'

'Sorry. Remember Archie Rice, Louise:

"No draught Bass in Canada"? No draught Bass in Tavira, either. This is as close as we can get. You didn't leave Portugal yesterday? Or you've actually been back to London and returned? Really? Too worried about us? We've had something like it happen before, haven't we, Clara? Once or twice. Remember Walter and May? People fret about our condition and show up like this when they're supposed to have gone. It's so well-meant. I certainly don't feel resentment. Clara somehow gets an emotional hold on visitors. Poor Louise, I can see why you fret. Aren't you stuck with two damned problematical deaths, Estham and your actor? Were they symbolism or mere sex?'

He tossed a concertinaed empty can into the air and nod-headed it like a soccer player towards the shrubbery. A drop of the beer ran down from his scalp and formed a brown arc for a moment on his temple. Then it dispersed and soaked into the collar of his shirt.

'Louise wouldn't see anything mere about sex, I imagine,' Clara said. She brought her gaze down from the sky and stared warmly at Louise now. 'This actor fellow, David Gale, killed himself because of you, did he, my dear? You'd ended it? Your inclinations prevailed? Men can be damn vulnerable, regardless. Emotional. He could not get feeling into his roles, but that does not mean he

195

lacked it.'

Deem rubbed half-heartedly at the collar. Louise thought the stain made him look degenerate and past caring. She knew he was not the second. He said: 'Naturally, the frustrations of love are a much more likely reason for doing himself in than identifying with Pax. And they're also much more ... oh, I don't know – much more *interesting*?'

Louise said: 'But, Cliff, be consistent: you do believe – make out you believe – that Estham killed himself because of the affiliation with Pax?'

'Oh, Estham,' Deem replied. 'You're confused, Louise. Estham was a poet. Different brand of poseur altogether. Have you read his Shorter Works collection, called *We'll Have To Let You Go*?'

He recited:

Sing to me of stone on stone on stone.
We live to celebrate and ante-date defeat.
I leg it, mealy-mouthed, choate, alone:
a Métro dash, an uncommitted street.

'Roy dwelt on guilt, wanted gestures, signs. You can't beat a crimson bath for resonance.'

Clara spoke hesitantly, softly, with a comfy Bass slur: 'I'm afraid I can't believe you, Louise dear, when you say no closeness between you and David Gale. There was

196

something, I'm sure. And, you see, I wouldn't want to be a lover you go to merely on the rebound? I'm worth more than that, even so late. Let's wait a while – see how your feelings clarify.'

'She's not here as a lover, dear,' Deem said. 'She's anxious for your physical safety. She's scared of what I might do.'

Louise nursed the can, took no more beer. 'Just tell me there are no names, no accomplices you can point me to, because Roy Estham really did take his own life. I'd be at ease then.' She was speaking to Clara. What point in asking Deem?

'Drink up,' he said. 'Things are getting solemn, don't you think?'

'Oh, other names? They're not crucial, you know. Clifford would have been entirely capable of seeing to Roy alone, Louise. I mean, capable technically and mentally. His training would have stressed the extra security in handling things solo, if possible. Cliff knew how to get into a property and wrists. And it would have answered so much better like that, wouldn't it? Cuckold does cuckolder. There's a proper symmetry and one-to-one pleasure.'

Fifteen

Maybe Pamela de la Salle did have it wrong after all. D.L.O. kept coming in to his suite every day, and to Burston he seemed as jaunty as ever, so cheerful and solid; nothing like that sad figure who had gazed lingeringly around his office. Surely if Panopticon were for sale D.L.O. would know, especially if he was to be let go. Could rumours that reached a London journalist from the States fail to reach D.L.O: D.L.O., whose ears were like a bat's for the least tremor in the business? Or did D.L.O. know it was just another bit of nothing, the way Burston had told Pamela it was just another bit of nothing? Pamela rarely fell for rubbish, but she was a profile expert, not a cinema expert. Gullibility would happen now and then to any journalist. The *'Hitler Diaries'*.

D.L.O. intercommed Burston and asked him to pop up. He found D.L.O. had a guest. 'Here's Stan Faldave from L.A., Ted,' D.L.O. boomed. 'I thought the three of us to lunch in that great spot, Taste Bud, you discovered.'

'Ideal,' Burston replied. This could be dicey. If Faldave was big-time, and he looked big-time in his tweeds, Darren would worry he might not like the restaurant, and so Burston could be declared responsible for picking it. But if Faldave approved, Darren would get the credit for having sent out this talented minion, Burston, to short-list good eateries, with Darren finally picking the perfect one: such gifted delegation. Darren – basically an unsatisfactory name for the top man in a business, even a business which was just a branch office, and even a business that might be up for grabs. Half the muggings in Brixton were by Darrens. Faldave had a different sort of name altogether: 'Stanley' was big in cinema: Stanley Kubrick, Stanley Donen, Stanley O'Toole, Stanley Baker. All right, not all were alive, but the name Stanley had built itself an aura, and plenty of the younger people in the game had adopted it, to proclaim inventiveness and power. Faldave was not much above thirty and probably his real first name was Matthew or Mel or Darren, but he sought the Stanley clout.

'Stan's over looking around, Ted. He was eager to meet you.'

'Yes, indeed, Ted,' Faldave said.

'D.L.O. is as keen on Taste Bud as I am,' Burston replied. 'We think you'll love it.'

'I know I will,' Faldave replied. 'I've heard

199

about your good work, Ted. The Dave Gale Life. Not to mention looking after so many aspects of *Broken Light* itself, of course.'

So what the fuck was Bayzone Stanley's status here now? How come, after knowing you for two minutes, he thought he was entitled to sing your CV? Yet his voice was very gentle, almost cautious. Now and then in the business you would meet Americans like this. Somewhere, Faldave had learned about mildness, or its semblance. And the same went for deference and boyishness. Burston was sharp on accents and he would locate this one Chicago way; educated Chicago, say Oak Park: Hemingway country once, Bellow country. Deep in it you could hear the street rasp, the one-time Pig City slaughter-house rasp, but it had been deliciously overlaid by something which at a push could be associated with culture, or even scholarship. Burston thought Faldave would be from a non-Ivy League college, though one with quite a reputation in its immediate neighbourhood.

Although so young, Faldave dressed county English. His shirt was small red, green and brown checks and his tie thick wool in brown and gold. The tweed suit was predominantly darkish green, in cloth radiating distinguished age, which he was definitely not old enough to have put it through himself. The suit fitted pretty well, might even have been built for him, or Burston could have believed Faldave bought it from some grandson of C. Aubrey Smith, after a few generations of considerate use.

Faldave would be about Smith's build, though his face was without the cragginess. Stan Faldave had tidy, even features – nose, chin, ears – and docile grey-blue eyes, or eyes he could make docile when that might be handy. His profile was extremely easy to get on with. He had done the whole thing and was wearing heavy brown brogues with the tweeds, and these helped give him solidity, like a farmer at a beast auction.

Waiters in Taste Bud never fawned over customers, but Burston noticed they seemed pally to D.L.O., and this also made him feel Pam de la Salle must have picked up dud info: staff here would know as soon as anyone who was due a fall. *Hors d'oeuvre* time Faldave said: 'So, Ted, when you look at *Broken Light*, boxofficing like *Ben Hur*, would you say you've hit an enduring public taste for what we might reasonably call *cause célèbre* topics from recent history? Is this a one-off, or might we be into a mode, do you think? Plainly the suicide or otherwise of the star is most likely a one-off – oh, yes, most likely – but my own feeling is that *Broken Light* would have grossed beautifully regardless of that factor, whose influence is, in any case, unclear. Might it be more interesting to ponder whether a lasting public appetite has been created for dramas that, as it were, rectify history? Plus, TV may have helped open up a probing interest in the past. Over here I've seen TV programmes like your *Rough Justice*, where court verdicts are questioned long after they've been given, often effectively. We've got similar shows in the States, though maybe not so forceful. And then, of course, movie-wise there's would-be forensic re-looks like Oliver Stone's *JFK*-hokum, sure, but what the trade Press calls "gravitas hokum". How do you see things, Ted?'

He was truly lovely with questions. They came backed by a frown of novice puzzlement, as if he were really keen to be improved, not just to sound you out. Was this meeting a viva? Faldave would probably despise anyone naive enough to try a straight answer. *How do you see things, Ted?* So fucking blatant. Burston got more crudities into his mouth to show how relaxed he was. 'Yes, *Broken Light* did seem to mean something to many people,' he said. 'And yet the tale has been available for an age.'

'Obviously, prevalent leftist sentiments demand this type of revisionism? How *Broken Light* has scored. Nobody would go for a whitewash movie on, say Lord Haw-Haw or Musso.' He did not laugh, though Burston had heard much worse jokes.

Faldave was doing dryness in the English style; or the Gore Vidal still drier style.

D.L.O. said: 'Ted's organizing a national, even international, campaign to get Pax officially cleared, perhaps awarded a posthumous decoration. It's a project Teddy thought up entirely solo. So brilliant, so typical.'

'Really?' Faldave replied.

Burston said: 'Well, I had half an idea, you know, Stan. D.L.O. gave it the shape and impetus only he is capable of providing.'

'Ted's been putting some real drive into creating this.'

'That's certainly ... well ... fascinating for a film company. To get unambiguously into politics.' He looked frightened, like hearing his daughter had married Michael Corleone.

'Panopticon would stay totally out of sight, obviously,' Burston said. Did Faldave think it was good these reappraisals of history came from the Left, or did he simply think they came from the Left? Plus – God, yes, plus – was he actually Panopticon now, in his squire gear?

'I expect from the company's point of view the real and prime requirement pre any campaign is good research on this Pax guy,' Faldave said. 'You would not want people to come up with new shit about him once you've got that sort of link, however discreet it might be. I say new shit, meaning shit extra to what is already on him from being a traitor, of course. Some people are going to think that's enough shit, anyway, to make him even now nothing but a liability.'

'Teddy's taking care of all that, aren't you, Ted? Ted's really scouring – family inquiries, archives, the totality.'

Faldave still spoke mildly. 'So interesting this constant pressure from the Left to make history look different. We all see why. Up to now, history was written to satisfy a clique. Reaction against that has certainly been a discernible public mood on both sides of the water. Is it going to last, though?'

D.L.O. twitched a lip or two to indicate this could be more than a negligible question.

Faldave said: '*Broken Light* was supremely timely – and opportunism is the essence of most great box-office works. Do you think, Ted, if you were just starting to put *Broken Light* together now for showing in, say, 1991–1992, that you could still rely on such a public response? When I posited movies to you that would praise Haw-Haw or Mussolini – that's a *reductio ad absurdam* crazy joke, of course. Of course. Things are not going to shift that far to the Right in our trade. No. But some shift is happening, isn't it? Might folk get tired of this Left, retrospective subversion? It's a difficult one, a sensitive one. I'm asking whether you think the public mood is still going that radical way, Ted, post demolition of the Wall and so on, because I, personally, think it might not be. However much that is to be regretted!'

D.L.O. nodded.

Faldave said: 'But, of course, Ted, I'm not at ground level, street level, like you. The job makes me remote – and very remote as far as G.B. is concerned, obviously. Nothing like as much in touch as you.'

Faldave had ordered sea bass in a bright yellow sauce, but he only nibbled at the outskirts of the course. D.L.O. chose kidneys on rice and something, and he ate about as much of it as Faldave took of the fish dish. Burston worked away enthusiastically at his steak and kidney pie. It was burnt and full of undefined lumps, somewhere between stringy and hard, but he had to stand by this place and this dish. It was 'his' restaurant. To back off from the muck would be traitorous; and, although it was not wholly clear, Faldave seemed set against treachery today. Had Faldave bought Panopticon? Was this lunch a short-list session to decide who would run it in Britain for him, his father-in-law and the Bayzone board? It *was* Faldave's father-in-law at the top of Bayzone, wasn't it – that kind of traditional Hollywood marriage arrangement? Someone audacious enough to wear that suit would not want a fucking kow-tower like Darren, would he, for God's sake? Could a business operate on such slimy leadership, even if it was the leader who helped put *Broken Light* together? Show some conviction, some confidence. Burston got the fork into two flint parcels at once, took an admiring glance as he lifted the load, then dragged them lovingly off the prongs with unflinching front teeth.

'I adored the Gale Life,' Faldave said.

Momentarily – perhaps because his chewing had to be noisy – Burston heard 'ordered' the Gale Life. He was going to cry out around the not-too-manageable stuff in his mouth that there was no need to approach a bookshop, he had spare copies. Or did Faldave mean it was he who originally gave orders for the autobiography to be commissioned? But surely to God Faldave was not running Panopticon then.

'Yes, really *adored* it,' Faldave said.

Did they do 'adored' like that in the States, the gush of it, or was this more of his donned Englishry? Didn't Faldave realize 'adored' was a Dickie Attenborough word and would not do for someone in old green tweeds and a wool tie? Foreigners should skip idioms.

Faldave said: 'That ghost – Louise something? – a weighty talent. She really knows about getting a pretty veil over things. Gale's broads, obviously, and the drinking. And his lumpy acting style. Summers' book – creatively vague. Brilliant.'

'Ted's instructing her to meaty up the suicide for the reprint.'

'Really?' Faldave said.

'Ted thinks there's mileage in it for Panopticon.'

'Really?'

'To get the film and the Life more profoundly connected with Andrew Pax and his death, so it has a recurrent Main Street theatre relevance,' D.L.O. explained. 'Sort of empathy?'

'What's she like this Louise?' Faldave replied. 'Fuckable? I mean, fuckable by a star, among all the easy pickings? Something very nice between her and Gale during the writing? The usual thing. You can feel it here and there in the text, wouldn't you say, Ted?'

'She's doing a life of Pax now,' Burston said.

'Fascinating,' Faldave said.

'It's sure to portray him – and justifiably portray him – as heroic,' Burston said. 'Why else do a biog? We're seeking a long-term spin-off benefit from this, too, for *Broken Light* and the Gale Life.'

'Ted thinks it could bring a depth, Stan. Just coffee, I think,' D.L.O. told the waiter. Faldave had said he did not want anything at all.

'I'll take the flan. With cream,' Burston said.

'It's all very, very problematical,' D.L.O.

said. 'But Ted is determined to orchestrate the various parts: determined, and so wholly certain he's right, one has to let him push on.'

Sixteen

D.L.O. disappeared. His PA thought he might have gone back to the States with Stanley Faldave for a couple of days. Apparently, there had been some talk of 'major boardroom confabs in L.A.'. She said she had no idea what about; and that could be half true, or even a bit more. Burston had known him drop out of sight like this before once or twice. D.L.O. regarded such sovereign impetuosities as a status perk, even *de rigueur*. In due course, there might be a phone call or a fax, possibly giving his location and checking that things were running all right.

In the past, Burston had felt it a compliment that Darren would leave him in charge without pre-briefing. During these absences, the PA automatically switched to Ted all problems she did not feel capable of handling herself: few. If there were important folk to see, she assumed Burston would use D.L.O.'s suite for the meeting. She showed them into D.L.O.'s waiting area before calling Burston down on the intercom from his preferred hutch and giving him the OK to instal himself temporarily in D.L.O.'s luxury.

Perhaps D.L.O. had been freighted back to the States to tell Faldave's colleagues in detail what they had bought with Panopticon, which would include Burston, so far. This might indicate D.L.O. was to be kept on in his job. Possibly the Taste Bud lunch really had been a feeler, and Burston failed to convince that he should/could replace D.L.O. Oh, Christ, should he have eaten with such audacious verve? Might flan and cream when the other two skipped dessert seem impertinent?

But possibly, too, D.L.O. was needed in the States to discuss with the board his terms of severance. If he fell in a takeover, he would have a stuffed purse coming to him, including, most probably, complex continuing percentage dividends on *Broken Light*, *Vain Tempest*, *Over My Shoulder* and other works. Bayzone might want to buy him out of those, and that could most likely be finalized best face to face, with in-house lawyers at the con. Film companies loathed permanent piece-of-the-action deals. These meant a movie did not wholly belong to them: every revival or special promotion of a picture leaked box-office coin because an employee or artist had far back somehow worked an entitlement.

'Did they actually leave here together, D.L.O. and Faldave?' Burston asked the PA.

'D.L.O. always keeps a packed flight bag in his suite for emergencies, as you know, Ted,' she replied.

'How did they seem?'

'How do you mean, seem?' She would know what he meant, of course, but Marie was what D.L.O. had made her: getting on for as slippery as himself, yet now and then warm with it, and even needy: a face of untidy moods and occasional tiny lewdnesses.

'Well, did they seem friendly? After the Taste Bud lunch, did they seem, yes, friendly? More friendly than before? Did they go from here together?' He did not rush the questions, but sought to put executive doggedness into his tone.

'Friendly?' she asked.

'This is two people who'll sit next to each other across the Atlantic, Marie. How did they—'

'Oh, seem,' she said. 'I don't know for certain they were going to cross the Atlantic together, Ted. D.L.O. might be in the States, he might not. And, if he is, he might have travelled with Stanley Faldave, he might not. Stanley Faldave could be still in Britain.'

This was fair, and Burston nodded. 'Did D.L.O. have the flight bag with him when they left?'

'I'm not sure if they left together. They were still talking in D.L.O.'s suite when I went home last evening.'

'Is the flight bag where D.L.O. usually keeps it?'

'It isn't there absolutely all the time, Ted, even when D.L.O. is not travelling. Sometimes, if he's been abroad he'll go home with the bag on his return, obviously, and perhaps neglect to bring it in for a day or two. There wouldn't normally be any urgency about that, because after he's been on a trip he doesn't usually do another for a while. As you know. And he needs to refill it with clean clothes and so on.'

'Marie, love, the point is, isn't it, is the bag there now?'

'I did as it happens look and it's not. But this is by no means conclusive,' Marie replied.

'And when they were here, around the office, after the lunch, before you went home, how did they—?'

'Seem together?'

'Yes.'

'You mean were they friendly?'

'Yes.'

'But why not, Ted?'

'They were?'

'I heard no shouting or fighting through the wall. Nothing's broken in there, Ted, and no spit on the dado.'

212

'How did he look?'

'D.L.O.? Oh, you know, as ever, sort of relaxed yet *puissant*.'

'Did he look as relaxed yet *puissant* as Faldave?'

'Faldave's quite a rare one in that suit.'

'And what would his background be?'

'These people come up very fast in the States. He's probably only about thirty. What did you think?'

'Are there night flights to L.A.?'

'Oh, yes, some. Or with changes. To take advantage of the time lag for meetings.'

He liked to think of D.L.O. being dragooned into the flight with Faldave. He recalled that now famed, touching scene in *Vain Tempest* where the anti-hero criminal, Cornelius Lowther, played winningly by Derwent Rich, is finally flown back to the States from Frankfurt, handcuffed to F.B.I. men. Burston found he could visualize Lowther, but with Darren's head and shoulders, in Club class.

'I'm going to Wales for a day or two tomorrow,' he told Marie. Burston suddenly felt he must behave independently, struggle out briefly from under the imperious hierarchy here and see what message Pax's sister could give.

'I don't believe D.L.O. mentioned Wales.' She looked imperious herself now, but keep it for the office cleaner, you middle-grade cow.

'Something's come up,' he replied.

Her body grew as solid as a road block. 'Well, Ted, I don't know. If D.L.O. calls he'll wish to talk, won't he? I can fill him in on most things, but he'll definitely want to speak with you, as a formality. You're nominally deputizing.'

'He's got my mobile number. Say I had to go into Wales.'

'On what account, Ted? I mean, D.L.O. is sure to ask. Somewhere like Wales.'

'The Pax campaign.' It was his. HIS.

Marie gave herself a pause and touched her lips with three fingers, maybe to make sure she enunciated dead right what would come next: 'Oh, Pax. I heard in outline of that fine proposal from you, of course, Ted, and I love Pax and love *Broken Light*, obviously. But are you confident that, in the circumstances, the possibly new circumstances, I mean, one way and the other ... can you be confident D.L.O. will be still as committed to it?'

'*I'm* committed to it. Some issues have unvarying worth.' People like Marie were unfamiliar with constancy. They considered everything relative: relative to what D.L.O. thought, or was thought to think, or what those thought to be possibly controlling D.L.O. thought, or were thought to think. Perhaps he, Ted, was like that once. He had emerged, for now. He must sound resolved. He found he rather liked the vision of D.L.O., frogmarched on to that aircraft with Faldave. Whatever the reason, D.L.O. came out of it looking damn passive: a cargo.

In contrast, Burston wanted Faldave to hear ... to hear that, regardless of all the uncertainties and shifts, he, Burston, had pushed on forcefully with a project he believed in: a good project which would lastingly benefit Panopticon, or whatever Panopticon might get turned into, and which had inherent merit, anyway, even apart from Panopticon. It was about justice in its biggest sense. He, Burston, did not waver, although Faldave had withheld outright blessing for the Pax campaign. They were all slimy. But Burston had to act with spirit, positivism, tenacity – central requirements of leadership, in his opinion. He had to trust this opinion: had to try to believe that if he stayed convinced of its value the value must be real and others would recognize it, too.

'If Faldave comes on, tell him I couldn't be more grateful for his hearty support in the Pax cause,' Burton said.

'If you say. But are you sure he approves of this, Ted? Oh, God, he ought to, no question, but are you sure he does? I thought I was picking up an undecided tone from him. At least undecided. Possibly sceptical.' She looked mostly frantic. 'I believe D.L.O. felt similarly. He was being very gradual with Mr Faldave on that, nothing too defined.'

'I'll travel down tonight,' Burston replied. Was he going to dispute with someone's PA, for fuck's sake? But, of course, she could worry him. Although Marie was not the voice of D.L.O. she was a voice that often spoke in place of D.L.O.

Burston asked them to re-run *Broken Light* for him in the viewing room. He needed to be garrisoned. He needed to suck in again the themes of sad injustice and brutality so thoughtfully exposed in the movie. A campaign demanded fervent convictions, and he must warm his up. A few – only a virtually negligible, mischievous few – said Gale was such a non-stop mess in *Broken Light* that nobody could get serious sympathy going for Andrew Pax. Never would Burston accept this. Gale hit several moments of authentic poignancy. Watching him, only the malevolent or biased would fail to feel that Pax had almost certainly been wronged. It was all so credible: a clever boy, but not a worldly boy, led by his fine beliefs, and by the strong and purposeful influence of Estham, into overwhelming perils.

Their first meeting in Cambridge was covered brilliantly by the film. Seeing it again now, Burston still thought so. Gale skilfully caught Pax's mixture of interest and suspicion at the older man's clear targeting of him. In 1930s Cambridge, Pax might at first have thought Estham a predatory gay. But then Gale ably showed Pax coming to realize that the bonds Estham wanted were only intellectual and political. Only! Only enough to kill Pax. To this kind of approach, though, he was responsive. Through facial mobility and subtle body language – almost unassisted by dialogue – Gale revealed the fine excitement of this growing rapport between the two men.

Burston heard movement at the back of the room and turned, expecting to see D.L.O. It was Marie, though. She came and took the place next to him, huddling down in her seat like in a slit trench. 'Whenever I can, I look at *Broken Light* again,' she said. 'I heard you were running it through. Do you mind, Ted?'

'Oh, I grieve for that lad,' Burston said.

'Which?'

'Well, both, I suppose.'

'Not that arrogant ram and lush, David Gale?' she snarled.

'I was thinking mainly of Pax, yes.'

'I can understand that, I really can. I weep and weep at *Broken Light*.'

'But – well, in the picture Gale is Pax. How do you separate them?'

'I don't see it like that. I can feel only the presence of Pax.'

'Yes, it's a fine performance by David.'

'Fuck dead David,' she replied.

'Oh? What happened with you and him?' Burston asked.

The film moved on. Pax and Estham were in someone's Morris, Estham at the wheel. The car had been turned into a kind of tank, with sheets of metal and wood covering the windows, only a small windscreen space clear, through which the camera viewed them. Estham drove the car fast at a gang of undergraduate hearties who were trying to break up a peace demonstration at the Cambridge war memorial on Armistice Day. They scattered. Pax and Estham whooped like children, faces ablaze with fight and righteousness.

'Good on you!' Marie yelled. She stood and punched the darkness a couple of times. 'That's based on fact, you know, Ted, though a different year. Justified licence. It was actually Julian Bell and Guy Burgess in the car.' When she sat down again she let her hand drift possessively into Burston's crotch, but kept it motionless. 'Don't mind me,' she said. 'I'm always turned on by distinguished cinema. I need basic reassurance.'

'Yes, distinguished,' he replied.

She did weep when the death-row scenes came and stuck her face into his shoulder padding, her hand still in place and still inert. 'Anything,' she muttered.

'What?'

'Anything to clear him must be right, even so long after. I see that.'

'Why I'm going to Wales.'

'I know. I do know, Ted, believe me. Please say that you believe me.' Now and then in this trade, people not on the acting or dramatic side at all would begin to speak like a script, because they saw so many and sat in on such a lot of viewings.

'Thanks, Marie.'

'I'll try to cover.'

'Thanks, Marie.'

'Wow,' she said, pressing down for a moment with the hand, 'do I feel you coming up to meet me? I think so. I do. Hanging gives you a throb? But I must get back in case D.L.O. calls.' She left before the cast list appeared, moving busily up the aisle, rubbing the same hand over her face now to get tears off.

He sat with Pax's sister, Elsie Gough, in a bright, single-storey, grant-aided factory where she had been tasting pickles when Burston arrived. Through a window he could watch hill sheep outside nibble the ornamental lawns of this neat little industrial estate, created by the Development Board for Rural Wales. Philip, her husband, ran the pickle-making business and would be in later. Burston did not know whether it was

219

Gough who had told him over the telephone to fuck off that time, but probably. Burston had not phoned again, but simply presented himself first thing this morning. Now and then in the past, when he was only a researcher, he had found this technique paid best. People were knocked off guard if you simply rolled up. Elsie had on a long, white, much-stained apron and was seated at a table full of shallow dishes of yellow-brown mixtures. An open box of small white plastic spoons stood alongside the dishes and she looked up with a spoon in her mouth when Burston was first shown into her glass-walled office. Bottles of tan pickle, so far unlabelled, moved slowly on a belt and on to trolleys in the open space area of the factory, like Lilliput's khakied troops queueing for innoculation.

According to the file, Elsie had been nearly twelve years younger than Andrew Pax and would be in her sixties now. The spoon stuck in her mouth made her seem less than that, like a child forcing herself to take tonic. Just the same, there was a large-scale stateliness to her, even when seated. She had a big, benign-looking face with a good narrow nose and grey, see-all eyes. Under a small, round white hygiene hat, her grey hair was worn long and tied with a fragment of grey ribbon behind. She put Burston in mind of the actor Finlay Currie, who did Magwitch in the Lean *Great Expectations*, though Elsie was nothing like so animated.

'To talk about your brother,' Burston said.

She took the spoon from her mouth and threw it into a bin. Then she stood and went to close the door. As he had guessed, she was tall, perhaps five feet nine or ten. Pax had been about that. Recalling pictures of him, Burston could see little other resemblance to Elsie, but this was many years on, time for a lot of change. Perhaps that moment of childlikeness when she had the spoon in her mouth had reminded Burston for a second of Pax's look of conquering innocence and bounce.

'Are you taking Andrew up?' she asked, still standing at the door.

'I believe an injustice may have been done.'

'Others have tried. Do you think it's necessary?'

'Necessary? Yes, I like that. Yes, it's necessary.'

She went and sat down again. 'We're up for a taste award,' she said, 'using only limes.' Filling a spoon from one of the dishes, she held it out to Burston. He lifted a hand to take it from her, but she grunted and nodded, signalling that he should bend forward and receive the sample direct into his mouth. He did: it seemed like a test of virtue and manhood. Was there something like it in the Old Testament, though reversed? Didn't

Jehovah tell Gideon to recruit only warriors who drank from a river using their hand, not those who knelt and lapped? The pickle was sharp and getting on for unpleasant. 'Don't say anything,' she told him. 'It's not necessary – that word again. But when Phil comes in he'll want to know if you've tasted and you can spin him a testimonial. It's best to keep him cheerful these days.'

'It's great,' Burston said. 'It reminds me of—'

'Don't say that to him, even if it was going to be a compliment. This is supposed to be new, new, new. We retire to Cyprus on this pickle.'

Burston moved a sack of brown sugar off a chair and sat down opposite her. 'Mrs Gough, I appreciate that Andrew's death must seem like another era.' He gestured towards the sheep. 'This is a long way from 1941 Pentonville.'

'I think of it every day for most of the day. I can think of it while I'm tasting and while I'm listening to Phil. He's a Social Democrat. He believes in the law.'

'I'm glad Andrew is still your concern.'

'If I'd been the older one he might not have turned out so errant,' she replied. 'How could I influence him? He had his scholarships and visions. Here's Phil now.'

Gough was fair, bedraggled and probably not quite as old as Elsie, though Burston could see why he might be thinking of a happy late-life income through his product. Tall and spindly he was nothing like what Burston thought of as standard Welsh. His suit would be fine in Llanidloes, though. He came into Elsie's room and shook Burston's hand. There was no obvious evidence of hate. 'You're the pictures man?' he asked. Burston had realized at once that the accent was not Welsh, either. The same voice as told him to fuck off? He could not accurately recall the sound of that now. Burston would place his intonation somewhere between Stafford and Lichfield. A Development Board seduction grant might have pulled him into green-field Wales. How nations were built.

Gough took a spoon, dug out some of the stuff from one of the dishes and put it into his mouth.

'Grand, isn't it?' Burston said.

'Elsie's given you a tour of them, has she?' Gough replied through the taster. 'Good. All at once Andy Pax is flavour of the month, then?'

'This movement has been forming itself for a very long time, Mr Gough,' Burston replied. 'Certainly more than months!' He laughed a little.

'It's a movement, is it?'

'We feel it should be,' Burston said. 'Must be.'

223

'Who sent you?' Gough asked.

'I felt I had to come.'

'Yes, but who sent you? What's the scale of this interest in Pax? Is the impulse major? In business you learn to ask, who's behind this or that. Which ballpark are we in? To be honest, I don't see an interest in a dead brother-in-law doing me much damage. But I'd still like to know the dimensions. I export quite a bit to Holland. Plus the award to keep in mind. We're almost there with this, I'd say.' He pointed into his mouth.

Elsie said: 'I thought the film could have struck a provocative note if they had given Barbara something of a tum in that jail gate scene. People are more liberated about babes in partnerships these days. I don't say it's good, but they simply are.'

'We didn't know about a child,' Burston said.

'Imogen Cruse is lovely but quite thin,' Elsie replied. 'She did the pain of it all so well.' Burston thought Cruse had been splitting up with Enid at the time parts of *Broken Light* were shot; and it was before she had the new thing under way with J.C.J. The misery in her face for these sequences was three-quarters autobiographical.

Gough said: 'These old battles, dogma battles – who cares now? I ask the question with all respect, believe me, in view of Elsie's feelings towards a brother and the general weight of the topic. But I think we need to look at living issues. Dogma's got whiskers. Religion's taken over, hasn't it? Islam. I have to think of possible business repercussions. I do get a bit of ribbing about Andrew. But the Labour people are sympathetic, of course. And the Welsh Nationalists: they see his death as another instance of the crush-all Brit State in action. Could be. In any case, one doesn't argue. I'm a guest in this country, Wales. On the other hand, the Con club can be damned harsh. "We were ready to fight on the beaches and he was opening the back door to them." That sort of thing from veterans. This is why I asked about the scale. They'd probably come round if someone big was in the campaign: not just titles but people with money. That might convince.'

'Shall we just say, I do not stand alone in this,' Burston replied.

'Should that be enough for me?' Gough said.

'You, only you, can decide.' Yes, damn easy to slide into scriptshit if you spent your working life in it.

'Right,' Gough said. 'But it would be great if you could get a big politician. One who does apologies for the past – say for colonialism.' Gough took another spoon and a scoop from a different dish. 'Which of these said the most to you?' he asked Burston.

225

'He was keenest on Number 4A,' Elsie replied with a big, joyful wink.

Gough smiled. 'I don't know if Elsie told you—'

'Nothing,' she said. 'I thought it would be better, if at all – I mean, the commercial security aspect – but, if at all, better coming from you, Phil.'

'Right. But I think it's all right: Burston, 4A is probably the one we're going to foreground. This will be our award contender.'

'He's most likely got a natural flair, Phil,' Elsie said. 'It can happen with pickles, as we all know. Or have you had commercial pickle experience – say before choosing the film trade?'

When Gough had gone and was watching them off-and-on through the glass walls of his own office, Burston said: 'I feel a guarded but very definite approval of the campaign. Certainly from you, Mrs Gough, and, yes, even from your husband. The journey here has been worthwhile.'

'Perhaps Andy's child is the one above all who should be consulted. If she/he is alive, of course. She/he would be going on sixty. Conceivably, the mother is extant, too.'

'But we can't find them,' Burston said. 'We've tried. And, in any case, the campaign won't make a thing of the fact that his girl friend might have been pregnant.'

'Oh, was. No, might.'

'We would focus on the execution, only that.'

'This kind of agitation can bring all sorts to the fore, you know. What is referred to as "out of the woodwork" in this day and age. People can be so evil.'

'The people who put him to death were possibly evil, yes.'

'Oh, most people have the potential, I fear. We are conceived in sin. Consider much wider. As Phil says, do your bosses and above favour this campaign? Or is it just a you thing? That would be very noble, but noble meaning likely to come unstuck for you, personally. I think of John the Baptist.'

Seventeen

Unannounced, Louise drove north to see Roy Estham's son: Ted Burston had told her once that, on occasions, it paid just to turn up when on a research assignment. She had an address from the *Broken Light* research file, but, there appeared to have been no contact for the making of the film. Probably it had seemed unnecessary: although Estham was significant in *Broken Light*, he had been nothing like central; and he had no family, no wife, at the period covered by the movie, though certainly a family later.

The meeting excited her. In Portugal she'd had those moments of longing for the safety of old, distant topics of biography like Hallam. The Deems had badly unsettled her, and still did to an extent. But she came to see that they unsettled her because a tale like the Pax tale remained alive and vibrant. It had to be worthwhile searching for the truth since the truth still mattered, with a possible impact on people now, this year, this week, today. Estham's son might be another instance of that. He was – ought to be – a means towards some aspect of that truth, but might also be affected, good or bad, by that truth, if Louise could only unearth it.

She said: 'I want you to tell me – now, really, please tell me – tell me if I'm asking about matters that are too painful even now. I'll shut up, I promise.'

'My mother refuses to see you, doesn't she?'

'Well, I haven't really—'

'I phone her now and then and she told me you'd been asking. She says she won't have anything to do with it. I expect you know she's fixed up with a man, maybe even remarried. You've looked into things, I'm sure. All of that other – she's put it away. And her partner doesn't want any of it dug up again now, so long after. It's reasonable. He doesn't even much like my phoning. To him, you see, I'm part of the other life. Especially as I'm coming from a booth on reversed charges. My mother thought I shouldn't talk to you, either. What's the use? Do you know what I mean – I mean – I don't mean to give offence – Louise your name, yes? – what's the use, Louise?'

Louise said: 'I can understand your mother's attitude. Of course.'

'But you come looking for me, just the same.'

'This kind of work – I must try everything.'

'You have to be hard, I expect. *This kind of*

work. What's – what's the use of it?'

'It might be important to tell people what happened. Part of a really quite big and important story, an era story.'

'Which people? People heard about it at the time. It was in the Press, wasn't it?'

'People now.'

'What for? What's the use?'

'We might be able to get closer to the truth than those Press reports in the sixties and the forties.'

'Oh, truth. Fine. But does anybody need it? I mean, digging old stuff out. Does anybody want that now? Andrew Pax and my dad – who cares? History.'

'Yes, history. It's to tell people of another time. It's to educate them, startle them when they realize what Britain was like then.'

He thought about this, or about something. 'Yes, most of it's painful, if I go over it much. That is, if I let it get painful. So, I don't. And I'm in the dark about such a lot of it. I was only a kid when he died. Eight.'

Anthony Estham lived on a big bare council estate on the Derbyshire side of Sheffield. To Louise, the terrain seemed delightfully, bleakly familiar. She felt a kind of welcome, a guarded, unlavish kind: she was brought up in the same sort of town-edge, narrow, modern streets, though in South West England. Her parents had moved out and bought themselves a place in

230

a private road soon after Louise left for good, and she had been away from these sorts of surroundings for a long while; but she could still respond here: was instinctively at home in this treeless symmetrical neighbourhood; huddled radii around tower blocks. Did things look a bit rougher than she remembered? Were shop fronts barred then, thick-barred? Was there so much broken glass about the streets? The Social Club building was tall scarred concrete, its windows narrow and set well up, perhaps for security, the high, swinging sign reduced to only its frame by stoning. Although the Club did not actually look anything like the besieged police station in *Fort Apache, The Bronx* – not so handsome – that's what it put her in mind of.

Just the same, Louise was at ease; knew that most people in these houses and flats and maisonettes would be making the best of things on very little, as her parents had done. Perhaps conditions looked rougher because times were tougher. Anthony Estham was the family-man son of a member of the Order of Merit, who had been also a professor of literature, a poet, political thinker and activist; yet ex-public school boy Anthony seemed pleased to get a few pounds and free beer on Friday and Saturday nights calling bingo numbers in the social club. Yes, times might be tougher. She was not clear yet whether he had any other job, but thought probably not. Why did she think so? Patronizing? Perhaps it had been something in his voice when he wearily repeated Louise's words about her research: *This kind of work*: as if work – the whole notion of it – had become esoteric.

Louise sat with him in the social club and worried a little about her clothes. She had on a black leather bomber jacket and black leather skirt. Most of the women were sparklingly dressed up for the evening, and she wondered if her outfit would seem too casual, insulting. She had not expected to go clubbing. There had been nobody in his house when she called but a neighbour told her that Estham did his regular bingo stint at weekends. He and his family would be there. When Estham finished and came down off the stage she went and introduced herself. He had looked uncertain, but found them a spot to talk.

Preparations began on stage now for a live musical show, to follow bingo. He and Louise sat at a table in the long ground-floor bar-cum-ballroom/theatre. His drinks were free but he had bought her a whisky: would not hear of her paying herself. 'My guest,' he said. 'Unexpected, but still my guest. I was sprucely brought up, you know. We're a welcoming lot here. They say I've got a sweet rhythm when I'm bingo calling, yet clear, too. Good enunciation and poetic. Comes from my father, the lecturing verse man.'

She had bought tickets for the bingo but did not win. Perhaps she missed a number or two through studying Estham as he sang-spoke the patter. If she had not known he was the caller, she might still have recognized him as Estham's son. The couple of photographs in Roy Estham's Panopticon file showed him as lean-faced, sharp-chinned, long-nosed and lively-looking, with a sweep of dark hair falling over his forehead. The son had most of these, though perhaps some of the liveliness was missing: but she had put this down to the monotony of his caller's role. Although he meant to mock himself, of course, when he spoke about the poetic rhythm in his technique, he did in fact have something like that. There was a dignity to him, an elegant, relaxed presence, even during that serfdom with the numbered balls, and regardless of his terrible cardigan. It was not that he looked as if he should be doing something different and better, but that he did this task as well as it could be done, with a bit of wit, a bit of warmth, a proper pace, a helping of excitement.

'Better'? What was 'better', anyway? Who said that was better? Was writing a biography better? Was ghosting? Of course they were fucking better: better paid, better esteemed, better skilled, better fun than shouting Legs

Eleven. She had to stop patronizing. She had to stop sentimentalizing from her childhood and consider how difficult it was going to be to ask this man of thirty-odd whether he thought his father had killed himself out of noble, principled regret; or had been killed because he was having it off with the wife of a dangerous man trained in violence, who could depute dangerous friends likewise trained in violence.

Estham had clammed for a while after their first words. Then he said suddenly: 'I think I remember coming back to the house with my mother and going to stare at the bath,' he said. 'It was empty and had been cleaned up, of course. This was a big bathroom, done Victorian, with lots of wood and brass taps, genuine tiled floor, not lino imitation. They were into all that, my parents. It's very graphic and exact, my recollection. The taps, the different colour soaps, heaped, folded towels on a shelf. But *do* I remember, or is it something I've built since, because I've heard what happened? Did I even know at that age he'd been found slashed in the bath? Would my mother tell me? Do I imagine it and repeat it because I realize this is the kind of thing people like you want to hear, and you've come a long way and into strange territory to hear it?'

'Not such strange territory. You were away from the house when he died.'

'You don't ask, you tell. Yes.'

'At your grandmother's. Your mother's mother's.'

'Yet if I'm imagining it, why do I see the bath empty? Why don't I see him there? Would the imagination tidy things up like that?'

'But you don't see him?'

He took little sips at his beer, as if it were a grand claret. 'You want to know why we were absent from the house when he died, don't you?'

'Oh, people do visit their grandmothers.'

'Who else have you spoken to?'

'All sorts.'

' "*You were away from the house when he died*," ' he said. mimicking the matter-of-factness of her voice.

'I find it unnerving, the way you pick up a sentence and say it over,' she replied.

'Oh, I'm listening to it, re-listening to it, getting the shape and the undertow. More of my poetic lineage, I expect. I think you're asking me why we were away that specific night. I guess you'd like to put that one to my mother.'

He astonished her. Wasn't it eerie to have her words examined with such subtlety in this rough-and-ready, noisy, crowded room by someone dressed like this and drinking freebie beer? Near the stage a couple of men tested the sound system for musical accompaniment to the stage performers. 'My wife and daughters are in this show,' he said.

'Oh, great.'

He looked at her over his pint tankard and said: 'Well, it *is* great.'

'Yes, it's great,' she said.

'This community's been knocked about, and is still being knocked about, one way and the other, but it can do things for itself, bright and boisterous happy things. This place, the Club, holds us together.'

'I can feel it. I'm sure your father would have understood that. His politics.'

He looked wrongfooted for a second. 'Oh, sorry. Yes, I forget it's my father you're interested in, not us. The great populist. You focus on Pax first, then my father a long way behind, and us, really, nowhere at all. But that's fair. Your job. My father? No, I don't think he'd understand. What I've heard about him, read about him – probably the same as you've heard and read ... he had that great intellect and his views and aims, and energy. But this was not the kind of spot where he could actually have lived, though it seems in line with his outlook. This would not have been his brand of club. I'm sure of that. Not for ten minutes. You know the sort, although they had quite good intentions they didn't really know people like those around here then, and now. It would be the same type who designed this estate and who'd be amazed now to find it doesn't work the way they hoped. They didn't cater for worklessness and drugs and arson.' The cardigan was slack and blue-purple. It helped age him. God, it put him in a class.

Someone made announcements from the stage about future shows at the hall, including a Christmas pantomime. 'Of course, you'll come back for it,' he said.

'Thanks for the invite. I'd love to.'

'Yes?' The public address system whined. People were urged to get raffle tickets in the last five minutes available.

Louise said: 'I expect when you grew older your mother spoke to you about things.'

'Things that bath night? Never,' he said. 'That's what I mean about useless digging. We've put it all away. She sold the house soon after. This was not about loathing the bathroom, though. A money matter.'

'I don't think I understand that – the silence on something so—'

'I heard the chatter later, naturally. I was at Stowe, the public school. You knew?' That would be where the clear-cut, laid-back voice with the numbers would come from. Perhaps he saw she was thinking this. He stared around the bar. 'How many Stowe boys make it to bingo calling?' he said. 'My mother believed in that kind of education. And so did my father, apparently, Red or not. I think one reason she sold the house was to pay the fees. She told me it would be his wish. Kids in that sort of place don't give a monkey's what they say. Some of them knew more about my family than I did myself. We had boys whose fathers were big in journalism or in Parliament. All the rumour on tap. The whole thing was years old by then, of course, so perhaps they thought it didn't matter any longer. They'd hear their sons mention me at home – mention me just as a schoolmate – and the name would set off the memories. "Estham? Estham? Related to Roy Estham – the one who?" ... You'll know the kind of stuff.'

'Stuff?'

'Oh, you'll have heard it.' He stared at her for a couple of seconds, as though trying to read what she knew. 'That why you're here? Is Deem still alive – the one supposed to have found him? Sorry, the one who did find him. The one on Her Majesty's Secret Service. Yes, naturally I've done a little research myself. But very little. You've spoken to him, I expect.'

'Yes, he did say he found him.'

'Of course he said it. And it's true, probably – he did find him. He said it in court. They let him be Mr X, because of his job. The Press liked that. Good for headlines – nice and short and sinister. But my mother knew his name, naturally.'

'She did talk to you about it, then? Where

else would you get the name? Boys at school knew it? That's incredible.'

A man singer appeared on stage and crooned some oldie numbers backed by the sound centre music, a microphone up to his lips. It became difficult to keep a conversation going, especially a sensitive one. Louise sat back, enjoyed the whisky, joined in remembered slices of 'Paper Doll', 'Yellow Submarine', 'It Had To Be You'. A comedian dressed in drag as a nurse followed, his act full of gags about club members, about dole and sickness benefit, about awkward illnesses, most of them midriffed. 'Here's my crew,' Anthony Estham said, when the comic went off. It was casual, but proud. A fattish dark-haired woman of his age played the guitar while two cheery girls of primary school age, also dark, danced and belted out beautifully a couple of Rolling Stone items, 'Street Fighting Man' and 'Wild Horses'. They were all dressed in dark T-shirts and jeans, their hair anywhere, probably to approximate Jagger and the rest. Energy fizzed. They were like people who had suddenly been given their chance to shine, and who nabbed it.

After they finished and took applause there was an interval for the raffle. 'They're grand,' Louise said.

'You don't have to say so.'

'I love it, love the attack, love those tunes –

239

glad they're getting a re-run from the 1970s or whenever.'

'We're part of things here.'

'I appreciate that.'

'Why I can't see the point,' he said. 'The excavating. They're on again in the second half, or they'd join us, I expect. Artistes! Saving themselves.' The woman and two girls came out into the body of the hall for the raffle, but at first stayed with the rest of the cast. 'A book could upset things here, upset things for my mother,' he said. 'My girls do well at school, for whatever good that might bring.'

'It will.'

'Oh?'

'Deem's wife is still alive, too,' she replied.

'It's a different tale from her?'

'Possibly unreliable. Oh, probably. She's quaint.'

'Or possibly not,' he said. He was following the raffle calls on a bunch of yellow tickets and seemed rapt. Louise remembered a journalist friend telling her she had once interviewed George Orwell's son, Richard Blair, and how distant he had seemed from all the fame and controversy of his father's life.

'Clara Deem might be afraid of him,' she said.

'Yes, I wouldn't be surprised. He's old, but ... Yes, she'd be scared.' Head lowered over the tickets he said: 'She gave you the story that my father had been removed because those two had an affair going, did she, Louise?'

'You've heard that?'

'School buzz. As I said. The Press printed one account because they had to, and thought they knew another.'

'And did the buzz give any other names?'

'Other?'

'Deem might have used helpers.'

'Oh, that would hardly be known to schoolkids, would it?'

Louise said: 'I wouldn't have thought any of it would be, but you tell me that they—'

Estham's wife and the two girls broke away from their friends and came to join them briefly now, his wife carrying the guitar. They were still full of the glow and fun of their performance, bursting with backstage information about missed cues and lost props.

'None of it showed. Brilliant,' Louise said.

'Thank you so much,' Estham's wife said. It was as formal and dead as it could be and spoken in the local Yorkshire accent. Louise longed to talk more with her, convince her that their act really had been a winner. The bloody three hundred quid jacket cut her off from these people. Most of the women here were smart, but none had three hundred pounds' worth on *in toto*.

'This lady is a spotter for a powerful West End impresario,' Estham said. 'She'd heard about you on the theatre grapevine. It's a surprise visit to book you up for London and Las Vegas if she likes you. And how couldn't she?'

'Oh, stop it, Dad,' one of the girls said. None of the three sat down. They were stars, on parade. They would give some politeness, then meet more fans.

'I tell you she's in showbiz. She knew David Gale.'

'Oh, did you? Honestly?' the younger girl asked. 'The one who ... who died?'

It was as if Gale's death had tipped them off. 'You're here to do with all that other business, are you?' the older girl asked.

'Oh, God, that,' the other snorted.

'Can't bear to think I might be a celebrity, too, can you, Sian?' Estham said.

'He's not just Roy Estham's son, you know,' his wife said. She looked sad, would have to pull back some gaiety for the rest of the show. 'Tony's Tony, with his own life and his own identity.'

'Oh, please, Mrs Estham, I do know that,' Louise said. She wanted to stand. It was not a levée. But she stayed as she was.

Anthony Estham said: 'Louise is mainly concerned with Andrew Pax, not my dad, love. This visit is just a formality.'

His wife and the two girls went to

242

circulate, bottles of Coke in their hands.

Louise said: 'I wondered whether—'

'Wondered whether my mother took me away from the house deliberately that night, to leave the field clear.' The raffle was ending. He threw his tickets on to the floor. 'I used to fight people at school for saying that. But there were too many, and I gave up. I never told her about it. Well, you wouldn't if you were brought up in that sort of school, would you? Ethos they call it.'

'I wondered whether, perhaps, an agreement between her and Deem to get your father thumped, only thumped, as a warning, so he would end the affair. Is this preposterous, slanderous?'

'Not as slanderous as if you said she'd wanted him killed and co-operated.'

'But the people Deem would use might not know how to go only so far and not further. They'd possibly had rougher training. That is, if there were such helpers.'

'Or if it took place at all.'

'There weren't any other names mentioned, were there?' she asked. 'Forgive me for persisting.'

'Here we go again,' he replied. The comedian came back on to get the audience receptive once more. Louise saw Estham's wife and children scuttling towards the rear of the stage in time for their next appearance. They all waved and Louise gave them a champ double handshake above her head. Estham stood to fetch another pint and a whisky for her from the bar. The comedian had a joke about 'Our Mr Caller making sweet music with a mysterious lady in leathers while his wife just makes sweet music.' People turned to look. Estham gave a slow bow with his feet splayed and spilled a lot of the beer on the front of his trousers. There were cheers.

'Just a beating? I've never heard that one before,' he said, sitting down again. 'Beaten then his wrists cut? Were there bruises on the body?'

'No. Lads like that – if they'd been told your father was a nuisance to Deem, and that the nuisance must end, they might have picked for themselves the surest way to end it.'

He said: 'Meaning, if Deem's people were turned loose on someone they simply could not do half measures – the way police are trained to shoot to kill, only to kill, not maim? Or like Bradman couldn't play a bad stroke? Possible. And you're also saying, are you, that Deem told my mother it would be only a beating but ordered the helpers to finish him?'

'Yes, I'm afraid that's possible.' It would make Clara's account of that night credible.

'Or, of course, Deem might have done it personally.'

'Yes, I'm afraid that's possible, too.' This would make Clara's account of the night less credible. 'And there are other features,' she said.

'Yes, there are, aren't there? You mean my father wouldn't be regarded by these hired hands – if there were hired hands – as just someone who was banging Deem's wife. He was a one-time traitorous enemy who had subsequently turned broken-down fink. They wouldn't be able to conceive of anyone much more contemptible: altogether a target who had earned whatever came his way, including belated execution disguised as mock-up suicide.'

Louise saw and heard the agony in Estham and knew she was about to lose him. Hurriedly, she said: 'Oh, I wouldn't put it like—'

'You'll see why mother wouldn't want to talk to you.'

'Yes, but—'

'Too painful,' he said. 'And too painful for me. You told me I could say when things were too painful. Well, they're too painful.'

The comedian gave himself an exit line joke about the sudden state of Estham's trousers, which she thought it best not to hear. The crooner was on again with 'You Can Roll A Silver Dollar'.

Eighteen

On the intercom, Burston had a call from
Marie, PA to Darren, asking Ted if he
wouldn't mind popping down at once to see
people in D.L.O.'s suite. The snap usually
present in her voice for this summons was
missing: she seemed guarded, almost cowed,
and did not say who the visitors were.
'Please, Ted,' she muttered.

'Of course.'

When she came through he had been
running an Internet surf of Church of England bishops, trying to work out whether any
of these loud, soft-palmed peacocks might
be up to snuff for fronting a Pax campaign.
The trouble was, if crimson shirts did fuck
something up they fucked it up on a tran-
scendent scale. Burston had had two damag-
ing experiences with bishops when he was
promoting those fine, woman-angled religio-
bio-pics, *Esther* for Panopticon, and *Ruth* for
Several Brilliant Enterprises, his earlier em-
ployers. Bishops were autocrats in their
dioceses, and imagined they could run film
companies the same way, if you once let the

fluting bastards in with their standard issue ethics. Pax might be too delicate a project for any of them: the Litany and similar chant slabs hammered clerics into a farcically simple view of life.

Yet Burston feared almost as much approaching someone from the House of Commons to head up Pax: bishops were all mouth and worthiness, yes, but MPs were all mouth and worthiness, too, obviously; and the booze element was probably a bigger hazard with them, though it would be damn close.

Burston felt relieved to escape these selection problems for a while and he hurried downstairs to help Marie. She could be bossy and snooty and prick-teasing, but, in his position now, if some company employee wanted support he had to give it. As he approached D.L.O.'s waiting area he could hear women talking. For people visiting Darren, they sounded remarkably mild and unegomaniac, and he wondered why Marie had panicked. He thought he recognized one of the voices and, when he turned a corner of the corridor and could see the callers, found he had been right. Charlotte, David Gale's widow, was speaking. With her were Mrs Dorothy Gale, David's mother, and Rosemary Paston, his agent, wearing one of her true outfits. They occupied armchairs around a low, circular glass table, on which as Burston arrived Marie was setting out coffee things. 'This is grand,' he cried. 'D.L.O. will be so sorry to have missed you.'

Charlotte said: 'Ah, Ted, before you arrived I told Marie that I wouldn't have objected at all – didn't object at all – at first – didn't object at all to her being at David's funeral. That could be seen as going with the Panopticon job. But the degree of her weeping, plus the kneading hands – oh, totally out of order, but OUT OF FUCKING ORDER.' Her voice soared and raged suddenly. Charlotte could do this. There was sometimes an almost oriental passivity about her supremely bland-looking features; but the passivity and the blandness she could ditch amazingly fast, if she considered the cause just. 'This was performance on a brutally possessive scale. This is a bird David slipped it to a few times, if that, and, my God, she's behaving like *Antony and* fucking *Cleopatra*. As I hear, she's going around most of the time slagging off David because he had her and dropped her – the standard tale – but for the funeral she switches to give-me-back-my-man wailing, at street-procession-Tehran, death-of-an-ayatollah volume. Now, listen, Ted, any memorial service, I don't want her there. You hear? I tell you, and I'd tell D.L.O. if he were in the office.'

Marie, jangling cups in self-defence, said:

'Really, Charlotte – Mrs Gale – I—'

'Just do the damn coffee,' Charlotte bellowed. 'I've a right to decide which pussy is excluded from a memo service, haven't I, Ted, for heaven's sake? I know churches are public, but we'd be chartering this place for the day, wouldn't we? Sort of a franchise. The purpose would be to display proper family unity. I'd bring the baby. So, some piece on the side claiming rapport with David and limelight I just won't have, Ted. This goes for that bloody ghost, too, Louise Summers. A bit of damn casual dick from David and some busy oral treatment gives them no such entitlement. God, there'd hardly be room if they all turned up.' She cried for a couple of seconds but then recovered.

'Memorial service?' Burston replied.

Rosemary Paston said: 'We weren't absolutely sure you'd still be here. I don't mean you, personally, Ted. Panopticon. There've been some changes made, I gather.'

'People outside hear more than we do ourselves,' Burston replied with quite a good chuckle given how things were.

'Do I understand Stan himself was over?' Paston asked. 'The three of you colloguing in Taste Bud, Stan decked out for Britain.'

'In fact, these reports account for our visit today, Mr Burston,' Dorothy Gale said. 'We are conscious of a certain urgency. Something might be lost if Panopticon is swallowed up.'

Rosemary Paston said: 'Mrs Gale and Charlotte feel there should be what Charlotte just mentioned – a memorial service for David. We were discussing it in my office – vaguely conscious of the shifts and uncertainties – and I said, damn it, girls, let's go over to Panopticon right now and see what exactly is what. But we find D.L.O. unhere and, what's more, according to Marie, there's no information on where he might be. So, can you tell us, Ted?'

'Where D.L.O. is?'

'What exactly is what,' Paston replied.

'We're frankly surprised that there has been no move by Panopticon to initiate a memorial service long before this,' Dorothy Gale said. 'One feels that so many in the profession and, indeed, outside it would want to offer a formal tribute to David's work. Actors of considerably less achievement have been given services. One sees them all over the *Telegraph* week in, week out. I note in the Press and on television pictures of distinguished colleagues attending. It is a mark of status, and one which I do think David deserves. Sir John Mills and Sir Anthony Hopkins – people of that eminence are happy to take part and to signal their respect for a departed colleague. For me it would be a comfort.'

'I'm utterly grateful you've come to put this suggestion to us,' Burston replied.

'My real point is, Mr Burston, that the suggestion should have come from Panopticon,' Dorothy Gale said.

'I'd want guarantees,' Charlotte said. 'The tabloids would be there and television. They'd know how David lived. They'd be looking for his women – women aiming to declare by their damn grief display that they'd fucked him. I'm not going to be made a monkey of all over the media, Ted. Yes, exclusivity is my due, at this stage. That's what widowhood ought to be about. A man can have a lot of girls, but only one widow.' She cried again briefly.

'My own feeling is that some stars might well come from the States to show solidarity with David at such a function,' Dorothy Gale said. 'He was truly international.'

'Indeed,' Burston replied. 'If Aeschylus isn't international who is?' He thought that had authentic idiocy, classic idiocy, you could say. He sat down with them in the waiting area, but it seemed wrong to be treating such topics on, as it were, a thoroughfare. And he did not like the group's disposition: Dorothy Gale immediately opposite him and too near, her miserably dark, dry eyes continuously poking into his poise; Rosemary, always liable to switch on hurtful, graphic rudeness, had a chair also too near on his right. Marie tried to disarm by remaining on her feet and waitressing with the coffee pot and biscuits. Charlotte sat hunched on the sofa to his left. Would it comfort the widow or cause more rage if Burston reported that Louise had probably refused to let Gale break his marriage for her? Would this make Charlotte feel only *faute de mieux*?

'Shall we go into the suite?' he suggested, standing. He would feel more able in there. He deliberately did not say 'D.L.O.'s suite'. There was uncertainty, as Rosemary Paton had mentioned. Conceivably – oh, at least that – the suite might very soon be his, Burston's. They should be made to know, though obviously without any crude direct statement. He stood and leaned forward to offer Dorothy Gale an arm as she rose. Mrs Gale Senior was getting on and looked thin and frail under a heavy woollen dark-green suit that seemed much too weighty, especially now she was in a deep armchair and had to climb out. She had a round, implacable face, perhaps with some traces of breeding. Burston must look that up. Her hair was cut short and not too cleverly dyed to a shade between tan and russet. The ugliness of this coiffure also suggested a well-born indifference to usual values. She wore on one side of her head, mistakenly leaving most of her hair visible, a small, felt, beret-type hat in beige, which would have looked very cheery on someone much younger. Generally, Burston liked this sort of mad valour in the elderly, but on Dorothy Gale the hat seemed malevolent, like part of terrorist uniform. Gale had often spoken well of his mother, and used to bring her to the set of *Broken Light* occasionally and make a show of asking her advice about period detail. Dorothy Gale's voice recalled her son's; it had that same pushiness and edge which were probably useful to a slightly built woman alone in a sharp world, but which meant a limitation of range in an actor. Of course, David had been aware of this defect, and when he was sober and his mind desentimentalized would fiercely curse his mother for landing him with such a speaking style. If he did kill himself his voice might have been one of the deficiencies that quite logically created his despair.

Although craving some distance from all of them, Burston did not get behind D.L.O.'s desk. They could reasonably have regarded that as jumped-up, bumptious. Despite her yelling, Charlotte seemed to him the safest of the three, and he took a straight-backed chair near her, with both Dorothy and Rosemary on his left and separated from him by a biggish world globe on a stand. With a pencil, D.L.O. liked to point to spots on that where Panopticon films were playing, particularly seemingly remote Third World countries, say Ethiopia or the Congo: 'In that heart of darkness,' he would say, 'usher-ettes are even now lighting patrons to their mud hut benches for our movie.'

Marie had not followed them in and Burston thought this wise. He said: 'Oh, naturally, a memorial service for your son was mooted, Mrs Gale.' It was true, but D.L.O. decided almost instantly that David Gale had not been big enough. 'We'd have a church scattered with nobodies, Ted. There's nothing more demeaning for an actor and his sponsors than a half-cock memorial service.'

'You say you looked to us for a lead, Mrs Gale,' Burston replied now. 'But, with respect, this was the kind of personal matter where we thought it best to see if suggestions along those lines came from the family. D.L.O. had – indeed, has – a phobia about intrusiveness. I think possibly it's natural when one works in an industry like ours. It is an industry which can take over the very life of its most prominent people, and especially of its stars. D.L.O. feels that at least in death our most eminent colleagues should enjoy a little privacy if they or their families wish it.'

Rosemary Paston said: 'In many respects D.L.O. might be a right prick, but I would be surprised if Stanley has the neck to get rid of him immediately. He's a little chameleon figure, Stanley. He likes to fit in – might have been the original for Woody's *Zelig*. I doubt he'll want to disturb the scenery for a long time.'

'Oh, is that how you see it?' Burston asked.

Dorothy Gale said: 'To us, to Charlotte and me, it appeared that Panopticon did not want to get too close to David's death because of that abominable early slur – the suicide slur. You feared a taint by association, did you not, Mr Burston?'

'But with respect that's preposterous, Mrs Gale,' he replied. 'At no time did we—'

'Well, it's immaterial now,' Dorothy Gale said. 'We know it was an accident, and we have a court's Open verdict. There is nothing to scare off you or the damn churches. It's as if David had died in, say, an aircraft crash: tragic but clean.'

Rosemary Paston said: 'Ted, I haven't spoken of this to Dorothy or Charlotte because I'm not sure about its – well, its authenticity – but one tale around is that Louise Summers has been asked to angle things rather more towards suicide in a new edition of the Life. Is this correct?'

'She's doing fucking *what*?' Charlotte screamed.

Now and then you could see why David looked for it elsewhere so earnestly. Burston said: 'Oh, some very minor amendments. This is the kind of routine tidying up that always takes place in a revised work. The first edition was prepared at speed. There are some small errors, fact and emphasis.'

Rosemary Paston had on a deep-blue tracksuit; or more like the kind of siren suit that Churchill wears in some wartime photographs. It zipped very high to a collar which folded against the underside of her bony jaw. Burston liked the effect. It put him in mind of ruffs worn by people playing courtiers in the Raleigh period and gave a mild raciness to Rosemary's businesslike face. She was tall and very lean, not at all like Churchill, and you could imagine her using a tracksuit actually on a track, after, say, pole vaulting. She had concocted an astonishingly progressive career for David Gale, and getting him into the Aeschylus tragedies had been a real coup, even for her. She could justifiably consider it casual of him to have opted out by suicide, if it was suicide. 'My worry is that no church will allow a memorial service if the strongest line about is that he killed himself, regardless of the court verdict. Not even the Non-cons could put on a big show for a suicide. All right, Ted, you'll say we could get the memorial service done before this revised edition of the book actually comes out. But the word's already around, isn't it? How else would I have picked it up?'

'Who suggested it?' Charlotte asked.

'Who?'

'What?' Burston replied.

'Who suggested bumping up the suicide aspect?'

Burston said: 'Well, we all—'

'Did this come from one of these fucking women?' Charlotte asked, bellowing towards the door which led to Marie's office. 'Her? The ghost?' She turned and spoke to Dorothy Gale. 'You see what a woman like that would be doing, do you? This is proclaiming that David was so unhappy with you, me and his child that—'

'Not at all,' Burston cried, 'believe me.'

'Which of them was it?' Charlotte whispered in reply. 'Or one of the others? "He killed himself to escape his wife" – that's their tale – and because he couldn't have this other one – whichever – except, of course, he could and did have her any time he felt like it, and when he was not too pissed. I'll kill her. Summers. The tale's around she was the one, the one he really wanted. I'll turn this fucking ghost ghost.'

Rosemary Paston said: 'Probably you would not want to offend the church, Ted – bishop level and above, I mean. You can't afford to put their noses out of joint by sneaking in a memorial service on the back of the Open verdict, can you? Not if the trick's sure to become obvious soon after. I hear you're hoping for a "vindicate Pax campaign", a very sweet idea. But you'll need episcopal backing, plainly. They're very touchy sods, bishops. They've got values. Could you reach the printers in time and tell them to scrap the alterations to the Life, let the accident version stand?'

'In a sense, and a very real sense, David's career is itself a memorial,' Burston replied. 'I think of a great novelist or composer where the works are sufficient to preserve the name of their creator. Possibly one might consider a church service superfluous. Panopticon is determined to keep before the world public all of our films that David so brilliantly played in.'

'Olivier had a service,' Dorothy Gale said. 'Wasn't *his* work also a memorial?'

'Panopticon?' Rosemary Paston said. 'Panopticon will need a memorial service itself pretty soon.'

Charlotte was crying again, quietly. She spoke now with a patient, sad tenderness and Burston would have liked to stretch out and touch her in consolation, her cheek or her hair. He feared she might regard it as impertinent, though: she was the widow of a star, he a stand-in functionary. 'Ted,' she said, 'don't you understand what we crave? In the heavy papers after a memorial service you get a printed list of who was present. It tells the world about the range of the remembered person's life and it tells it in a form that can be cut out and kept. Yes, a kind of permanence and dignity. It says, Mrs So-and-so, mother, Mrs So-and-so, wife, then maybe a headmaster and friends – people with a truly personal connection. It gives depth. Following that come the professional colleagues. As mother says, you can gauge the achievements of someone that way. Yet it's the personal and family side that to me is so important. I would get a frame for a list like that and put it on the wall at home.'

'As a matter of fact, the *Telegraph*, *Times*, *Guardian* and *Independent* all gave him appreciative obituaries,' Burston replied. 'Quite apart from the tabloids, some of which was certainly distasteful.'

'Obituaries are fine, and they used quite decent photographs of him. It's just one writer's view, though, isn't it? Whereas with the memorial service, yes, it's those small-type long lists that are crucial,' Charlotte said, still with lovely constraint. 'The roll call. This is where his real self would be reflected and contained. And then at the end, after all the names, comes "as well as many other friends". That "many other" has something so warm and limitless about it, don't you think, Ted?'

'Well, I do see—'

Abruptly, Charlotte went into a savage howl: 'Normally, I would not mind if Marie or the sodding ghost, Summers, were buried under that little formula among the also-rans, but in this case, because of their fucking behaviour, no, fuck them, keep them out.' Burston glanced towards the door. It was not good for Marie to hear abuse of this kind. He felt a responsibility for the morale of all staff. 'Please, oh, please, Teddy,' Charlotte continued, her tone sliding effortlessly back to winsomeness and deference, 'you would not deny my Davy his little posthumous moment, would you – would not starve him of his list?'

Nineteen

So, it had become necessary to doorstep Roy Estham's widow. From her chats with Ted, Louise recalled that charmingly brisk term: it meant doing what she had done to Mrs Estham's son: arrive and confront, without warning. What Anthony Estham said was true: three times Louise tried to arrange an interview with his mother – twice by telephone, once by letter – and always nothing doing. The receiver had been put down immediately Louise said who she was. In fact, on the second call Louise did not say who she was but the woman at the other end seemed to guess anyway and cut the call; or she had Caller Display for the number.

Louise assumed it was Mrs Estham who answered each time: a weary, on-edge voice, pretty cultured. She appeared to have retained that name, although the letter came back unopened with 'Not known at this address' printed on it in purple crayon. The research notes for *Broken Light* referred to her as Mrs Roy (Gloria) Estham and gave an address and the Hereford telephone number. The entry said 'possibly in business', though without details. It was not clear whether anyone at Panopticon had approached her; had tried to approach her. As with the son, it might have been considered unnecessary; unnecessary and liable to produce trouble.

In the car Louise did ask herself, and did keep on asking herself, whether it was brutal to pursue people about immensely painful matters in their past. Honestly debating this, she went on driving west, though; did not turn around. She had a duty to truth, didn't she, a unique duty to truth? In the last three or four years hadn't she lost two good relationships because of the heavy devotion and exhaustive time she gave to a biography once under way? That was her work style, and her work always mattered most. Or was it all bollocks and fancy to talk of a duty, and of truth? Who wanted to know whether Roy Estham killed himself decades ago or was killed? His son did not appear to care. Anthony thought nobody would care now. Was Roy Estham so important to the truth, anyway? Chewy, chewy questions. Her book was about Andrew Pax. Of course, Estham had to figure in it, but only as a side factor, an influence. Was he beginning to grow too big in her mind, because Clara and Clifford were such dominating characters and had had some kind of dubious involvement –

some kinds of dubious involvement – with him? This could always turn out a nasty hazard for a biographer when there were living witnesses: forceful personalities might push the direction askew.

She detoured a little and stopped for lunch in Cheltenham. It was the end of October, coldly sunny and heartening. It looked a fine moneyed town, built around wide, stately, tree-lined roads of capacious Georgian houses, and hardly any dog shit on the pavements. Culture was about. She saw many posters for classical music concerts and a theatre would be doing *Antigone* and *Top Girls*. People in the town centre looked as though they knew what was what and meant to go on getting plenty of it. They dawdled in and out of classy shops, loud-hailing one another in gifted, slump-proof accents. She saw a lot of Barbour jackets and tweed suits – on men and women – and a lot of first-class black ankle boots and brown ankle boots, on men.

Would these smart folk want to know the ins-and-outs of Roy Estham's death, or of Andrew Pax's? Were those two deader than dead now? Hadn't Pax and Estham and what drove them been proved hugely irrelevant? The Wall was down. In Britain, rich and poor continued; even richer and poorer, and many of these shoppers would no doubt drink to that in something vintage. Cheltenham remained Cheltenham.

Yes, it did, but ... but ... Perhaps one or two of these nicely shod pedestrians might in fact respond if she suddenly whispered Pax's or Estham's name in their ear. After all, the Government's secret communications centre, G.C.H.Q., was here. Spies and spy-catchers strolled these smart streets among the landed and loaded, and some would have studied important episodes in the history of their trade, and have an academic interest in discovering more about ancient enemies. Christ, perhaps they already knew more than Louise – from handed-down professional gossip in the espionage labour force. If she could not tell them anything new, would even insiders like this want to buy her book? What value would her bits of 'truth' be to them, supposing, that is, she could get any bits today?

Oh, fuck all that. Truth had to be, and could be, its own justification. If not, where were we? The past made the present, so get the past right. As right as it could be got, which, admittedly, was not very.

She ate quickly and then drove on to Hereford. Her work was important, was important, was important. And the manner of Estham's death was important as many times as that, too. Her book would be about an era, about a passionate, positive, dodgy and probably dirty philosophy; just the same, about authentic bonds between brave people which sprang from that philosophy. If Estham killed himself out of self-disgust it would say something about the power of those bonds, and the seriousness of the philosophy behind them. But if he had been merely removed for banging Cliff Deem's missus, his death would be only a sordid murder. It could offer no insights on the strength and stricken grandeur of his political history, and the political history of so many of his contemporaries.

So, Louise asked herself, should one roll up to Gloria's place in this nice, border-country cathedral town and politely inquire, Did you and Deem have a scheme for Roy to be beaten shitless one night, with you tactfully out of the house? This would be to convince him he really should stop fucking Clara Deem and get loyal to you, just as he had got loyal to his country late in the day. And did this happy stratagem go wrong because Cliffy chose people whose aptitudes ran away with them?

That is, if one got the chance to ask her anything at all.

And one did not, not at once, anyway. Mrs Estham would be at her shop, a neighbour said, and the Brigadier with her, definitely. The house was detached, quite new, mock-Georgian on a clean little private estate with wide streets and a lot of greenery.

'Shop?' Louise asked. Brigadier? But did not ask.

'The books.'

'Oh, yes. Which?'

'Rare.'

'She sells rare books?'

'Hereford's hot for rare books. This is a busy little industry, and not one run by Japs, yet. Mrs Estham's shop is called Font, which is a printing term of some note, apparently. And the Brigadier's. Shop, that is. Joint. He'd have capital from a golden bowler when he retired.'

Louise went there and, loitering at a section of modern Firsts, took an occasional gaze around Font. It was not badly stocked and she seemed alone for a minute or two. Then a short, lean, very nimble man of about seventy-five appeared out of a room behind the shop and stood watching her from a few yards away. He looked thoughtful enough and untwitchy enough to have been a brigadier. Louise reached up and took out a copy of C. P. Snow's novel *The Masters*. She studied the date on the copyright page.

'1951,' the man said. 'It's a First all right.'

'Oh? I thought it was written earlier. The thirties. Wasn't there some factual basis to it?'

'An election at Christ's, Cambridge. 1936. Snow was at Christ's as a Fellow. He knew vitamins, or was supposed to.'

'Some say that's all he could do, report what he had seen and heard in the dons' common room.'

'Combination Room.'

'No creative imagination.'

'Rot. But he did write up the situation, with other names, of course. Finished 1938, probably. He had to sit on the book because of libel threats from one of the protagonists – called Raven. Jago in the book. Actually, in an interview Snow said he wrote it later than that just after the war. But this was probably to counter the kind of accusation you've made, about his work being only instant reportage.' He had a very small, brilliantly assured voice, useless for shouting orders above a regimental band.

'I'm fascinated by this period,' Louise said.

'Yes.'

'Cambridge in that decade. The whole aura,' she declared.

'Oh, yes.' It seemed to her like the technique of an interrogator: he let the subject talk, to clear the formal irrelevancies, and in a minute would turn to what mattered. She sensed he knew why she was here.

'I've met someone who was at Christ's at that time and I know of another,' Louise said.

'This is interesting. A personal connection often brings a book added appeal.'

'How do you mean?' she asked.

'Like a painted landscape of somewhere one has been oneself. There's the appeal of the actual work, plus an autobiographical element. One is, as it were, in it, whether picture or a volume.'

'Well, I wasn't actually at Cambridge myself in the thirties,' she replied, laughing a bit.

'Hardly,' he said, also giving this a chuckle. He would go along with her until he was ready. His face was round and fattish for his spare body, but not boyishly round and fattish, more cockily round and fattish. She saw aggression there, and even malevolence: but maybe she added that to him herself, because of what she was coming to suspect. Unquestionably, though, it was a careerist face, a bright, purposeful, less than friendly face.

'May I say how much I like your greatcoat,' he said.

'Thank you.'

'You're not around Hereford much, I believe. I would remember a greatcoat like that – the cut and the wonderful colour. Not quite grey, not quite blue? It's what one can say so often of the sea, I suppose. And you are just the right height for it. Greatcoats are not always the thing for shorter folk. Myself, I stay out of greatcoats of any tint, on principle.'

She looked at the price pencilled on the

front endpaper of *The Masters*, £15.

'I could knock five off,' he said. 'For you. In the circumstances.'

'Which are those?'

'I can't pretend it's all that valuable. Snow's quite skilled, but he doesn't altogether rate with collectors. Same as Angus Wilson. Remember that abuse of Snow from F. R. Leavis? Of course you don't. But you'll have read of it. Yes, the slur lingers. And *The Masters* was a biggish edition. Not scarce. It would be useful for your aura studies, though.' He came forward and took the book from her hands. Carefully, he flicked through the pages, checking for defects, and he tested the binding. He said: 'Listen, I don't think she'll even see you, let alone talk. It's not worth taking your greatcoat off.'

'Is she here?'

'Oh, yes, she's here.'

'Could you ask her?'

'Of course I could ask her,' he said, chuckling again. He handed the book back to Louise. 'Have it. A gift. Then just fuck off out of the shop, perhaps? Best not return or ring further. She finds phone calls from nowhere so threatening.' He spoke this gently, as though it were an item put up between them for discussion, the 'perhaps' a genuine cue. Louise decided to take it like that.

'Could you ask her?' she replied.

'She put down the phone on you. That was

269

Gloria's own doing. I didn't advise her.'

'I'm surprised she answers at all, then.'

'She wants to tell you she's at home – that it's not just No Reply – she's there, but she's not going to speak. It's an anti-message.'

'You do advise her on some things?'

'We're a partnership. There's reciprocity, I hope.'

'What kind of partnership?'

He gestured towards the shelves. 'This and a bit of home life. She'd be alone otherwise.'

'Brigadier is quite a rank, isn't it?' she replied.

'It depends where you're looking at it from, below or above. Brigadier wouldn't do for Prince Philip.'

'Yours must have been a notable career.' In this kind of research or hunt you come across many seeming nonentities, difficult to sort out or remember, sometimes, but they all had significant lives – significant to them, anyway.

'Keep your nose clean and talk brisk – the way to promotion. It's all centred around this area.' In the air he drew a circle that took in the lower half of his face and his throat. Swiftly, then, and soundlessly, he went to the door of the shop, closed and bolted it, and pulled down a blind. 'In case she should agree to talk to you despite everything. The matter might be confidential, I suppose. This is the thing about dealing in rare books. It's rather dilettante. Nobody expects you to be open very often. Do you know that impolite Driffield guide to these shops? He's got a code for people like us: N.O.E. – not open enough.'

'I spoke to her son, and saw her grand-daughters in a fine stage show.'

'She's heard about that, I think. Your name's Louise? He rings up, you know. His career has had a blip, a very long blip, but a blip. I don't despise him. It takes some resolve to go total prole and make one's self comfortable at that level. "A fine stage show." Yes, I'm sorry I missed that. It must be quite wearing for you, tracking down all these people from another age. I mean, Gloria, thirties Cambridge folk, plus some government personnel of that era, too, I imagine.'

'You?' she replied.

'Deem's a name Gloria mentions now and then.'

'I've heard of him. Did you know him yourself? Possibly work with him?'

'It's *them*, I think. A wife, too. Influential and intelligent. I'd have thought you'd have started with them, more or less.'

'They're abroad.'

'I think I'd heard that,' he replied. 'The Algarve?'

'Certainly Portugal.'

'So, then,' he replied, 'are you going kindly

271

to get lost now with your book or do you really want me to go through with speaking to Gloria, your intrusion possibly upsetting her so badly, poor duck?'

'I wondered if you ever met her first husband?' Louise replied.

'Her only husband. As I said, this is a partnership, not more. She wouldn't want more. She's got a down on marriage following those events. I don't suppose you're married? The sheer ... well, elderliness of most of the people you have to interview must be off-putting. The cracked old tones and possibly cracked old brains and powers of recall. I don't think I envy you your kind of work.'

'Generally I don't have anyone I can interview at all. Everyone's history if you're doing a Life of Hallam or Dryden.'

'Ah, yes, we make a good change for you, do we?'

'We? Are you part of the Estham story, then?'

'I'm with Gloria so one has become part of it, willy-as-it-were-nilly,' he replied.

'No, I meant more than that.'

'Yes.'

'Do you mean, yes, it is more than that?'

'No. I meant I knew you meant more than that.'

'And was it more than that?' she asked.

He moved a little closer to her, too close

she thought. There was a smell of wool from his thick, grey and beige tweed tie, and a smell of perhaps glue or marmalade from his small-checked thornproof suit coat. He raised a hand. 'Let me have *The Masters* again for a moment, would you? I'll put a protective plastic cover on the dust-jacket. Even book jackets have to be condomized in this age of destructive bugs. It's the jacket that gives a First most of its value. The illustration declares its period, you see, whereas hardcovers are just hardcovers for ever. But you'll know all this, I'm sure.' She wanted to shift away from him, but felt it would be ludicrous and rude. She remained standing on that spot. He took the book and went to a table where there was a roll of transparent plastic. He removed the jacket of *The Masters* and laid it flat on the table, then enclosed it in a double length of the plastic. He picked up a large pair of red scissors to cut the length from the roll. Glancing over to her he said: 'Guard your jackets, do. A First *Brighton Rock* without a jacket – say £250. With a jacket, £3000.' The book was in his left hand and the scissors in the other. He held the scissors against his trouser leg, pointing towards the ground, as she had seen police in crime dramas carry handguns in readiness. He stood staring at her. 'Clara's talked all that hysterical crud to you in Tavira, has she?' he asked. 'What I mean

273

about your job – having to deal with batty cows of that age.'

'Tell me, were you implicated in—?'

'Why, here's Gloria now,' he said. 'The rumble of chat made you curious, did it, darling?' He half turned to greet her, nothing lavish or especially warm, but probably more amiable than not. 'She's been to see the Deems. Well, inevitably.'

Louise said: 'It's a courtesy call, really, Mrs Estham. Not much more than a formality.'

'She thinks I only made it to Brigadier because of some notable service I did along the way. Kind of Order of the Bath.'

'Why have you closed the shop?' Gloria Estham replied.

'It seemed only Louise's due,' he said. 'One didn't want interruptions, in view of what she brings. She's not just some customer.'

'This is a book shop, for God's sake, Leslie,' Gloria said. It was between a hiss and an enraged whisper. 'I want nothing like that here.' She went and raised the blind, then opened the door. 'Nothing like that,' she said again. He put the scissors back on the table and handed Louise the book.

'You can fuck off now,' Gloria said.

'He's already told me that,' Louise replied.

'I know. I heard.'

'I get a lot of it,' Louise said.

'So fuck off,' she said. She also was small, but slighter than Leslie, still pretty in a pale,

274

solemn way. She had on new jeans and a new denim jacket over a denim shirt. Perhaps she had recently decided to look younger. It was a decision Louise often took herself, though something more than willpower and denim was needed.

'What intrigues me is how you two met in the first place,' Louise said pleasantly.

'In the first place?' he asked. 'I don't think I follow.'

'The circumstances.'

'Oh, those,' he replied.

'This was why I asked whether you'd known Roy Estham,' she said.

'Ah, was it?' he replied. 'I wondered if it was. Where are you staying?'

A couple of middle-aged women entered the shop and told Gloria they were looking for a factual book by Anthony Powell about a publishing house's search for a missing author. They didn't have the title but thought it had been taken from a poem by Robert Browning.'

'*What's Become of Waring*,' Louise said. 'I read a lot of Powell. He gets it right. But not factual. A novel.'

'Without a question mark after Waring,' Gloria said. 'Very scarce as a First. Immensely valuable in the jacket, by someone called Barbosa, I think. Many copies were burned in a blitzed warehouse.'

'Oh, I was sure it was fact,' one of the

women cried. 'Didn't Powell work in publishing?'

'He did,' Gloria said, 'but it's a story, all the same. There was no real person called Waring.'

'Not Waring but Browning,' Leslie said. 'People do get mixed up about what's true and what's make-believe. The novel this lady is holding now, *The Masters*, is similar. And, in fact, she's possibly writing exactly the same sort of mixed, pot-pourri mess herself, aren't you, Louise, dear, though this time supposedly fact? Supposedly, yes. A strange word, pot-pourri, isn't it? From the French, meaning rot pot, would you believe?'

Twenty

'They give an annual prize over there,' D.L.O. said. 'It's no great amount of money and, true, it's not in the Academy Award league. But it does rate, Ted. This is a prize for what they term "Mediating Autobiographers". Meaning ghosts. Stanley has had an impeccable tip that the Gale Life is going to win it. I mean, *Louise* is going to win it. She will be the industry's supreme "as told to" this year. Everything's going for her. You know what books and publishing and prizes are like in the States: women have to win every fucking thing, to compensate them for those centuries of second fiddledom.'

'Great,' Burston replied. He was analysing the words, all of them, not mainly for what they said about *We're Rolling* or Louise Summers, but as an indication of where D.L.O. had managed to get himself in the new company structure; and of also where he, Burston, therefore was.

He fixed on the way D.L.O. had said 'Stanley'. Burston probed this. There was an intimacy about it, but also respect. If he had

277

said 'Stan' it might have suggested bogus familiarity, and would have proved D.L.O. uncertain of tenure. If he had said Faldave, or Stan Faldave or Stanley Faldave, there would have been a hint of distance and possible resentment of Faldave's status and power: fear part disguised by the formal. But 'Stanley' seemed to mean D.L.O. was all right and thought Faldave was all right because Faldave had made sure D.L.O. would be all right. So, no fucking changes. Marie handling him briefly through serge and boxer shorts was as close to sway as he was going to get in Panopticon.

She had intercommed Burston quite early to say D.L.O. was back and wanted to see him. Her voice had that hop-to-it lift around the edges, plus all the traditional battering aloofness, so Burston could almost forget that only yesterday he had helped defend her from Charlotte Gale and the other two; and that only the day before she fell into that bracing little familiarity.

'I mean great for the company and for Louise,' Burston said.

'Certainly. Stanley is delighted for her. And, naturally, for us in that we commissioned her, Ted, and hatched the half-and-half deal with her publisher on costs and profits.'

What 'impeccable tip' meant in D.L.O.'s announcement was that Faldave had fine contacts in the industry over there and that he was prepared to share with D.L.O. the boons they brought. Well, of course, of course, Faldave had fine contacts. Would he be in that job so young otherwise? This was another son-in-law also rising, wasn't it? Hadn't he heard somewhere that Faldave married very cleverly?

D.L.O. looked as gaunt and short of sleep as ever, yet there seemed a disgusting poise about him, as if he thought he *was* Panopticon: was *still* Panopticon. Perhaps it had turned out as Rosemary Paston said, and Faldave and his crew felt afraid to get rid of him after *Broken Light*'s triumph. And this award for the book would help him, too. He said Faldave had praised both of them for using Louise and for the deal. But, of course, D.L.O. would have made it so clear that *he* had been the impulse; with Burston far behind in a flunkey part, witnessing signatures and doing the word-count on Louise's stuff – just clerking.

'The first edition – this is the version that's won, obviously,' D.L.O. said.

'Oh, God. The un-self-destruction issue?'

'Apparently. According to Stanley's tipster, it was her skilled demolition of the suicide "slur" that impressed the judges most. I gather "humane" and "sensitive" are words prominent in their report. As praise. This is some fucking situation, Ted.' His head slumped forward in the style heads did slump forward to signal despair. D.L.O., also, had seen a lot of acting. 'How far on are we with those new edition changes fattening up the suicide aspect?'

'The publishers have had the amendments for quite a time. They'll be with the printers by now. Whether they've actually begun rolling off copies yet I don't know. I haven't checked lately.'

D.L.O. tugged at the little finger of his left hand with all the clenched fingers of his right. This was always a sign of rattiness with him, and his own personal thing, not borrowed from screenplays. 'Well, you should have,' he said. 'This is forty-five thousand copies at what, £16.99?'

'Fifteen thousand for this country, twenty for the States, ten for general export.'

'Christ, we're actually printing the States edition this side? How come?'

'Now and then they do that, apparently. On a big run it's cheaper.'

D.L.O. hit a sort of anguished croon. 'Oh, this fucking Gale. He could wipe us all out, not just his poxy self, the craven sod. We've got to stick, stick and stick again with non-suicide. The award is not a gaudy thing, but full of prestige, and it always produces a hell of a lot of publicity and revived sales, apparently. Biography and autobiography boom, here and in the States. How's it going to look if we fill the shops with books that say the opposite of what the judges gave the prize for? Where the fuck did the notion pro-suicide come from anyway? All right, so Monroe killed herself and got super-iconized as a result. Good luck to her. But Monroe fucked the President of the United States. We can't count on the same process for David Gale. He'd fuck anything, anything but Imogen, obviously – Marie, Kirsten, the three Sarahs, Louise, Griselda. Plus Charlotte. This is not comparable cachet. You'd better get on to the publishers and tell them to stop the rejigged volume. We'll want a new print of the original instead. Same quantity.'

'It's going to cost, D.L.O. Possibly cost a lot if they're far on. You realize this could mean pulping? I mean, pulping on one hell of a scale. And we'll have no way of checking how many they've actually done. They could really sting us.'

D.L.O. was striding about his suite. Burston had the chair that Gale's mother, Dorothy, sat in yesterday, full of sadness and grave dignity. D.L.O. came quickly towards Burston and punched him in the temple, a long-armed, incompetent blow, yet one which Burston was not ready for. He was hit from the seat and fell sprawling but conscious on the carpet. 'You shit-house,' D.L.O. screamed, kicking his shoulder and chest with his suedes. 'You always take the worst fucking scenario. You want to persecute me, don't you, you bastard?'

Burston stood up, enraged, mainly with himself. Twice before in this suite D.L.O. had struck and kicked him at crises in Panopticon business, yet he had still been off guard just now. Although he had noticed the little-finger drill, he was not ready for violence. Burston rushed him and went for a karate chop at D.L.O.'s neck but landed just below his ear, a little too high for possible dislocation of the vertebrae. D.L.O. yelped and flung a hand up in pain and Burston swung from far back the point of his black slip-on into D.L.O.'s balls and then, when he did not immediately go down, mashed him there again. D.L.O. fell and huddled himself against further kicking, his hands and arms around his head. He sicked up a little and groaned when he could. Burston kicked his knees and shins instead of higher and then, when D.L.O. pathetically put a hand down to try to guard these, gave him two in the Adam's apple. D.L.O. vomited a few dismal strands more. Burston wiped the toe of his shoe clean on D.L.O.'s sleeve.

Marie might have felt the impact of the falls in her outer office and came in now without knocking. 'Oh, God,' she said, 'people are so damn committed in this firm.' Between them they lifted D.L.O. and got

282

him laid out on a sofa. Marie wiped down his face with pages from an old script taken from one of his wall shelves. She had spotted the sick on the floor very early and dodged it easily. D.L.O.'s eyes were shut but he seemed aware of Burston and Marie. As they bent over him, asking if he was going to be all right, she moved her left hand into Burston's crotch and gave him that little upward moving fondle again through his clothes, as though not certain D.L.O. would survive.

Then she started talking, perhaps to divert D.L.O. from concentration on his injuries: 'Did Ted tell you we had Charlotte here yesterday, plus Mrs Gale senior and the agent? They want a memorial service.'

'They fucking what?' D.L.O. muttered, his eyes still very shut.

'Exactly,' Marie replied. 'That Charlotte. So damn rude and dictatorial, D.L.O.'

He seemed to sleep for a while, his appearance serene and childlike except for the shoe weals on his throat. Marie released Burston's dick and went to open a window for more air. When D.L.O. came to again he said: 'A memorial service might not be bad, though.' He sat up. He was opening and closing his lips, a squeamish look on his face, to signal a hellish taste in his mouth. Marie went back to her own room and brought a glass of water. His eyes were closed even now and he felt along her arm to the glass and drank a little. 'A memorial service is status,' he said. 'They're right on that. And it could be done, as long as we're going the full bundle on non-suicide. Suicide's a very fluctuating item. Churches don't mind accident, provided it's official, even if there's doubt. We've got the Open verdict, and the Life won't be contradicting that now.'

Burston said: 'But have you thought, D.L.O., how much we need the suicide aspect for our Pax campaign? Gale's despair was such a splendid lead in to that. Those two factors are complementary pillars.'

'Stanley's against, I think.'

Burston had, of course, thought this about Faldave's reaction, too. It would have taken a zombie to think anything else. But he said: 'Against what?'

'The campaign.'

'But we're already involved, D.L.O.,' Burston replied. 'It would be one of the best and most selfless things Panopticon has ever done.'

D.L.O. opened his eyes. 'Our *films* are the best things we've ever done. We're a film company, Ted, not a Centre for Sucking Up To Rats.'

'Is that what Faldave said?'

D.L.O. stood and did a couple of steps, testing his legs. Burston watched the lout carefully now. D.L.O. did not seem too shaky. He came back and lowered himself

284

gently on to the sofa. 'I see what you mean about the cost of pulping, Ted,' he said.

'We'd probably have to meet the full bill. This would be our sole decision. We couldn't ask the publisher to chip in.'

D.L.O.'s lips were pulled back hard, exposing all his teeth. He was obviously raging against Burston again for blackening the black. But he did not try to get up and attack. 'I suppose it would be impractical to propose we keep the noble suicide version for Britain and let the States stay with the first. Would it, Ted?' He sounded plaintive, feeble.

'Certainly impractical, Darren,' Burston replied.

'Yes, probably.'

'Some journalist like Pamela de la Salle gets wind there are two contradictory versions around and where are we?'

'Jesus,' Darren replied.

'She'd set the warring paragraphs alongside each other across a couple of columns.'

'Jesus. When you say "involved" in the Pax campain – How? Have you spoken to anyone – bishops and so on? Harold Pinter?'

'Not actually.'

'No, but—?'

'I've done a bishop shortlist. That involved taking some soundings, obviously, D.L.O. It had to be done professionally.'

'Fuck professionally,' D.L.O. replied.

'The word is around, I expect.'

'I don't like it around.'

Marie said: 'I think you're all right now, D.L.O. Yes, sounding and looking grand.' She left the suite: 'Do try to keep it all at the discussion level, boys.'

'And Stanley wouldn't like it around, either,' D.L.O. said. 'Take it no further, Ted. If bishops or other stirrers ring up inquiring tell them we're no part of such a putative campaign and never have been. A misunderstanding, possibly deliberately and maliciously promoted. Yes, maliciously. By a rival company wanting to damage us through association with off-colour causes. Get a list of such bishops if they do make contact and possibly I, or even Stanley, will write to them personally, explaining the error. I know Stanley and I would agree that we have no wish to alienate opinion-formers of the status of bishops and so on. Stanley is especially keen to give ample and clear respect to British institutions. And call the fucking publishers. Call them today, Ted. Stop the reprint. Stop it in the hail-to-suicide form.'

'If—'

'Stop it. And don't come with some lies about it being too late – because you think that might save the Pax campaign. You've got yourself emotionally embroiled with that, I don't know why. If any of the bishops who

286

calls is local, I mean London – how many bishops do they have around London, anyway? – but if one of them's from London, explain politely we're not interested in the Pax campaign but what would he say to a memorial for Panopticon's late star David Gale, whose death by tragic accident is well known about and officially confirmed. This would be a real boost for his church. Glossy names attending.

'Yes, by the way, Stanley says the name Panopticon will continue, at least for the present. This is the kind of thoughtful person he is, Ted. It doesn't have to be a church bang in the middle. We would not mind going out a bit. The media would still cover, given David's shagging *réclame* and screen work, plus the kind of congregation we'd get. The tabloids are going to want to see which women turned up in tribute to what he did for them. You could say it's quite probable Stanley Faldave would come himself to such an occasion. Then, Ted, get on to Louise and pass Stanley's congratulations. He specifically asked they should be conveyed. And give her mine, too, naturally, and your own. It's important she is told immediately that her pro-suicide revisions will not be used. We clearly do not want her talking about these around the trade. It could mean confusion. And she will gather, won't she, that virtually a condition of the ghost award is the hearty denial of suicide, as in her unsurpassed first edition? She will not want to endanger her success by indulging in talk with friends and folk in the game generally about the alterations she was asked for. Such tales spread, even across the Atlantic. You'll be able to make it clear to her, won't you, Ted, that the award is not confirmed yet – though certain, if there are no slip-ups or stupid rumours – and that she has a duty to David, as well as to herself, to accept the properly-arrived-at view of the death?'

Twenty-One

'Retired as lieutenant-colonel,' she said. 'But I keep up membership. It's nice to stay in touch, don't you think? I finished in military Intelligence, ironically enough, protecting secrets, seeking spies.'

'You liked the Army?' Louise asked.

'Loved it. Loved its craving for perfect organization. Loved its essential broadmindedness. Could put up with being called "Ma'am". Did you ever read Osbert Sitwell on his time in the Guards? Now Osbert was quite an Osberty sort of cove, very arty and independent-minded. All that. He found Guards officers entirely purposeful in military matters, but at the same time able to understand – and, in many cases, to share – to understand the cultural concerns so important to Sitwell. One runs into officers who can play the cello beautifully or who write poetry – and I don't mean whingeing-type stuff like Wilfred Owen's. He was just a duration of hostilities commission. I mean real officers, career people.'

'Owen was a very brave leader in the field,

surely,' Louise replied.

'That goes without saying, doesn't it?' she replied. 'Any officer.'

Lord Chate said: 'It began so early. Even as a small child Veronica talked Army and more Army.'

'So tell me what you think of this place, Louise? Not quite the Groucho, is it?'

They were lunching in the Cavalry and Guards Club in Piccadilly. Waiters did call her Ma'am. The room was long and handsome, with high arched windows, grand mahogany furniture and large unsmiling oil paintings of famed military leaders, one or two in long cloaks, though not famed enough for Louise to recognize any of them. Conversation from other tables was brisk, officerly, but apparently civil, and less than blaring. Veronica spoke rather in that style herself. These folk were used to getting obedience, and yet were also used to giving it: they had voices that knew how to shout and knew how to defer. Louise found she liked the club, which was certainly not quite the Wig and Pen, and no worse for that. Louise treated Veronica very carefully. She was small and podgy-faced, without diffidence and rich in vigour. Her lips looked ready for insolence. She wore no rings.

When Louise returned from Hereford there had been a message from Chate on her answerphone asking for a call back. She did and he suggested lunch at the club. 'I'd no idea you were commissioned in the Cavalry. Or the Guards,' she had said.

'Not in your research? You're right. I wasn't. By the end of the war I'd made it to corporal in the Royal Army Service Corps. It's my daughter, Veronica, who's hosting the lunch. Her home ground.'

Now, Veronica leaned across the table, grinning: 'So, has he put you in the picture, Louise?'

'I make a guess,' Louise replied.

'I bet you do,' she said. 'Your trade.'

'Guesses are no good in my trade,' Louise said. 'Or only as start points. Officially, you are still what I understood at the beginning, Lord Chate's daughter.' But there was a silky aggressiveness to Veronica and a sly shine in the eyes that Chate did not have.

'And it's true, in a sense,' she said. 'I *am* his daughter.'

'Of course it is,' he said and himself leaned across the table to grip her forearm lovingly for a moment. 'One of them. Who else's if not mine?'

She grinned at him. 'Well, yes, who else's?' she asked.

'There's something wonderful about it,' Louise said.

Chate considered that for a few seconds, frowning: 'No, I wouldn't say wonderful. Something tidy, perhaps. And something comradely – just comradely comradely, not political comradely. Cambridge comradely, but not Red Cambridge comradely, Christ's Cambridge comradely. Same staircase comradely.' He passed a hand over his long, narrow, completely bald head. He seemed much older than when she last met him. Perhaps it was the effect of London, or of this dignified club. Perhaps he was never at his best when away from 'Embate' his manor house and acres, despite his contempt for the pool and fountain. Elderly people could get like that: moved from their own setting, they grew troubled. 'Veronica's very much in favour of this vindication campaign, Louise. Well, as you'd expect.'

'Campaign? I don't know anything about it,' Louise replied.

'Oh, stirrings,' Chate said. 'Bishops. That sort. Rumour level, but I believe authentic. We'd very much like to help. This has become quite central in our thinking.'

'Well, as you'd expect,' Veronica said.

'Probably it would mean things being brought into the open,' Chate said. 'But Veronica is prepared for that. And if she doesn't mind, I don't.'

'It would be different if I were still serving,' Veronica replied. 'Revelations and a kerfuffle might have damaged the Army. Not now.'

'She graduated top in her commission course, you know,' Chate said. 'Distinctions in Strategic Planning, Personnel Care and Counter-terrorism.'

'And I do crave an official recognition that he was innocent,' Veronica said. 'Well – as you'd expect, again: I'm trained to believe in official statements, aren't I? They are order and decent continuance.'

'We both feel the film company are to be congratulated for this initiative,' Chate said.

'Your information comes from Panopticon?' Louise asked.

'Ultimately,' Chate replied. 'Though they'll stay out of the limelight, I imagine. Their motives might look doubtful: there could obviously be a publicity advantage for their film about Andrew. A man called Burston?'

'Yes, it could be Ted.'

'Is he the head there?'

'Not exactly the head,' Louise replied.

'But influential?' Chate asked.

'He's thoughtful,' Louise replied. 'Pretends to be ignorant, sometimes.'

'Of course, I read in the business pages of changes affecting Panopticon,' Chate said. 'But I would hope a campaign of this kind might lie outside the usual hardnosed board-room concerns and that it would continue unimpaired. We are talking here about justice itself.'

They had met early at the club and before apéritifs and the meal Veronica showed them around. She had lingered on the first landing near pictures of Captain L. E. G. Oates of the 6th Inniskilling Dragoons, who walked out to his death in a blizzard during Scott's South Pole expedition: frost-bitten feet made Oates a liability. A painting showed Oates leaving the tent. The caption read, 'a very gallant gentleman'. Veronica had said to Louise: 'I believe in gallantry.' Nearby was a large silver cup alongside kettle drums. The Kadir Cup was prize in the Pigsticking horseriding contest begun in 1869. Fixed to the wall was a list of winners from that time on.

'You see, I don't mind Britishness,' Veronica said. They had passed a statuette entitled *The Last Call*. It was a fallen horse, the rider brandishing a trumpet high. 'I can't really believe that anybody born in this country would seriously want to undermine Britishness. No, I can't.' The three of them were making their way downstairs at the time, and perspectives changed frequently; but Louise thought that for a second she saw a tear hover in the right eye of that sword of honour face. This might have been the moment when Louise began to wonder at full lick about her.

Now, eating ice cream as dessert, Chate said: 'What else could I have done? It was to have been only a temporary thing, you know, to help her mother at a very tricky time. There was another man, and she was trying

294

to start a career. All that seemed reasonable, seemed admirable, to me. Andrew was a fine man, but he had been dead four years by then. This was a woman still not twenty-five. She was right not to let the past control her. As a babe, Veronica had been in and out of institutions during the war. I could not let that go on, could I, not once I had a settled home? Could I?'

'And being billeted with you became permanent?' Louise asked.

'Something like that,' Chate said. 'What else could I have done? I'd married in 1944 and we had two children of our own. One more didn't seem any odds. Veronica became part of the family. Then, after a while, my wife and I would have been distressed to let her go.'

'Do the reference books list you as an Hon., now your adoptive father is a lord?' Louise asked.

'There's never been an official adoption,' Chate replied.

'Ma'am's bad enough,' Veronica said.

'And your mother, your natural mother?' Louise asked her. 'Is she still alive? Do you keep contact?'

'Ah, the researcher! You're thinking of your book about my – about Andrew Pax. We did keep in touch, yes,' Veronica said. 'She died in 1986 in the States, where she'd gone to live with her husband. Oh, yes, letters. An occasional phone call. Even a visit.' She laughed and waved a hand to embrace the club. 'I expect hearing this you'll understand why I prize tradition and order – why I revere stability, continuance. And why I admire people who fight and die to guard those traditions.' She laughed again. 'Is this heavy? A corrective of my genes?' It sounded as if she did not care whether it was or not.

'Heavy*ish*,' Chate replied. 'But excusable, darling.'

'I'm an institution person, you see. I will not believe my ... I can't believe Andrew Pax wanted to destroy all the structure and system of Britain. How could I have grown to be what I am if he had really been so?'

She seemed to have answered her own question before she asked it. Louise said: 'Did your mother ever speak to you, write to you, about him, about what he wanted?'

'Ah, again the book!' she said. 'Sorry. Never. That part of her life seemed to have been shut down. My father died in the war – this was all she ever said. True, of course. For all I knew my father had been shot down facing fearful odds. A hero. Well, for all I knew until I was quite grown up.'

'One can help with this campaign, Louise,' Chate said. 'A little money, some wire-pulling, perhaps.' He held up a hand and a waiter came at once. Service was almost frantic here. The officer corps knew how to get what they wanted when they wanted it, and an ex-corporal could take advantage. Chate ordered a bottle of Sauternes to accompany what was left of their desserts.

Louise said: 'I can't say what will happen at Panopticon. I'm only a hired writer, you know. I'm instructed. I don't instruct.'

Chate said: 'A lad called Stanley Faldave's big there now, I believe.'

'I'd heard that,' Louise replied.

'Quite young?'

'Thirtyish.'

'This would be about right.'

'Do you know him?' Louise asked

'I possibly know the father-in-law. Donman Capel.'

Louise said: 'Oh. Well, of course everyone in the trade has heard of Donman.'

' "Donman", I bloody ask you,' Chate replied. He tasted and approved the wine. The waiter filled their glasses. 'But that's how they are over there. Bayzone his firm? But besides the studios he does quite a bit in shipping. I've used his vessels for freight now and then. Still do. Could do more. And I had a freebie cruise on a luxury craft of his. He was aboard with his wife and what might be the daughter who married Faldave. Emily? Not pretty, though prettier than Donman.'

'I love the whole idea of a campaign,' Veronica said. 'Such a stirring word. Like something powered by the Iron Duke.'

Twenty-Two

Ted Burston decided he had better see Louise and let her know about the ghost award she was tipped for; and also say her suicide rewrites, although approaching magic, would not now be used; and that it would be wisest not to talk about them. It mortified Burston, the need to backtrack like this. What would she think of him as he relayed this latest policy switch and demanded secrecy? Wasn't she bound to see him as a piffling minion: someone who obediently passed on one order today and its opposite tomorrow, because D.L.O. or those behind D.L.O. had decided things that way?

God! Cornered in his degrading little room, surrounded by posters for dead and dying films, Burston grew positive. Why didn't he just forget all the fiddling about here, get on a plane and go to see Faldave one-to-one, face-to-face himself in Los Angeles? Late in the day, yes, but not too late, why didn't he demonstrate to Faldave the kind of man he, Ted Burston, truly was? Or could be, if provoked. Why didn't he corner dear Stanley out there and prove to him with quality passion that the Pax campaign was not like other bits of workaday Panopticon policy, liable to be picked up or put down or picked up again according to caprice? This was a mission, a cause, a duty. Its qualities did not, could not, vary. They were sturdy, worthwhile, almost timeless. And, if Panopticon undertook that mission, that cause, that duty, those sturdy, worthwhile, almost timeless qualities would be reflected at least in part on Panopticon's productions, and particularly *Broken Light* and the Gale Life.

Yes, yes, why the devil didn't he do that – the quick plane, the meeting, the self-elevation into a figure Faldave was bound to see as full of conviction, full of grit, full of ... full of, why not say it, full of a kind of grandeur? Why didn't he? Why? Well, because probably he was not that kind of man and knew it. Grandeur? He winced. Jesus. So, what kind of man was he? He was the kind who waited tamely around the office for D.L.O. to return to the office from the States and name all the new-from-the-horse's-mouth policies. He was the kind who passed on other people's contradictory instructions to people like Louise Summers, and hoped they would at least conceal their merriment and contempt. He was the kind who had their cocks fondled too briefly by women

299

through two layers of clothing, and that was as far as it went. He was the kind who could make a shot at placating widows or mothers or agents, but who could initiate nothing that would last. He was someone who, when it suited, acted dim and crude and did it shamefully well.

He was ... Oh, Christ, could it be true he was really so? And could it be true that this was really the kind of fart Faldave would want helping to run one of his companies? Burston had been out to Los Angeles and Hollywood twice before on Panopticon business and would not feel overwhelmed by the sprawl and the driving and ugliness and wealth if he landed there on impulse tomorrow. He would not land there on impulse tomorrow, though, would he? His impulses lacked impulsiveness and were heartbreakingly strong on checks and balances.

In his little room he gave Louise sherry and all the congratulations and warnings due after the Life award. He sketched how this had caused amendments in D.L.O.'s thinking on the suicide theme. At once Louise said comfortably and apparently without sarcasm: 'This sounds all right, Ted. By which I mean, there's nothing I'm supposed to do, is there?'

'Not at all,' he replied. Often he would find her coolness dismaying. It more or less de-sexed her for him. He prized commitment, though exercised with tact, obviously.

Louise said: 'It's all done and double done, isn't it? All that's necessary is forget the double done bit, chuck it out.'

'You take a very reasonable attitude.'

'I'm a ghost. Ghosts don't have backbones. Do any of us?'

'What?'

'Have backbones,' she said.

But, now, there it was – irony on its way, exposing its unpleasant teeth. This girl no longer even tried for humaneness. She didn't know he had changed, that he lusted for the worthwhile, at least as an interlude. Well, that was all right. How could she? 'I'll probably go out and have a direct word,' he replied with really good brusqueness. 'It's often the only way with these *arriviste* people.'

'A word?'

'With Faldave.'

She took time to reply, doing astonishment. *'You* – go to L.A.?' she asked.

This almost infuriated him. 'That's where he is.'

'Go there with what in view?' She was not staring at him, but he could feel she wanted to. Sitting opposite Burston in his room, Louise had her eyes down towards the desk some of the time, but now and again she lifted them to do an estimate: to see if he still looked like Burston, maybe.

'There are a whole complex of matters,' he

301

replied now with plenty of crispness. 'Inter-linked.'

'The campaign?'

'You've heard of that?'

'A murmur here and there.'

'The campaign might come into it. Does he understand this country?'

'Faldave?' Louise said.

'That's what one has to ask. I mean, in his own interests I ask that question. Does he realize how much he could damage his personal standing, and the company's?'

'D.L.O. has told you to go and beard him?' she asked.

'D.L.O.'s is not the only voice here, Louise.'

This time she replied too fast: 'No, no, of course not. But you'd go to L.A. off your own bat?'

'You find that strange? I'm familiar with the town, you know.'

'I'm sure, but it doesn't—'

'Doesn't seem like me, right for me: isn't what one expects from Ted Burston? Why not, Louise?' Politeness still, though.

'If it's a sort of individualistic, sort of you as you, gesture, would D.L.O. sign the expenses?'

Now, Burston roughed his lips together. She was not the only one who could register contempt. He knew actors and body language.

'I heard Faldave is Donman Capel's son-in-law,' Louise said.

'Someone's, anyway. But one can't get hung-up about names in a case like this, can one? This is not a matter of contacts within the business, however eminent. This is to do with justice.'

'I've heard someone else say that.'

'Oh?'

'Someone who mentioned the campaign.'

'This is what I mean: justice is a concept that reaches out, that naturally enlists support. It's what living in a democracy still implies, despite everything.'

Louise said: 'Well, I hope you're lucky.'

'Thanks, Louise.'

'I'd say you could have a better chance with him than you realize.'

He liked that. Yes, she could josh him, but she would have an intelligent respect for his battery of flairs, too. 'I'm confident. I know I can be convincing, inspiring, persuasive.'

'Right.' She nodded a bit, perhaps gathering some ideas. 'If you talk Faldave around to your thinking, might it mean that the suicide rewrites could still be useful in a subsequent edition, a third or even fourth edition? I've put them on disk now and I'll keep it, shall I?'

'They might have a place. It has to be possible,' Burston said. 'Once the award has actually been made and you hold the prize, I

think we could reasonably consider adjust-
ments, to chime with shifts in public opinion. I see nothing dubious about that. There
are no holy, unchanging truths when dealing
with matters like these.'

'Not many.'

'Louise, you do seem to stay so damned
detached.'

'These, also, are essentials of ghostliness.
My habit.'

'But ... well ... you and David.'

'Yes?'

She sat smiling, uncommunicative, un-
troubled. OK, so she would not help him,
the scribbling sow. 'That ... well ... *connection*. It makes things less impersonal, one
would have thought, Louise. With respect.'

'You'll know that Edna St Vincent Millay
sonnet,' she replied.

'I doubt it. Who? Is that one person?' Oh,
God, Burston thought, this cliché queen was
going to give him 'I, Being Born a Woman
and Distressed'.

'Called "I, Being Born a Woman and Distressed". Goes like this:

'I, being born a woman and distressed
By all the needs and notions of my kind,
Am urged by your propinquity to find
Your person fair, and feel a certain zest
To bear your body's weight upon my breast.'

'Saucy,' Burston said.

'And it finishes thusish:

'Think not for this, however, the poor
treason
Of my stout blood against my staggering
brain
I shall remember you with love, or season
My scorn with pity, – let me make it plain:
I find this frenzy insufficient reason
For conversation when we meet again.'

Burston said: 'I see. Paraphraseable as:
"Don't imagine that because I momentarily
required a fuck, sir, I need you on a
continuing basis." '

'Of course, you knew it damn well already.'

'David Gale wanted something more?
Something serious continuing? What, he
longed for permanence? He'd definitely have
left Charlotte for you?'

'Look, there's a sort of kudos in having it
off with a star, Ted. Even a star like David.
There are worse. He could keep my name in
mind even when pissed. Have it off thrice.
You know Erica Jong's "zipless fuck"? Or it
could be fucks, if not too many. It, they, just
exist for themselves, can enliven a few dull
days, nights. Some closeness, some warmth,
some merriment. And no messing about
with a relationship. What was it the actress
Margaret Leighton said – "On tour it doesn't

count." Hanging about locations and sets was like being on tour.'

'He couldn't bear that notion? I mean, literally could not bear it?'

'He might have been more sensitive than you realized, Ted, and more sad.'

'And you thought bedding Dave kudos? Well, I suppose so. Even if he went everywhere and anywhere?'

'It would have been more hurtful if he hadn't gone to me, too, then, wouldn't it?'

'Insulting,' Burston replied.

'One day I might show you a letter,' she said. The cow made it sound unlikely.

'What letter?' he asked.

'I might.'

He found himself beginning to shout, and, after a few words, forced himself to bring his voice down a bit. 'You mean a letter to you, to you personally, privately, that would explain the death? A plea? Look, with respect, Louise, this is important, isn't it?'

'Of course it's important. But not relevant.'

'It would be relevant to a coroner's court.'

'It might have been. We're not a court. It's not relevant to a Life. After all, we have to be able to shape that the way we want, don't we?'

'He actually wrote and said what he was going to do and why?' Burston asked.

Marie came on the intercom with full surliness: 'To see him now.'

'Or I'll keep it back for my autobiog,' Louise said. 'I've got a title: *Ghost Rides.*'

It took Burston a while to get through Customs at Los Angeles airport. Did he look like a drugs courier, for God's sake. 'Purpose of visit?' a girl in uniform asked.

Justice? Self-realization? 'Business,' he said.

From a booth downstairs he phoned Faldave at work. The call seemed to go right through to him – no preliminaries with the outer-office. Perhaps it was the Freedom of Information Act here: you had a right to speak to the chief, or, at least, the chief's son-in-law. 'Sure I remember you, Ted. Taste Bud. You discovered it.'

'Oh, it has good days and not so good.'

'Piquant, I thought. Look, you'd better come to my house. It's nicer.' He said the place was called 'Semblance', in the Hollywood Hills, off a street called Alta Vista: 'not so very, very far from the Neutra-designed Loring house. But just tell the driver Alta Vista.'

'Ah.' That meant it was very, very far from the Neutra-designed Loring house. Neutra must be an OK architect, and Faldave prized the association, even if didn't exist.

'I'll leave for home now. I thought you might show. I've got to regard myself as always accessible, and to worldwide inter-

307

ests, Ted. It's what company management means to me.'

'You thought I'd come?'

'Sure.'

'But why?'

'What do you mean but why?' Faldave said. 'You're here, aren't you? That's the why. I see people as individuals.'

'This is heartening. I've come here as an individual.' Holding the phone, Burston felt a kind of abject loneliness, and a kind of distinction.

'Sure you've come as an individual, Ted. And I couldn't be more grateful.' Faldave never seemed to consider asking whether D.L.O. had sent him. Burston decided that Stanley or whatever his real name was could easily turn out to be someone of true instinct and judgement. The fact he was Capel's son-in-law might be of only incidental significance. Burston wondered whether Faldave would offer to send a car to the airport for him, but no. In fact, he seemed to assume Burston would take a taxi. 'The driver will know my house,' he said. 'Just tell him "Semblance".' On second thoughts, this absence of a car pleased Burston. It showed that Faldave really did think of him as someone of individuality, who would not want to be cosseted and made to feel obliged. A cab would cost God knew how much, but to fuck about with public transport might take some of the sweetness from the visit. He was here to get a young man unhanged and you did not handle something like that by bus.

He liked L.A. airport. You knew straight away you were in another culture. Well, the rows of palm trees would tell you you were not at Heathrow or Copenhagen; and the amusing white Theme Building with its circular restaurant hung high between arched concrete legs. First sight of the town outside could depress you if you looked too hard, and he had learned not to. No town was at its best near the airport. L.A. had a jumble of concrete two-storey factory build-ings, scrap dumps, warehouses, transport yards. What the hell were they turning out from so many factories? Guns? Gas masks? Graffiti sprays?

On the freeway things improved fast. The taxi made for the 405 going north to the Sunset Boulevard offramp, then east. The driver did not talk. This must be another difference between California and New York. Burston could enjoy the journey now and grew even more confident in the case for Andrew Pax. He felt what he was: someone on a mission, a valid mission. The freeways were as busy as ever, but he soothed himself by gazing at the banks of ivy and iceplant edging the road, and the occasional splashes of pink oleander.

They turned off at Sunset Plaza Drive and kept going but north now, into the hills that look down on to the Los Angeles plain, the 'flats'. Despite the forecast, his driver could not find 'Semblance' at once, and they drifted about for a while among mansions in every style except bijou: rococo, hacienda, French château, English baronial, Italian palace. Burston saw one vast place completely covered with a mural of sandstone hills, a lake and distant skyscrapers. You wouldn't call much of the area witty, but a lot of these people obviously liked a laugh. And, what you'd expect in movie town, they were strong on visuals.

Faldave lived in something wooden. Burston could smell preservative before he opened the taxi door. A dog waddled forward to greet him, a stout, aged, liver-and-white spaniel, its tongue hanging low and obviously too weighty on a close day for hauling back. The dog looked older than Faldave and Burston wondered whether it had been taken over with the property. This seemed the right sort of dog for a wooden house, not just the colour but the dog's shakiness on the ground and overall crumbling quality. Faldave and a very sober-looking, dark-haired, pregnant, formerly slim woman of about his own age or younger followed the dog into the driveway. They were both in denim shorts and individual T-shirts. The woman's had a motif in yellow italic: 'Beget A Life'. Burston was paying the taxi.

'He's already fond of you,' Faldave said.

Burston glanced at the driver. 'The dog,' the man muttered.

'I've never seen anyone look less jet-lagged,' the woman said. 'Marvin promised you'd be like that. He knew you were the type who'd resiliate. The British type, and then a bit more for luck. We've got nearly the same style gym in the basement here as Jerry Bruckheimer – you know Bruckheimer who made *Top Gun*? Of course. And Marvin does a lot in there to toughen the frame and myself too when in a different condition, but you Brits seem to have it by nature. The Battle of the River Plate, was it?' Thin in the legs and arms, she had a softly cornered squarish face, full of her own certainties. The voice relayed a brisk, quiet informativeness, like someone capable and very good-hearted giving street directions to a stranger. Probably that came when your father was powerful.

'This home,' Burston said, turning to gaze at it as the taxi pulled away, 'it's in the style of an English country house, yet of timber. Lovely.'

'Do you know a property called Chatsworth over there?' the woman asked. 'It's ducal. Many who have travelled regard our house as a kind of representation of that, though miniaturized to a degree, of course, and, as you say, of wood. And so the name. It's a semblance. We thought it would be ... well, like sneaky to call it Chatsworth. Wood's probably more a mode here than over there with your icy winters. When I say Marvin, you'd think of him as Stanley, which is also quite fine.'

They went inside. The house was furnished modern, not at all like Chatsworth, and barely. Burston liked the style. Big windows looked out upon a wide and very blue pool and a garden shaded by bamboos. A butler, also dressed in shorts and T-shirt, brought vodkas and lime on a wooden tray. 'Marvin was telling me about the campaign for giving this young boy, well, like another chance after all these years.'

Faldave said: 'Emily was really moved.'

'This is someone you cross an ocean for, Mr Burston, and cross a continent for,' she said. 'Aren't I bound to be moved?'

Burston said: 'I know your husband wonders whether we're getting the politics of it correct, in the present aftermath mood, yet...'

'I don't dismiss politics,' she replied.

'One can't, one can't, I appreciate that,' Burston said, 'yet I—'

'Yet you have come to contest this view with Marvin. This cannot be dismissed, either. Unneeded, but not to be dismissed.'

'Unneeded?' Burston replied. 'I don't follow.'

'I must acknowledge the force of your gesture, too,' Faldave said.

'I couldn't see I had a choice,' Burston said.

'That I can appreciate,' Faldave replied.

'When Marvin said you would be the kind who would concede no fragment of energy to jet lag, the British kind, I remarked to him that, if this Britishness were so strong and positive in you, Mr Burston, it was going to be better if he listened to you upon arrival when you spoke to him on what the general British thinking was on Andrew Pax.'

'I did not resist this logic, Ted,' Faldave said.

'I believe the country is ready for it,' Burston replied at once. 'I come here as an individual, yes. Yet I believe I can speak for my nation.' Jesus. Easy, easy, Ted.

'It's clear to me, Mr Burston, that you believe this, or you would not have flown an ocean and crossed a continent,' Faldave replied.

Burston said: 'I feared I might seem presumptuous.'

'Individuality and confidence are brothers,' Faldave replied. 'Emily's father instilled that notion in me. There are certain central tenets we try to live by.'

'My father is clearly an influence,' she said.

Burston sipped and savoured. 'I am happy now. I have the feeling that Andrew Pax is, as it were, safe.'

'I hope I believe in forgiveness and, yes, in humanity, whatever the political background,' Faldave said.

'Thank you,' Burston replied. Emily sat back on her wicker chair to make the weight of her pregnancy more comfortable. She had refused the vodka and was drinking juice. 'This hanged man had a child, you know. It's another factor that moves Marv and me, as you would expect.'

'I heard rumours of a child,' Burston said.

'Oh, fact,' Faldave replied.

'Really?' Burston said. Of course, this California fucker in his shorts would have discovered more about it than he could himself back on the spot.

'Father knows the father of this child,' Emily said.

'Not the father of blood, you understand, Ted. Well, no, hardly. The effective father. You know Donman Capel, do you, Ted?'

'Never directly met.'

'Donman's *eminence grising* this whole Panopticon deal, as I know you'll have guessed,' Faldave said.

'He's at the core of our profession,' Burston said.

'A Lord Chate,' Emily said.

314

'I beg your pardon?' Burston replied.

'Raised the child,' Emily said.

Burston considered this: 'Lord Chate knows your father, and has spoken about the need for a campaign?'

'This is not a title like say the Duke of Devonshire in Chatsworth,' Emily said. 'This is one of your life peerages. But a genuine lord. Plus Cambridge.'

'Hey, Ted, I don't want you thinking this was already decided before you even appeared here. I mean, big influences, out of sight. This impulse of yours, this is valuable, this is a soul and a conscience speaking. And able to confirm the mood of the British nation. Where else do we go for that? "London Letter" or whatever it's called in the *New Yorker*? Great as far as it goes, but you hear those special drum beats when someone like you talks. Donman's really impressed by the drive you've shown on this Pax, and he's thinking of putting one of his own people in temporarily at Panopticon to – well, to *eminence grise* it, the way he personally *eminence grised* the Panopticon negotiations. That's what we kind of call this guiding-hand control over here, *eminence grising*, after a famed French statesman, Richelieu. There's a bond, Donman-Chate. Donman wants to be sure things are suitable for Chate. The child is a girl.'

Emily said: 'When Marv came home and

said you would be soon here, I asked him did he send a car and he said no, because sending a car would look like we thought you must be suffering from jet lag, which someone of your resilience never would. But I thought he should have sent it, all the same. Then later again I was thinking Marv could be right and it would be something like, well, devilish to rush you up here in a studio limo just to be told the whole trip needn't have been, because father and Marv had already settled the Pax thing so typically.'

'I still love the individuality in Ted's untiringness, Emily,' Faldave said.

'Oh, sure, there'll always be a place for that,' she replied.

Twenty-Three

Louise was glad now that she had come. She had wondered about it, even after the invitation. Well, of course she had wondered. The invitation might have been forced, almost certainly was. But this was a good memorial service, even a happy memorial service. It made David Gale seem worthwhile, and this had to be heartening. She thought it was achieved mainly by the attendance – by the support of his colleagues and family and friends – but also by some words spoken from the pulpit.

They were words which did manage to isolate several of David's genuine strengths: he had once in a while hit an acting part exactly right; and there had been about him off and on an undoubted bounce and humour and amiability. The clergyman was decently briefed on those qualities and referred to them well. His words – these pulpit words – did occasionally stray from David himself and mixed his own personality with those of some of the characters he had played, including the tragic figure of Andrew

Pax. That blurring of identities was, perhaps, inevitable, even in a church service: the campaign for Pax's name had begun to stir by now, and it had some stature, especially among a particular group of Church leaders.

But to confuse Gale with Pax was, of course, ultimately ludicrous. Louise knew why Gale was dead and how; and it had nothing to do with latter-day fellow feeling for Pax. Gale had feelings, yes, but not centred on people he played and not stretching back to someone dead for more than fifty years. His feelings had reached out to what was close and immediate, or they would have liked to. Yet this phoney merging of the two men by the vicar was a comforting notion and one that elevated Gale. She could respond to it, as she might respond to any capably presented theatrical fiction.

The hymn-singing and the Scripture and other readings and the prayers seemed richer for this lovely touch of nonsense. Would his widow like it? She must feel perplexed to hear her husband described as if he had been in part someone else, like a service for Olivier where he was spoken of as Heathcliffe and/or Othello. Well, memorial services were show business.

Charlotte and David's agent, Rosemary Patson, had called on Louise at home a couple of days before the service with the invitation. 'Please, I want you to come,

Louise,' Charlotte said at once, fondly catching hold of Louise's forearm: after all, Charlotte had done some acting herself, in smallish roles.

Rosemary Patson boomed: 'She does need you there, Louise. Not previously but now, yes.'

'Oh, it grew to seem absurd – any attempt to limit those entitled to remember him. Can I put a fence around recollections? You, too, loved David. All right, that should not have been. No, it should not! It did happen, though.'

No, it bloody well did not. Not love, nor anything like. Or not love or anything like from Louise, at any rate. *Making* love a few times, sure. That was in the way of friendliness, newness, passing need, and a hell of a relief from listening to him talk about himself. Different altogether from love. But Louise did not speak these corrections to Charlotte. Instead, she smiled and nodded once, to signify thanks for Charlotte's large-mindedness.

'You knew him, Louise,' she had said, her face vivid with friendliness and acceptance. 'I don't mean merely as a lover, but you knew his life. Well, obviously: you actually wrote his Life. All right, they call you a ghost – so damn dismissive. But I know you were more than that. You entered into David's very self. I have to recognize that there may be a sense in which you knew him even better than I.'

'Oh, no, Charlotte,' Louise cried. 'Never.' It sounded like modesty. She hoped it did, at any rate. This, too, was different, though. She resented what Charlotte had said: would never have sought to know Gale at such intolerable depth, and with the intolerable reciprocities this implied. She grieved over his death, naturally, but grieved only as any friend might. She felt no guilt for his death, because she was certain that she would never have been able to offer what he wanted: long-lasting love. Louise knew his Life but not his life, and that was enough. They should never get mixed. A ghost was a ghost and could be content with that. Louise had an idea that it was the Life, and the award for the Life, that had made Charlotte change. How would it look if the writer who had given him such posthumous eminence were excluded? To many – including the tabloids – it might appear as if Louise had been kept out because there had been more between her and Gale than a Life. A life, perhaps. So, they *would* be mixed.

Rosemary said: 'I'm so glad Charlotte has decided this way. It's entirely her own impulse, of course.'

Ah, possibly Rosemary had advised her, then: perhaps mentioning the Press and their way of seeing what they wanted to see.

'It would have seemed so wrong for the wife of someone like David Gale to appear narrow, vindictive,' Rosemary said. 'People might have been disappointed to find this was the kind of woman David Gale had chosen. That would have run counter to their idea of him, I'm sure.'

'Oh, yes,' Charlotte had cried. 'David was a shag-mad, self-mad piss artist, but he did have these little moments of inner light. God will know what to make of him.'

Or, God knows whether God will know what to make of him.

The memorial service produced some fine readings. Louise had expected this: such a gathering of word-power pros, of course. But what Louise liked was that these performers for the most part kept the show decent, did not ham beyond and try to make the clergyman sound drab. Barry Wight gave that James Mason 'Though I speak with the tongues of men and of angels' piece from *Odd Man Out* and the New Testament; and George Moben – or Lord Moben now, of course, since his Social Theatre achievements in roughest Liverpool – George gave them a few paragraphs from *We're Rolling*, paragraphs which were creepy, like any ghosted work, but which Louise thought had a bearable phrase here and there.

David would admit to a degree of dandyism, yet also confessed to times when clothes bored him and he was content to put on whatever came first to hand. These would often be very worn and unfashionable outfits, to the dismay of the public-relations people entrusted with his image.

George gave the words a good cheeriness and pace. Louise considered it not a bad way of saying that quite often Gale was too rat-arsed or hungover to dress properly.

Stanley Faldave had flown over to the service from the States. He sat with Charlotte and the child, D.L.O., Ted Burston and D.L.O.'s PA and so on, and Marie. For Marie to have been asked suggested that perhaps, after all, Charlotte was genuinely all-round forgiving. In his closing sentences, the vicar spoke of Gale's dauntlessness, optimism and verve, as if determined to end with a strong dismissal of rumour about suicide. Fine. Kind, perhaps. 'Though I speak with the tongues of men and of angels and have not charity...' And, in any case, required by church policy.

But, listening to him, Louise thought of Gale weeping alongside her in bed, terrified for his career, certain he would lose her and aware at last that she could not think of him except as a nice, short-time adventure, among her own short-time adventures and his. She had wept herself, and wept a little now during the memorial service, because the situation with Gale had made her so helpless. It was impossible for Louise to give what he wanted. There was something bewildering about his needs: as if he thought that by taking on his Life she had taken on his life, rather as Charlotte suggested. In the *Daily Telegraph* not long ago, Louise read a ghostwriter's account of how she helped on the Life of George Davies, founder of the fashion chain Next. The writer's boyfriend complained that she was so immersed in Davies's personality she had actually become him, as a good actor might move totally into a part. There was nothing between her and Davies – even less than between Louise and Gale – but that writer and her boyfriend broke up not long afterwards.

Louise could understand how such things might happen. A version of it had overwhelmed David Gale. He seemed to think he had delivered himself so entirely to Louise that he was incapable of continuing without her. Yet she told him he must. She had not become him, and did not wish to. This memory of Gale, defeated, abject, even suicidal, was not something to be disclosed. He deserved to be thought well of, and Charlotte and the baby deserved to be considered the people he cared for above all, and to the last. Louise had decided even before the service itself that she would never blow apart Gale's memory by revealing the agonizingly prescient letter he wrote her after that third evening. In fact, she had destroyed it, and quite possibly all the photocopies, before leaving for the service. The gesture had seemed inescapable.

Twenty-Four

D.L.O. said: 'It would not have been so bad but for this damned epilogue.'

'The thing with Louise is she's fierce about keeping the two sides of her professional life separate – the ghosting, the other,' Burston replied.

'This fucking epilogue more or less undoes everything that's gone before,' D.L.O. said.

'It's a kind of scholarly tentativeness, I suppose,' Burston said.

D.L.O. stood up from his desk. Burston tensed on his chair and hard-clenched his right fist and half-clenched the left. There was no actual danger yet. Partial readiness was enough, probably.

'I know about scholarliness, I hope, and about tentativeness as well,' D.L.O. replied. 'But we've got a campaign under way here. It's flagging. This bloody book could have helped.' He flicked the copy of Louise's Pax biography with the ends of his fingers where it lay alongside his table lamp. The beam from the lamp spotlighted the dust-cover picture of Pax, a Cambridge portrait, which showed him youthful and bright-looking, and wearing the kind of scarf Wardrobe had given Gale for those early *Broken Light* scenes. The prevailing background colours of the dust cover were muted green and silver. This book was a prestige production. Louise's name featured large, with 'author of *Hallam* and *John Dryden*' underneath.

'I like the title,' D.L.O. said. *'The Judgement of War* gets it beautifully right: suggests that judgements taken in a time of crisis could be wrong judgements. Isn't this all the campaign wants to prove? Yet here we are, what is it, eighteen months on, and no real move towards a vindication of Pax. If anything, the contrary – a hardening. No Russian verification he acted for them, yet still this impasse.' D.L.O. punched the volume this time. 'And now here comes this fucking book with its fucking epilogue.' He bent and opened it to the page. 'This pious stuff about the trade of the biographer – its holy fucking rules, its reverence for provable truths, its chaste limitations. Fucking *truths.*'

'As you say, though, D.L.O., the general import of the book is that Pax was wrongly executed.'

'It was a mistake for us to go any damn where near this campaign,' D.L.O. replied. He began to pace and Burston himself stood and got his back against a wall. 'What's in it for us?' D.L.O. yelled. *'Broken Light* has had its main street life, and a good life. Is this campaign going to resurrect it – I mean, even if the campaign was getting anywhere as campaign?'

'A film of this quality and significance can remake public mood, D.L.O. Think of the way *Twelve Angry Men* gets a fresh run out whenever there's a trial scandal.'

'You've been talking to Faldave again?' D.L.O. snarled. 'He says all that sort of shit. Or his father-in-law says it, so Faldave does. And Donman Capel says it because he does business with Chate, who brought up Pax's kid. I detest this kind of self-interest and pressure.'

The size of the conspiracy against him seemed to weaken D.L.O. suddenly, and he sat down and began to read from the epilogue of *The Judgement of War*. Listen: ' "British libel law is very kind to the living but takes no account of the dead." '

'She's referring to the death of Estham, Pax's possible recruiter,' Burston replied.

'I know what she's referring to.'

But now that D.L.O. was seated again and looking sick, Burston felt he could keep going: 'It might well have strengthened the vindication of the Pax campaign if it could be shown incontrovertibly that Estham killed himself in a state of regret and shame for having connived at his execution. And I'm sure Louise would have wanted to help.

But she's restricted. What she's saying at the end is that Estham might have been professionally slaughtered merely because he was conducting an affair with Clifford Deem's wife. She's saying it, Darren, and yet she can't say it, not outright. Deem's still alive, and, as far as I understand from talking to her, so is the man who actually did it on Estham and later shacked up with his missus. Consequently, in the epilogue, Louise puts herself in the clear, and comes clean on the impossibilities of biography.'

'So why write the fucking things? So why write the fucking things and do damage to a damn well-rated film? Hasn't she any respect?'

'Modern biographers stress that truth is elusive, various. They offer a version of someone's life.'

'And suggest there might be others! Christ! "I swear to tell the truth, a fragment of the truth and possibly nothing like the truth, so help me God – i.e., God, help me to collect my ten per cent royalty for this slab of hit or miss."'

'They aim to suggest the plenitude of existence and character,' Burston replied. 'Plenitude' was one of those words that came to him suddenly from nowhere. Perfect. Lovely ample final vowel sound and rich in gorgeous bullshit. 'She has to show that events of apparently supreme stature in the past – Pax's death, even Estham's death – may be overlaid by, and subject to, matters of quite appalling banality. Biography these days does seek to highlight these lowlights, as it were, D.L.O., and so reveal the ironic jumble of things.' Wow, but fucking wow!

'You studying Existentialism with the Open University, you wordy sod? So, Summers is trendy. That's what you're saying, yes?'

'D.L.O., this epilogue is a kind of apology for being bound both by regard for likelihoods and for all the possible contradictions in all the possible situations. That is, likelihoods as she sees them, of course – or half sees them, Darren.' Burston had begun this explanation in a D.L.O. mode, but grew confident in the argument towards the end and switched to 'Darren'. He tried a bit of buttering: 'There's even a hint there of what you suggested once: that Estham might have been a double-agent, a plant. But, obviously, she can't prove it because she could not get to independent witnesses. Deem would not cough.'

'Of course Deem wouldn't cough. Would you if you were Deem? He's got children, hasn't he? He has to stay looking as decent as he can in their eyes. The past viewed by the present, with the present the important bit: it's exactly what we've been talking about. For God's sake, Ted, Louise did a

329

good helpful job on the Gale Life, didn't she? Why does she have to piss us about with this one?'

'That's what I mean – the way she divides herself, her roles.'

'Does she give a twopenny fuck about us?' Darren asked, near a sob. 'Does she worry about this foundering campaign and the present's indifference or worse to Pax in 1941?'

'The Gale Life is going sweetly still,' Burston replied.

Darren nodded, reluctantly at first, but then managed a minor smile. 'Yes. Perhaps it's time to encourage the campaign to go gentle into that good night.' He tugged at the fingers of his left hand, but remained safely seated. 'Kill it, Ted,' he snarled. 'Donman Capel can be quite reasonable. He'll see we've done all we can for him and Chate but that it isn't working. Can't work. You're used to talking to Stanley Faldave. Pop over to L.A. again and explain. Do you suffer much from jet lag?'

'Never. I resiliate.'

'It's an asset. Tell Stanley we'd like, instead, to think about a retrospective, a season, of David Gale's films, with *Broken Light* the centrepiece naturally. Yes, let the Pax campaign go fuck itself. We'll talk to the publishers and get a further edition of the Gale Life out. Push things along.'

'Will you want to incorporate Louise's

suicide rewrites now in this version?' Burston asked.

'That's a point,' D.L.O. said. 'I'll have a mull. It might give a new edition a freshish buzz, mightn't it?'

Twenty-Five

Louise flew out once more to Faro and went on to Tavira for Clifford Deem's funeral. This trip's fare would *not* be reclaimable from the Revenue. The service was in a small Protestant church. About twenty-five people attended, including some teachers from the English centre school, but not the football star. Afterwards, Louise accompanied Clara to the cemetery in the big, old hired limousine driven by a Portuguese mute. Clifford had died from one of those strokes Clara spoke of, perhaps during an evening of special excitement and din. Louise did not ask the circumstances, and Clara never said. The little procession and service around the grave made Louise think of Harry Lime's funeral at the start of *The Third Man*, although the weather was kinder here and Clifford definitely in the box, presumably. Perhaps sparseness of turn-out suggested the comparison. Only a few of the teachers came to the cemetery. At no point did Clara weep. She wore a dark seventies-style silk suit, and a black tam.

Later, back in the Deem villa, Clara said: 'I'll stay on here, of course. All that malarkey about coming away with you – that's what it was, malarkey. I owe it to Cliff to stay. We've established something here. It's worth continuing. Yes, we had our periods of hate one for the other, more or less equally, I suppose, and there were those times when I might have killed him, given the chance and ability. But we got to some sort of mutuality at last, didn't we? And, as I've said, he murdered for me. This is bound to rate with a woman, isn't it?'

'He definitely did Roy Estham, or had him done?' Louise asked. 'And out of jealousy, nothing to do with the Pax case?'

Clara giggled. 'I'm going to say jealousy, aren't I? It raises my value.'

'And it's true?' Louise said.

'You more or less said it in your book, anyway, didn't you?'

'Only more or less.'

'Because you feared the libel laws. Now he's dead, you needn't.'

'Oh, I'm fed up with rewrites. I'll leave it so, even if there's a reprint.'

'You disappoint me. I'd have liked to see a proper account of Roy and me – how we met on one of his calls to our house, seeking Cliff and reassurance, and then ... and then so on and so on until...'

'It didn't trouble you he—?'

'Had been regarded as an enemy?' Clara said. 'All so shifting and relative, isn't it? He had the O.M. He was Deemed an enemy – capital D – that's all, and for very mixed reasons. All marriages have their little tangles and mysteries, don't they, Louise? But you'll say you don't know, you've never been in one. Been close to one, though, haven't you? David Gale's? Didn't he ever tell you what was wrong there, and write to you that he was going to end himself?'

'Wrote.'

'Wrote what?'

'I don't talk about it, you know.'

'But you've dug into my life, haven't you? Isn't a bit of reciprocity called for?'

'Possibly.' Yes, possibly. 'He wrote: "Louise, my ghost, I can't reach you – the way one can't ever reach ghosts. Maybe I'll get to be a ghost myself, then. David." '

'Clever – for an actor,' Clara replied.